PROMISE ME ANTHOLOGY

by

Tara Fox Hall

Published by
Melange Books, LLC
White Bear Lake, MN 55110
www.melange-books.com

Promise Me Anthology ~ Copyright © 2013 by Tara Fox Hall

978-1-61235-711-9 print

Cover Art by Caroline Andrus

Promise Me Anthology
Tara Fox Hall

Table of Contents

*These stories link together to tell a wider story

Thank you to Dark Moon, my fellow WAH authors, and Melange Books, who helped launch the Promise Me series in these short stories. And to fellow authors Jenny Twist, Tori Ridgewood, and Jodie Pierce, for all your help. To Deb the most wonderful hairstylist in the world, for requesting a story about Terian. To my wonderful childhood friend Lynette, who asked for a story on Sarelle. And as always, to Mom.

With Every Goodbye

"Make love with me."

I blinked, then turned over in bed. My husband Brennan was lying next to me. Daylight streamed through the double windows, giving his short light brown hair reddish highlights. *Damn, but he always looks sexy in the sun.* "What time is it?"

"7:23AM; the perfect time." His warm blue eyes blinked once, his facial expression teasing.

I stretched, yawning. "Have you been awake long?"

"I don't usually get up before you do," he said, chuckling. "I was watching you sleep."

I snorted. "And you were suddenly inspired to lust?"

"Something like that."

I slipped my hand beneath the sheet, searching. Brennan straightened suddenly, grunting.

I stroked his hardened flesh. "Tell me you love me."

Brennan made an attempt to look stern. "I wouldn't have married you if I didn't, Sar."

I let the corners of my mouth curl up just a hint, my hand not stopping its motion. "Come on. Say it—"

"I love you. I'd go to the ends of the earth for you." He grasped my free hand in his, threading his fingers through mine. "Don't stop."

"Sorry," I said cheerfully, straddling him. "Like you just said, it's the perfect time for making love." I brushed my lips over his, then pressed harder. Brennan groaned again, then pulled me close, rolling over onto me. I giggled, then sighed in bliss, feeling his lips kiss their way lower.

God, it was great being married

* * * *

"Slowly! Go slowly," Brennan shouted at me, as I bore down on him atop my 55-HP John Deere tractor.

"I have things well in hand, just like I did this morning," I said loftily, easing past him through the doorway with a foot to spare. "I'm getting very good driving standard."

"Like hell," Brennan called, as I parked the tractor inside the woodshed. "You nearly drove over my foot."

"Maybe you should have stepped back," I teased. After shutting the tractor off, I began to unload the wood from the tractor bucket, piling it from one end to the other across the length of the woodshed. Brennan came up beside me and began helping, dumping wood in armfuls onto my neatly begun row.

Don't tell him he's piling it wrong. It'll just start a fight, and it doesn't matter that much. "Thanks for helping."

"I'm your partner," Brennan said, matter of fact. He deposited another armful. "I'm supposed to help. Besides, it's not as if you're going to be the only one sitting by that woodstove come December. I'll be right next to you." A log slipped through his fingers, landing on the dirt floor. He picked it up with a grimace, tossing it haphazardly onto the stacked row. "It was a good idea to put it in. That saved us a ton on heating last winter."

Heating with wood was a lot of work, between the stacking, the splitting, the chainsawing into pieces, and lugging trees out of the forest in the first place. "It does. I don't mind the extra work, knowing we don't have a mortgage on the place." My words were awkward, like they were any time that I brought up finances.

"I wanted you to be okay, if something happened to me," Brennan said, just like he'd said a hundred times before. "I didn't mind putting all my savings into the house, along with yours. And we got the life insurance policies together, too—"

"Your mom thought it was too soon for us to think about dying," I said darkly. "She still thinks I forced you into getting them. That I forced you into paying off my house."

"Let's not argue about my family," Brennan said, his tone both defensive and supplicant. "My mom will come around in time, then so will the rest of them. It's our house now, Sar."

We stacked wood in silence, both of us unwilling to bring up the matter that neither one of our families had exactly embraced our marriage. Most days it was enough that we had each other, and we were making a new life for ourselves together. I reassured myself again that Brennan was right. It would just take a little more time.

* * * *

"Why do you have to go?" I asked for the second time.

"Andy," Brennan said with false patience, his jaw muscle twitching. "My best friend from high school. He flew all the way down from Alaska for our wedding, remember? He's getting a divorce and he needs a friend."

"I'm not talking about that," I said, shooting him dagger eyes. "I'm talking about the climbing expedition—"

"You're making it seem like I'm going to Everest or something—"

"You told me it was a dangerous climb," I said louder, determined not to be dissuaded. "Now you're acting like it's not. Which is it?"

"It's not dangerous," Brennan said. "He's done it before. And I've done a lot of climbing myself—"

"Not in the last year you haven't."

"Because I moved here to the East, to be near your family and my new job," Brennan said, irritated. "How am I supposed to stay in shape climbing mountains when there are no mountains, Sar? I'm not a novice. I've climbed most of my life. I have close to a decade of experience—"

Go for the big guns. "I just became a wife. I want a few more years before I'm a widow."

"I'm not going to take any risks," Brennan assured, hugging me. "Just because we took all those legal safeguards doesn't mean I want to test them out! I just want some time with an old friend. Plus I can stop out West on the way back home and see my mother, Sar. My family has been making noises about me coming out there to see them this summer. I know you don't want to fly out there—"

3

The truth was that we couldn't afford it right now, not for both of us to go. And he did have a point that this wasn't his first climb. My husband had been a climbing guide in both Wyoming and Colorado in his college days, even if he'd never climbed in Alaska before. "You win," I said reluctantly, hugging him. "Just come home to me in one piece, okay?"

* * * *

"Be careful," I said, hugging Brennan in the airport lobby. "Remember you're climbing for two. Four if you count Ghost and Darkness. Six if you count Jessica and Cavity."

"I'll be careful," he said solemnly. "You be careful, too, okay?"

"I'll be fine," I said, rolling my eyes. "I'm not going to be hanging off the sides of mountains on thin ropes."

"Accidents happen," he said ominously. "Just be safe, okay? No chainsawing by yourself. And no splitting either."

"All right," I said reluctantly. It wasn't as if I could get my chainsaw started by myself anyway; Brennan always had to start it for me.

"I love you. I'll call you as soon as I get there."

"I love you," I said, then hugged him tight, finishing with a passionate kiss. Brennan returned it with ardour, then shot me a joyous grin, and headed into line, placing his bag on the scanner as he walked through the metal detector. He went through, then paused once to blow me another kiss before heading into line to board. Then he was gone, vanishing down the retractable tunnel to his plane.

Brennan called just like he said he would. But I had terrible dreams that first night, waking from nightmare after nightmare. I spent the next day in a fog, getting up only to walk our two German Shepherds, Ghost and Darkness.

They were really my dogs, but Brennan had known them their whole life, from our selection of them as puppies to their gawky adolescence to their sleek adult selves. Ghost was white as snow—so long as he stayed clear of mud—and Darkness was black as onyx. She was just as glossy, too, when she wasn't mud covered from digging holes looking for mice. I'd done most of their training myself, and they knew several commands beyond the usual "sit," "down", "no," and "stay."

4

Our two cats, Jessica and Cavity, had also been mine. They were cats I'd spent my college years with, back when I'd lived with my mother. After she'd gotten remarried to my stepfather Chris, I'd sort of inherited them. When she'd found me a home in the country only a few miles from hers, I'd jumped at the chance. I'd always felt like I didn't belong in the city, with its obsession on trim lawns and nosy neighbours. Now Brennan and I had our own place. We were building a wonderful life here. It was normal that the first years would be a little rocky.

I smiled, then got on my laptop computer, paging through to the classifieds. It was past time to look for a job. Brennan kept telling me that there wasn't any rush, that he was happy being the breadwinner. But I knew that was just another strike his family held against me. They didn't understand that I'd spent the last year painting, sanding, spackling, laying floor tiles, and doing other remodeling to our new home; they only saw that he worked a job and I didn't have one. Now that most of the refurbishing work was done inside on our new house, I was going to find something to bring in some money. I'd held a full-time job after college, and I had my chemistry degree. There had to be a lot of jobs I was suited for.

* * * *

The clock struck ten, chiming. I blinked, then remembered I was on the couch waiting for Brennan to call. Rain was pouring down from the noise on the roof.

Better check the cellar. In heavy rain, the cellar always had a little water seep up through the floor cracks. Brennan had been down there moving boxes when he'd packed a few days ago. If he'd forgotten to move things back, there might be problems.

I roused a disgruntled Jessica from her spot on my lap, then walked downstairs. There was a little spot of water near the stairs, but nothing else. Relieved, I headed back upstairs and let the dogs out. With a flurry of ferocious barking, they descended on the plastic doghouse in the backyard.

"Hey! Stop!" I yelled as I ran toward them, wincing as the rain rapidly soaked my pyjamas. The dogs backed away, and I peered into the house, expecting a rat or a rabbit. Instead a forlorn white and grey cat stared up at me in utter fear, shivering.

I stripped off my robe, then wrapped it around the cat, which hissed and swiped at me. With difficulty, I let the dogs back into the house, then managed to get the cat to the cellar before it broke free of my arms. It promptly ran into the darkness at the far end of the basement, disappearing beneath some boxes.

"Asher," I said tiredly, standing. "You must be blessed by God. You lived up to your name, facing down the dogs like that. What possessed you to decide to finally join the family tonight of all nights?"

There was no answer. I trooped upstairs, gathered some food, water, and litter for an extra litter box, then set out my offerings with a small plate of wet food. Asher came out as I was working, watching me.

Brennan and I had noticed the stray cat living in the barn when we'd first moved in late last fall, but all efforts to trap her had been foiled. We'd been feeding her since then, and calling her Asher. "I'm going to have to go get your heated bed from the barn tomorrow," I told her. "I'm glad you came in. Brennan's going to be upset he missed it."

Asher mewed at me, the sound almost inaudible even in silence. She came over and sniffed my fingers, then bolted away again.

* * * *

I woke in the stillness of dawn, the half-moon windows above me pinkish with the rays of the rising sun. I shifted, then groaned at the sudden dull ache within my lower torso. "God how I hate my fucking period," I muttered, staggering to the bathroom. After cleaning up my mess, I got an early start on the day, knowing that it was useless to try to sleep. I was just downing two aspirin with breakfast when the phone rang.

It was the right area code for Andy, but the wrong number. Worried, I picked up the phone. "Hello?"

"Sarelle?" a female voice said. "It's Susan."

"Hi," I said as friendly as I could for not knowing who Susan was. "Can I help you?"

"There's been an accident."

"There wasn't a boat," I replied foggily. I flushed, realizing how dumb I sounded. *There had been a dream last night about a boat accident. I was standing at the edge of the water, looking down at the lapping waves.*

"You need to come out here," Susan said. "I've called the airport, and they're holding a ticket for you to Wyoming—"

"What happened?" I asked. "Did Brennan get hurt?"

"It's your duty to be out here," she said, then hung up.

My shock at her abruptness cut through the last of my cobwebs. Angrily, I pushed *69, then 1. After a few rings, a woman answered.

"I'm not flying anywhere until I know what happened," I said angrily. "Do you hear me, Susan? Now who in the hell are you and what is going on?"

"Your husband died along with my soon to be ex," Susan said grimly. "They fell off a cliff on Mount Foraker. Brennan's family is holding a funeral as soon as possible. If you want to be part of it, get the hell out here!"

My tongue felt like it was stuck to the roof of my mouth. "Why did you get me a ticket?"

"Andy asked me to," Susan said. "He was found alive, and he asked that I get you a ticket. He said you'd never come out otherwise and that Brennan would have wanted you here."

I put the phone down, hearing it click. But the sound had lost meaning.

In my dream, there had been a boat. Brennan had sailed off in it. And I had come down to the water's edge to greet him and found only wooden shards floating on the water.

I would have stayed there for days, if the phone hadn't rung again. This time it was the Alaskan police, calling to advise me that my husband of exactly one year and a few days was dead, victim of a broken neck.

* * * *

I arrived in Wyoming hot, jet-lagged, and exhausted. After renting a car, I found my way to my in-laws home. The place was packed. I rang the doorbell. A woman answered. It took me a moment to identify her as Brennan's mother. She looked so worn.

"You made it," she said politely. "Please come in."

"Where is he?" I asked, coming inside.

"Coming in a few hours," she said, guiding me to the couch. I sat, looking around at all the people chatting. "That's my knitting club, my bridge club, and the local Lionesses club," she said, her tone containing a note of pride. "I'm very active in my community."

My eyes narrowed. "Where is Brennan? I want to collect him and take him home. I have to make arrangements."

"You don't have to do anything of the sort," she assured me. "We're his family, Sar. We've got it under control."

I looked at her with hostility. "He's not staying out here with you."

She stared right back. "He wanted to be cremated and scattered out here in the mountains. With all your death arrangements, I thought you both went over your last wishes."

I had never hated anyone more than in that moment. "He's coming home with me."

"No, he's not," she said coolly, handing me a paper. "This is his will. In it he stipulated what I just told you quite clearly."

I snatched the paper out of her hand and read it. Yes, it was Brennan's will, the one we'd signed a year ago. He'd left his worldly possessions to me, along with his SUV. Written on the bottom in longhand was a paragraph long notation in his handwriting, asking to be cremated, and "cast to the winds." It was his handwriting, no question. But that didn't mean I was going to roll over for her. I stood up. Holding the will, I walked to the nearest phone and called the police.

* * * *

All told, it took me a week to do the necessary paperwork, get death certificates, collect Brennan's things, and board a plane for my home. My now-estranged in-laws got their way, in the end. I was there on the helicopter they chartered to cast his ashes in the Rocky Mountains. I agreed that it was what he'd wanted. After it was over, there was nothing really more to say, or so I thought. But his mother had said plenty on the trip back to the landing pad, about how I'd used her son for his money, how he'd died because I'd let him climb that Alaskan mountain, about how I should give up my false grief now that I'd gotten what I wanted. Some of what she said cut me to the bone, before I tuned her out, knowing she was grieving just as I was.

It didn't really hit me until I was on the plane home. I was a widow now. That life Brennan had hoped to build with me was over at the close of our first chapter. The rest of the story now fell to me to finish. *Where the hell was I going to start?*

* * * *

I cleaned out Brennan's clothes immediately on my return, purging our bedroom of them and then all traces of him from the house. My wedding rings I removed and put in my jewelry box. As much as it was painful, feeling a pang every time I glanced at one of those formerly filled spaces, it did make it easier to get through each day. Because that was all I was doing, really…getting through each day in the hopes that one day I wouldn't feel like I was going through the motions of living.

The pets helped, of course. They were constant company without judgment.

My new job also helped. When a part time position at a metal fabrication shop was advertised in the local Pennysaver, I applied for the job. At first, the owner acted as though he thought the job was going to be too dirty for a woman, that he wasn't sure I could take it. But after I explained that my inclination lay more in machinery and hard work than staying at home baking pies—even if I was handy at that, too—he agreed to hire me.

The work was tough at first, as I'd had no experience working in industry before, much less knowledge of all the governmental rules and regulations that required compliance. With a lot of research and help from the local Department of Labor, I rapidly built a rudimentary network of safety and health programs, and began enforcing them. At first, the guys on the floor didn't respect me. But with my persistence—and more than a few batches of my special chocolate chip cookies—I slowly won them over.

My mother and stepfather liked my changes in lifestyle. The only trouble was that for them, the modifications weren't encompassing enough. "You're by yourself too much," became my mother's most used comment. That morphed to, "we want you to be completely happy," a.k.a, "you need a man." When I challenged that for its sexist attitude, she began saying, "it's dangerous for a woman to live alone. So many things can happen." Insisting that I was safer as a single woman in the country than a single woman in the city, fell on deaf ears. To shut her up, I finally contacted a local shooting range, purchased a used .38, and got some training to handle it safely. My stepfather was pleased with my interest in self-preservation, buying me a side leg holster like Lara Croft's that Christmas. I admitted that having the gun that winter did make me feel braver about being there alone, even if I never used it except in target practice. While I had used my old shotgun before to scare away trespassers, there was something about having a handgun that made me feel more self-sufficient.

That first spring, I learned how to start my chainsaw myself, with a lot of swearing plus trial and error seasoned with some bitter tears of frustration. As I slowly gained upper body strength working with wood, starting the chainsaw became easier. But I did keep my promise to Brennan, either asking my friend Kat up or my mother to help me when I used the chainsaw. My pets had only me now. I wasn't going to risk an accident claiming my life, too.

That was the only thing that really bothered me: most of my friends had moved on. Brennan hadn't made a lot of friends; he hadn't been in this part of the country long enough. His family was out West, and they'd not spoken to me since his funeral, not even at Christmas. I'd never had a lot of friends, but I'd had enough at my former job to give me a big send off when I quit to marry Brennan. None of them had contacted me since I'd left there, except Kat. I'd never had many friends in college; I'd been too busy studying. At my new job, most of the guys were married; I didn't think their wives would appreciate a new widow trying to strike up a friendship with their husbands, even an innocent one. Outside my mother and Chris, I had no other close family. That left religious and local associations, and my neighbors.

I'd never been big on associations of any kind, and I preferred that God's relationship with me be a private one of prayer. So it was time to meet my neighbors.

I made friends with Henry, who lived to the north of me, did construction and plowing, and offered me the use of his quarry behind my home for target shooting. I forged a partnership with a local farmer, who agreed to farm ten acres of my land in return for helping me manage other jobs too big for me to handle. And I met Flora and her grandson Ken. The former was to become in the last year of her life one of my best friends.

* * * *

I stood at the door and knocked hard. The doorbell didn't work, so there was no point in trying it. The curtains fluttered the tiniest bit, then the door opened.

"Sarelle!" A frail voice cried softly. "Is that you?"

"Yes, it's me, Flora," I said, smiling down at her small twig-like frame. "I've come to visit you. I brought you some flowers."

"Come into the kitchen then, dear, and be sure to close the door behind you," Flora said sternly.

I obediently followed her into the kitchen and put the arrangement down on the table.

"Leave it right there, so I can look at it," she said firmly. Her wrinkled face creased itself into a gentle smile. "How have you been, Sarelle? I know it's getting close to a year."

I sat down heavily, letting her take one of my hands in hers. It was wrinkled and frail, the bones showing through her papery skin. "I've been good."

"You shouldn't have, dear," she said gently. "I know your money situation is tight."

My work at the shop was bringing in cash, but not enough to live on. I was steadily using Brennan's life insurance money up, even though I'd cut my expenses as much as I could. "You're going to be ninety-eight. That deserved flowers."

"Thank you," she said, laughing coarsely. "Why aren't you at work today?"

"I have a doctor appointment later today," I supplied. "I wanted to come and visit you. I'm meeting a friend for lunch, too."

"Good. I hope it's a male friend."

My mouth twitched as I tried not to laugh. "No, it's a girlfriend. Her name is Kat. We've been friends for years. I'm not dating yet."

"Sarelle, you have to get back out and meet someone. I know Ken's had his eyes on you for a while now, and truthfully, much as I'd like you to be a granddaughter to me, he's too old for you. You need someone your own age." She drew herself up in her chair, her expression exasperated. "I'm old enough that I can say what I like."

I didn't like being pushed, nor to be reminded of her grandson's more than friendly affection for me. "Flora, I don't really want to discuss this."

"You never want to discuss it, Sar. I've been bringing this up every time you visit me for the past four months, and you always say that this isn't the time to talk about it. Brennan is dead, and he'd want you to move on."

I swallowed hard. "I know he wouldn't want me to feel like this. But I'm better now, really. I'm used to being alone now. I'm not sure I want another relationship anytime soon." That was a bald-faced lie, but I was making it alone, and that was what counted, right?

"People come in and out of your life," Flora said gently. "It's the time you have with them that matters, not that they might not be around forever."

I looked at her, vowing silently if she pressed any harder at me, I was going to leave.

As if sensing she'd gone too far, Flora let out a small sigh, then smiled happily. "How's your mother?" she asked. "How are your pets? Do you have all your firewood in for the winter yet? Tell me all your news."

"They're all fine," I said feeling relieved that she was dropping it. Then I launched into a tale of rescuing a baby turkey from Ghost, and the heavy moment passed.

I stayed for another forty-five minutes. After hugging her quickly, I hurried outside to my Explorer, looking at my watch and swearing that I was late.

Ken was there by the SUV door, waiting for me, holding a plate that I'd given him some cookies on a few weeks ago.

"Hi, Ken," I said, trying not to sound false.

"Hi, Sarelle," he responded shyly.

Ken was dressed in some ragged cutoffs, and on old T-shirt, with sneakers that had holes big enough to poke a toe through, even though a gas company that leased his land sent him a hefty check each month. He was pretty tight with money, but free with his smiles and always ready to help a friend or neighbor with a project that needed doing. I'd considered him a good friend, until I discovered he wanted more than my friendship. I was also annoyed that he'd recently begun letting his two beagle-hound mixes run loose so he could stop by my house looking for them.

"I wanted to return your plate," he said, handing it to me. "Flora said you would probably be stopping by to see her for her birthday, so I was going to leave it with her. Then I saw your Explorer, and decided to wait for you."

"I hope you both liked the cookies," I said, edging toward the door of my SUV. "I'm late for a lunch appointment."

"Well, have a good day, Sar." He remained standing where he was.

"You, too," I said, opening the driver's side door.

"Sar, could we go out some time?" he asked hesitantly.

I turned to face him. "Ken, I like you but only as a friend. I'm sorry."

"Don't worry about it," he said with a forced smile. Have a good lunch date."

* * * *

"So he finally asked you out?" Kat said in surprise. "What did you say?"

"It happened kind of fast. I told him I wasn't interested. That's it." I shrugged, downing a fry. "Tell me all the dirt from work. Are things as bad there as they used to be?"

"It's the same as when you worked there, except that the bullshit is getting deeper, and the shovels are getting smaller."

We laughed together. "Tell me how everything's been going," Kat asked. "I know you weren't into Ken, but is there anyone else new?"

I sighed a little inwardly. *From where?* "Not yet. Don't push, okay?"

"Hey, I'm here to do my part to tell you to stay single," she replied. "You won't believe what Brett did this past week. You know we've been trying to finish that house we're building."

I listened to her, nibbling my remaining fries. "I'll help, if you need me to," I said when she finished. "I've got ladders, circular saws and other tools, and I've put up drywall before, and I know how to shingle a roof—"

"Sar, you amaze me," Kat praised. "I should be used to it by now, but all the things you know how to do still surprise me."

"Hey," I preened. "I can't help it. My grandfather wanted a boy, and he raised me like one. I was driving a lawn tractor when I was six, and de-nailing boards when I was ten. I learned to like knowing how to do things, because then I could depend on myself, and not need anyone else." I was proud that I could do things that most women weren't able to do. That most women might not want to know how to run a chain saw or shoot a gun had never occurred to me.

"I know, I've seen the pictures, from when you were young," Kat teased. "You even had a boy haircut!"

"Hey!" I frowned at her. "It was a short style, but it wasn't a boy's haircut!"

"You made up for it as you got older," Kat said, smiling. "Your blond hair is to your waist now."

"Almost," I said, smiling again. "When I got to be a teen, I wanted to be a girl, and not a tomboy anymore. But I still like knowing how to do things."

"We all get older," she said a little sadly.

I understood that. Our culture praised youth in women, not experience. "All too fast."

"Sar, I'm going to be thirty-six this year," Kat said hesitantly. "I look sometimes at myself, and I think how the time has gone by, and I wonder how I got to be this older woman—"

"You are not 'older' yet, not really. Neither am I," I said, scowling.

"You're just thirty, Sar," Kat said wistfully. "It slips away so fast. I still feel twenty-something inside. What about when I'm fifty?"

"It matters how you feel," I said staunchly. "If you feel young, that's what matters."

Kat gave me a sad smile, as if I couldn't understand. I quickly moved the conversation back to work, describing a funny incident with my co-workers. Soon we were laughing again. Nevertheless, a sense of mortality settled on me in that conversation and stayed with me, even as we pretended it had flown.

With Every Goodbye

* * * *

I cranked up an old Def Leppard Album on the way home, listening to "Make Love like a Man."

Maybe it was time for me to start dating. My sex drive was certainly strong enough.

I sang at the top of my lungs with the song, and the sun peeked out from behind the clouds, making me reach for my sunglasses. In the sudden warmth, I decided I felt really good. Maybe I was ready to finally get out there, and meet someone. I was a widow, and I had lost someone I loved. I wasn't dead, and it was maybe time to stop acting like I was.

One song switched to the next, and the next, and I decided, yes, maybe this weekend, I would go to that singles dance that they were holding in the next town over. I was due for some fun. It was time...

Then "Have You Ever Needed Someone so Bad?" came on. Though I turned it off immediately, its first few lines popped the happy thought of my day, and left me feeling deflated. As I pulled into my driveway, the sight of the big blue barn and the sagging corral made me melancholy as I drove past them into the garage.

There were no horses in any of the stalls. We'd talked about getting horses someday, as we both had liked to ride, but Brennan's life had ended before someday had come. I had no time for horses now, anyway.

I parked next to Brennan's vehicle, a red SUV like mine. I'd kept it, as I couldn't bear to sell it just yet.

I walked inside, and my dogs ran up to greet me, Darkness with a toy in her mouth to let me know she had been thinking of me, Ghost just with his usual happy grin. After changing my clothes, I told them it was time we got to work.

* * * *

The chainsaw bit deeply into the wood, severing the branch in seconds. I eased up on the throttle, so as not to hit the ground with the chain and dull it. I didn't want to have to waste time changing it today. I had enough to do getting this last little bit of wood in. I opened the throttle again, and finished the log, the 16" cut pieces falling in a line. The cuts weren't quite as straight as I would have liked, but they'd do well enough to split the pieces anyway. I decided to call it a day after this last piece.

I'd gotten up early to get to my doctor's appointment, and started the wood work when I'd gotten home a few hours ago. There would be time enough tomorrow to take care of some of this work. Rain was forecast for overnight, but that wouldn't impair my gathering up the wood. I could also get some splitting done, too…

When did you stop asking people to chaperone you using the woodsplitter?

I finished cutting, and cleaned off the saw, thinking hard. It bothered me that I'd broken my promise to Brennan, even if nothing had come of it. But what bothered me more was that I couldn't remember when exactly it had happened or why. I'd always respected the inherent danger and power of my machinery. I was always super cautious. *Wasn't I?*

Somewhere this last summer, I had begun chainsawing alone. That wasn't cautious. That was asking for trouble of the worst kind. *You don't even have your cell phone.*

Disturbed, I stored the chainsaw, the gas and oil mix used to fuel it, and the chain lube in my barn. As I closed the door, and walked back to my home, I thought to myself that there was really no need to push myself so hard. I really had enough wood for this winter. What I was cutting now was surplus, most likely to be stored for next year. My mind shied away from continuing the thought, knowing that I had been pushing myself to work until I was exhausted so I wouldn't have to face an empty house.

You would never have done this when Brennan was alive.

I stopped suddenly and looked at the forest. Part of me wanted to go in there, to leave all this behind, and just walk for a while. But my reason said that was stupid, that bears had been sighted in the woods, and night was already falling. *Don't do it, Sar.*

I trudged inside and poured myself a glass of wine, petting Jessica and Cavity. Rain lashed the windows, the sudden pounding startling me.

Why had I been tempted to take a walk in the woods, when I knew that I shouldn't? Was I really getting better? I didn't think of Brennan as much as I'd done last fall, but it had been a year and I still felt a weight on me, a heaviness that always seemed to return when I was alone. I wasn't happy most days, not like I'd been once. Kat was right, that there were only going to be another ten years before I turned 40. It seemed urgent suddenly to make them count.

Putting one foot in front of the other, to keep getting up and trying to make what had been a great life into a passable one had gotten me functioning. Maybe it was time to seek help from others to finish my healing.

My mother and stepfather had been there for me all through that hellish first month. It was at the request of my mother that I had met with a grief counselor for a few sessions. When I had talked about my feelings during the sessions, he said only that my thoughts were normal. I replayed the last conversation I'd had with the counselor again in my head, searching for some clue as to what I could do about the way I felt. Stymied, I resolved to call him tomorrow and make another appointment.

* * * *

"When am I supposed to feel alive again?"

"Sarelle, it's different for everyone. Some people take longer than others to grieve. You just need to keep trying."

"But I still feel hopeless, like there is something missing in my life. I need that to go away. I want my joy back."

"Sarelle, it's not going to go away all at once."

"I understand that, but when am I going to feel like associating with my friends? My family?"

"Have you been seeing your friends or family?"

"Yes. We have a good time together. But I used to look forward to visiting, and now I have to make myself go."

"What about Brennan's family? Your in-laws? Do they still blame you, Sarelle?"

"Yes. Not for the accident itself, but for the fact that he was there at all. We don't speak. We haven't since the funeral."

"You believe that you were not to blame though, correct?"

"Of course!" I said, raking my hand through my hair. "Brennan was stubborn. He was going to do what he wanted regardless of what I said."

"It's true also that you talked about him dying, that he knew he might not come back?"

"That still hurts me. We talked about it the way a travel agent talks about crashing on an airplane trip. He didn't really take it seriously. Neither did I." I felt a sharp pain again, thinking of Brennan laughing about how he had climbed so many mountains, and this was just one more.

"He loved the danger. He thrived on it, and it led him to his death."

"Sarelle, I know it might not feel this way, but you are out of the worst of your grief. In fact, you are handling it better than most. You have a new job, you're making new friends, and you're keeping busy. I don't think you need to come and see me anymore, unless you began to feel depressed again."

"But there is something wrong with me," I persisted. "Since the accident happened, I've been less, um, cautious."

I had his attention now. "What do you mean?"

Mentioning that I chainsawed alone now seemed unremarkable. "I mean I find myself thinking about things that I never would have before."

"Such as?"

Like walking into my forest and being okay with not coming out. "Just odd thoughts. They don't seem like they're mine."

"Elaborate."

"I always used to reach for the phone to call 911 as soon as I got scared, back in the city," I said reluctantly. "But now I don't think I would call, if there was trouble."

The counselor gave me a stern look. "You aren't threatening them with your shotgun, are you? I thought we discussed that was not a good thing for a woman living alone to be doing."

I colored slightly. *Illegal hunters don't count. And you wouldn't say that to me if I were a man.* "Of course not. No one's bothered me, really."

"If someone does, call the police and stay inside."

Why? They would never get there in time, just like for Brennan. "Okay."

His expression remained unconvinced. "Have you had thoughts of suicide?"

"No," I said quickly. "Just thoughts of getting older, and wondering if this is all there is for me. I want there to be more than working and being alone all the time."

"I'm sure you've got a lot of living to do," he said with a smile. "I know it doesn't seem possible now, but this time next year, you may be amazed that you ever felt this low. Life has a way of changing." He handed me a piece of paper from his shelf." Have you ever read this poem?"

"With Every Goodbye," I read aloud. "I think I remember this vaguely from my youth. Isn't it about coping with loss?"

"Yes," he answered. "Take it home and read it. Think about it a little. Then if you want to schedule another session with me, I'll be happy to see you again."

I'd done as he asked. The poem was cheesy in its way, but I did like its message of self-sufficiency. I already knew I was strong and that I had worth. But I'd learned all I wanted to of heartache and loss. I just wanted to find someone with whom to share my joys. That was the lesson he'd wanted me to get; that to really be ready to date again, I had to accept that I might find myself back in this same position someday.

I wasn't ready to do that now. I wasn't sure I ever would be. I was okay with that. The rest of the world would just have to be okay with it, too.

* * * *

I was conveniently curled up on my couch one night in September, cats plural sharing my lap, reading the latest DeMille thriller. Asher was in the basement, which had become her home this past year. She still ventured outside, but only at night. She'd relaxed her guard enough for me to pet her and pick her up, but she still didn't enjoy being held.

My work at the metal shop was going well, and I was looking forward to a slow autumn, instead of the usual rush to the wire to beat winter's harsh descent. Maybe I wasn't all better, but I was going to survive. I'd written my second chapter already this past year, and made a new life from the ruins of the old one. The rest of my story lay before me in the years to come. Maybe there would even be a cowriter. There was plenty of time for a great love to enter stage right. And if it took a few more chapters for that to happen, that was okay, too.

Heart's Bells

(Previously Published in Bedtime Shadows anthology 10-2012)

"Don't you wish we could stay here forever?" Casey murmured softly. She leaned her head back on Theo's broad shoulder, her hopeful sea blue eyes meeting his.

Instead of the loving, or even lustful look she expected to see, Theo's eyes were overcast, his grey-blue eyes dark as storm clouds, his expression grim as he looked out over the quiet mountain lake and surrounding trees nearby. "You know I want that," he replied tersely, even as he shifted her into his arms, hugging her slight body to his muscular one under the thin blanket that covered their entwined bodies. "But it's the end of the semester. With how things stand now, my dad's not going to let me come back next semester. He wants me to pursue 'real work', not 'that art crap'."

"You don't have to listen to him," Casey soothed. "We don't need his money. We've only got a semester left, then we'll graduate. We can start a new life together."

"With what?" Theo scoffed, though he was secretly pleased at her faith in him. "Do you really want to be married to a starving artist?"

Casey turned in his arms, suddenly nervous, scared hope and shock on her face. "You want to marry me?"

"If you'll have me," Theo said with a boyish grin. His smile became wider. "Not that you haven't already copious times, but—"

"Jerk!" Casey said, giving him a good–natured shove. "Don't make light of this. Now are you proposing or not?"

"Yes," Theo said, his smile wavering as he fumbled a small box from his pocket. He cracked it open to display a small diamond ring. "Will you—?"

"Yes!" Casey yelled, her call loud enough to send the birds on the lake into the air, their wings beating frantically as they shouted their annoyance on the breeze.

"I guess we don't need an audience," Theo said, slipping the ring on her left hand. "Do you like it?"

"I love it," Casey gushed, then grabbed Theo's head in her hands, bringing him in for a smoky kiss that consumed them in its passion.

Eagerly, Theo moved atop her, wishing that they never had to leave the mountains, or face the worries of the real world. They'd fallen in love here, he and Casey. This was their special place, near the shore of the lake at Heart's Bells.

* * * *

Hours later, their ardor sated, Theo hugged the sleeping Casey to him. It felt like the best day of his life, and yet, he was scared to death.

His father had threatened to cut his college funding. He wanted Theo to be a lawyer, like he was. Theo's mother was on his side—her father had been a carpenter—but she wasn't willing to stand up to her husband, not even for her son.

Casey had also glossed over a lot of details. Yes, she was close to finishing up her nursing degree, but he would only have an associate's degree by the end of next semester. While he'd saved some money at his part time job, there wasn't enough there for a down payment on a one room apartment. His father would be against this marriage just as he'd been against everything Theo had ever loved...

Theo took a deep breath of mountain air and looked around, trying to forget his father. Maroon Bells, Colorado had never seemed so much like home. Some of that was because his best memories were here, his memories of Casey and falling in love with her. She had always called this place Heart's Bells since they had claimed it for their own.

Theo hugged her close, then closed his eyes, remembering.

21

It had happened two years ago, in fall. He had come up to hike Maroon Lake after moving all his stuff into his dorm. His father and mother had left almost immediately, after a few encouraging words to make sure he was going to attend all the freshmen activities scheduled. Theo waited until their car had disappeared from sight, then taken off in his own small Plymouth Neon. He'd be damned if he was going to attend any stupid orientation. He'd always been a loner, and he was happiest in the woods. That day had been a beautiful one, far too beautiful to waste inside with strangers. Not when the mountains he'd come here to see were finally his to explore.

He'd planned to hike Maroon Lake, and maybe work on a sketch of the famous mountains. The Maroon Bells were some of the most famous mountains in Colorado, and the most photographed, with Maroon Peak being the highest mountain Colorado boasted. If anything was going to inspire him, this would.

The view didn't disappoint. The reddish mountains loomed over the glacier-sculpted lake, perfect and timeless. The hills were awash in fall's vibrant colors, the leaves surreally vivid, as if they had to be a painting, not living breathing nature. But far more interesting was the girl Theo saw before him on the trail, her attention so focused on the view that she didn't hear him approach.

Theo walked up discreetly, sure at any moment the girl would turn, or give some sign she had seen him. Yet he managed to get within a foot of her unnoticed.

"Boo," he said softly in her ear.

"I heard you," she said easily, as if they were old friends. "Don't think you scared me, because you didn't."

"You've got nerves of steel," Theo replied, cracking a smile.

She turned and looked at him, her friendly smile enough to make his breath catch in his throat. Her short blond hair was up in a tight ponytail, her blue eyes teasing. "Don't I know you?"

No, he didn't know her. But God, how he wanted to. "I'm Theo. I'm taking courses at the Colorado Mountain College."

She took his proffered hand and shook it. "Hi. I'm Casey. I'm going there, too. Are you taking EMT classes?"

Theo shifted, suddenly uncomfortable. That was what he'd told his father he was taking. "No, Visual Art."

Casey nodded approvingly. "So you're an artist."

"I'd like to be a sculptor," Theo elaborated, encouraged. "I plan to get an Associate's Degree here, then transfer to a School of Visual Art."

"That's so cool," Casey replied. "You must be really good. I love to draw, but my parents refused to foot the bill for art classes. We settled for EMT, with a longer goal of an Associate's Degree in chemistry." She held up a pad and graphite pencil, an artist's eraser looped around the black painted wood. "Not that I've given up all hope."

"They don't know," Theo blurted out, turning away to look at Maroon Bells. "I lied, told them I was signing up for EMT classes. But I registered for art. They're probably going to make me leave when they find out. But I don't care."

Casey looked at Theo a moment, then at the Maroon Bells in the distance. "You know why they call them the Deadly Bells?"

Theo shook his head. "I've never heard that name for them."

"They're made of mud stone," Casey said. "Not granite or limestone, like other mountains here. That gives them their color. Mudstone is weak and fractures easily. A lot of people have died here in climbing accidents over the years, when the rock they trusted with their life crumbled away."

Theo was silent, unsure if his teasing comment that Casey seemed a little too into tragic events would be welcomed.

"I call them Heart's Bells," Casey continued softly. "Not just because of their pretty color, but because of their nature. Hearts are like that—easily broken." She touched his hand gently. "You should do what you want, Theo. If you think that art is what you were meant to do, don't let anything stop you."

Theo swallowed hard, not trusting himself to respond. Instead, he just clasped her hand in his, looking out over Heart's Bells.

* * * *

It hadn't taken long for Theo to fall for Casey. They'd become fast friends, spending most of their time together, even as Casey introduced him to her circle. Theo had only taken note of one of them, a jock called

Henry who seemed to find any excuse he could to touch Casey. Theo ignored it for the first month, then couldn't stand it any longer.

He and Casey had been hiking around the lake when he'd suddenly blurted the question that had dogged his mind for days.

"Are you in love with him?"

Casey had turned to him, bewildered. "In love with who?"

"Henry. Are you?"

"Of course not, Theo," Casey answered with a smile. "He and I have known each other since grade school—"

Theo was so relieved he grabbed Casey in his arms and kissed her, his desire to possess her and make her his irresistible. Casey kissed him back, her mouth devouring his eagerly as he pushed her back to a tree.

Finally, they separated with a last soft kiss.

"I'm sorry I cut you off," Theo said shyly. Then he straightened and looked her in the eyes. "No, I'm not actually. I'm not sorry at all. And I'd do it again because I've wanted to kiss you for weeks now."

"I know," Casey said coyly. "It's been obvious."

"Why didn't you say anything?" Theo demanded.

"I was hoping for a kiss like that," she said hungrily, tracing his lips with her finger. "It was just as passionate as I hoped."

"Then let me give you another," Theo murmured, covering her mouth with his own.

* * * *

The next year and a half passed like water. Theo loved his art classes, excelling and getting A's, even as he fed the EMT information Casey passed to him about her own medical classes to his parents on his infrequent trips home.

Theo and Casey became lovers within months, that first encounter—like so many of their firsts—near Heart's Bells. They had driven up in the early spring before the tourists, the road slushy with late winter's snow in places. But the area around Maroon Lake was dry. Parking in some trees to the side of the parking area, they had walked to the amphitheater in late afternoon. There, their sleeping bags zipped together, they had made love under the mountain's shadow.

24

Theo had wanted that night to never end. Many other times that summer, they had recreated it together, grudgingly giving the tourists the days and claiming the nights for their own. Theo had found a solace in Casey that he'd never known before. But no one had ever told him before that he was free to be himself, that his art was not only a worthwhile endeavor, but also an exceptional one.

All winter, he had waited for this night, eager to propose to Casey, but wanting to do it here, in this place that had come to mean so much to both of them. She'd agreed to be his. Now there was nothing that could ruin their lives together.

* * * *

When they got back to his dorm room the next morning, Theo's parents were there sitting on his bed, waiting for him with cool expressions.

"How long did you think you could hide this?" his father said angrily, before Theo could say a word. "I didn't pay thousands of dollars for you to play with clay and paint—" His eyes looked scathingly at Casey. "—or to stay out all night. Start packing, Theo. We're leaving."

Casey's hand tightened on Theo's, giving him strength. "No," Theo replied, his blue eyes flashing. "I'm not leaving."

"I've paid for the classes this semester, but that's all," his father answered, not backing down an inch. "You're dropping out, unless you can foot the bill yourself for this room this summer."

Theo's mother was already at his dresser, quietly folding his clothes and putting them into his duffel bag. Theo looked around, startled to see most of his personal affects had already been removed and packed into boxes.

"Have you ever even looked at Theo's work?" Casey accused, her eyes flashing. "He's talented—"

"I'm sure you think he is," his father countered, his double meaning clear. "You must think so, to help him lie to us."

"I didn't want to lie," Casey said quickly. "We were going to tell you—"

"We're getting married," Theo stated, his hand gripping Casey's tightly.

25

"You do, and you'll lose your trust fund," his father threatened. He turned to Casey. "You have enough to worry about on your own, missy. Your parents were the first ones I called when I found out Theo had been lying to us. They're waiting for you at your room right now."

Casey's eyes narrowed. "I've done nothing wrong—"

"Your brother's in the hospital. He was in a car accident," Theo's father said, his tone gentler. "They came here to tell you and found you missing. They called us first, hoping you were at our house—"

Casey's face went white, then her desperate eyes sought Theo's. "I'll be right back." She dashed from the room.

Theo's mother finished packing the last drawer. Without a word, Theo's father grabbed the two full duffel bags and strode from the room.

"How can you let him do this to me?" Theo said brokenly to his mother. "Don't you know how happy I've been here? And I love Casey."

His mother patted his shoulder. "It's for the best. Now please, grab the two boxes. I'll get the last bag."

* * * *

Theo didn't speak to his father for weeks. He tried several times to call Casey, but her parents refused to let him talk to her. His letters were returned, unopened. Finally, he went to the airport, determined to buy a plane ticket to see her. But his card was declined at the terminal, and he was detained by security. An hour later, his father arrived to take him home.

"You can't keep me a prisoner here," Theo said angrily. "I have every right to see Casey—"

"I agree," his father said, then gestured to the road in front of the house. "But you aren't using my money to do it. You want to go, start walking."

Theo cast his father a hateful look, then stalked inside.

* * * *

Before long, it was mid-August. Theo, desperate to see Casey, gave in.

"I'll enroll in the chemistry courses," he said grudgingly, forcing the bitter words out. "I'll take any courses you want me to. Be anything you want me to be. But I have to be near her. I love her, Dad."

26

His father looked up at him, his cold gaze suddenly softening. "I know you do. I just hope she loves you enough." He gestured to the chair. "Sit."

Theo sat, his heart relieved even as he steeled himself to doing his father's will.

"I loved art when I was young, too," his father said. "My parents encouraged me, and I got an art degree. Your mom worked down the street, at a bakery. She got pregnant right after we got married that following spring, after I graduated."

Theo blinked. *His father had loved art?*

"I was good," his father continued. "Very good. But no one would hire me. Sure, I got some small jobs for signs here and there, but that was all. That wasn't enough to support a family, much less you. We ended up moving back in with your mom's parents—your grandparents—right after you were born. I went to work for your grandfather. Over the years, I moved up the ranks in his company. I took over that company when he died a decade ago."

"I know all that—about the company," Theo said. "Why are you telling me like I'm a stranger?"

"Because I don't want you to have to learn the hard way like I did," his father said. "You can do art. I've seen your work, and it's very good. But if you want a life for you and Casey free of handouts, then you need a reliable job. You can't be a dreamer. You have to be a doer."

"Casey isn't like Mom," Theo said, hoping his mother wouldn't be offended, if she was eavesdropping outside the door. "She has a good degree—"

"Do you want her to support you?" his father said bluntly. "How long do you think it will take Casey to decide that working full time while you indulge your love for art isn't her version of happily ever after?"

Theo didn't reply, his conviction wavering.

"You've been rich your whole life," his father said. "Your mother and I spoiled you, because we wanted you to have everything we did as children. But there's going to be a day when we won't be there for you to lean on. I need to know you're prepared for that. I need to know that you'll not just survive, but that you'll have a good life, son."

27

His father had been hard on him his whole life. How much more would he have understood, if his father hadn't waited until he was nearly twenty to tell him all this? But would he have understood if he'd heard this when he was younger, before he'd loved someone? Probably not.

"I booked us a family trip to the Adirondacks next week," his father went on. "I know how much you like the woods, especially as a muse. Your mother is coming with us. We'll hike and talk this over." He paused. "I know that you've completed your two year art degree, for the most part. I want you to think about transferring to a four-year school to pursue graphic design. Computers are essential now to most everyone. With an additional degree, you can pursue your art interests in a career that has a good chance of keeping you and Casey comfortable."

Theo could live with that scenario, if not embrace it. He knew a little about computers, and his father was right. He had to take a more active role in his future, something he had always naively considered would take care of itself. However, he didn't want to agree without inserting a term or two of his own. "So you aren't against us getting married?" Theo challenged.

"Of course not," his father said, irritated. "So long as you are ready to be married. Right now, you aren't." He nodded once. "But in a few years, yes, when you both graduate. In fact, we want to throw you both an engagement party this fall."

"She probably thinks I've forgotten her or something," Theo grumbled. "She might have moved on. We haven't talked in weeks."

"If she can forget you and move on, then she isn't worth marrying," his father said. Then he flashed a small reticent smile. "But I have it on good authority that she is just as much in love with you as you are with her. I wasn't the only parent that stopped their child from getting on a plane this summer."

Theo was silent, considering. His father was trying to make amends. He had to try, too.

"Go get packed, son," his father said. "We leave at noon, sharp. And don't forget long sleeves. The most dangerous things in the woods aren't the bears. They're the ticks."

"All right. I'll pack. Can I call Casey first, though? I want to tell her about the party."

"Yes," his father said, handing him the phone. "I'll be outside."

* * * *

"Theo?"

Hearing Casey's voice after months of just imagining her soft tone was enough to bring tears to Theo's eyes. Immediately he wanted to see her, which just made knowing it would be several more weeks before he could that much harder to bear.

"It's me," he said, closing his eyes. "I'm coming back to school this fall. My father and I have worked out a deal."

"How?" Casey stammered. "Did you give in?"

"Yes," Theo admitted, "But he did, too. He's right that I should be able to help us out financially. I never thought beyond creating, and I needed to. I needed to think about your happiness, not just my own."

"I would have been happy with you," Casey protested. "We would have made it work. I never cared about your family having money or about you leaving it behind."

"We will make it work, Casey," Theo said with conviction. "We're going to have a good life together."

Casey didn't reply.

Theo had a moment of panic. Casey had used the past tense. Had she met someone else over the summer? "Do you still love me?"

"Of course, you idiot," Casey snapped. "I've been waiting for you to call me for months now. I hoped every day to get a letter, a postcard even to tell me that you still cared about me. I was about to mail back the ring."

"Your parents wouldn't let me talk to you," Theo retorted. "My letters all came back."

"I thought you might say that," Casey said, sounding tired suddenly. "My father acted guilty every time I asked him if you'd called. My mother was the same way when I asked about the mail. But I made sure to get the mail most every day. I believed them. I can't believe they lied to me."

"I understand my parents, but why yours?" Theo asked. "I thought they liked me?"

"My brother Carey is still recovering. His back was badly hurt, and he's having to learn to walk again. I've spent most of the summer at his bedside, encouraging him to keep trying, even when it hurt." She paused. "Carey was covering for me that night he was hurt, so I could be with you that last night we had together. He was in that car crash because of me."

"I'm sorry," Theo said, abashed. "Please tell Carey I never wanted anything like this to happen to him."

"It's not your fault. My brother doesn't blame you and neither do I," Casey said vociferously. "Come see me as soon as you can. I'm leaving for school next week."

"I'll be there," Theo said passionately. "Our usual place?"

"Yes," Casey said eagerly. "I'll be there where you first saw me, wearing your ring." She paused. "I love you, Theo."

He would wait to tell her about the engagement party. He wanted to see the look on her face. "I love you," Theo said tenderly. "I'll see you in two weeks."

* * * *

The trip to the Adirondacks was gorgeous. That first week was heaven to Theo, not just for the scenery, but for the extravagant lake house his father had rented.

They fished, went canoeing and then midweek went for an overnight camp out near Tupper Lake. That night, as they sat around the campfire, Theo and his parents discussed not only probable careers for him, but also the upcoming engagement party, which his mother was already in the midst of arranging. Dubious that Casey would want such an elaborate or formal party, Theo almost spoke up a couple of times to tell his mother that she should consult Casey before going farther with her plans. But she was so happy he put it off, reminding himself with a secretive smile that Casey had never had a problem speaking her mind.

That night, as Theo lay listening to the crickets, he again felt at peace. This was going to work out. Maybe he wouldn't be able to use his hands to create sculptures, but he could still use them to make art. Maybe it wasn't everything he had hoped for, but his father was right; he couldn't live in dreams. He had to think of Casey.

There was a noise in the tree line, a rustling too big to be a rabbit or a raccoon.

Theo sat up, then waited, listening and watching.

The rustling came again, closer this time, then a long throaty snort.

Was it a bear? They'd hung their food over there in the tree.

Theo shook his father to his left. "Wake up," he whispered urgently. "There's a bear."

His father woke, registered the words in a split second, then reached for his shotgun. His mother slept on behind them in her sleeping bag, oblivious.

Silence stretched, as Theo and his father waited.

A roaring erupted, a lanky shadow throwing itself at the hanging food. With a snapping sound the branch broke, the food cache falling to the ground.

"That's no bear," Theo's father said in disbelief. "That's a cougar."

"There can't be," Theo protested. "There haven't been cougars here in a hundred years."

"Tell that to him."

The cougar roared again. Theo's mother awoke with a scream. Immediately, Theo and his father turned to comfort her. As they did, a long-limbed shadow burst from the treeline, heading straight for them. It was a cougar, tawny fur matted with blood, its yellow eyes angry.

It launched itself with a howl, tackling Theo's father, knocking him sprawling. The gun went off with a boom. The cat screamed again, this time in pain, its back legs digging with claws, shredding his father's jeans as it ripped with its front paws at his neck. His father grunted, trying to push the monster away and protect his throat at the same time.

Theo grabbed at the cougar, trying to get it off his father, his hands slipping in the bloodied fur. Desperate, he grabbed its ears, trying to pry its jaws away from his father.

The cat let go, then turned, its long fangs sinking into Theo's arm. He shouted in pain, beating at the monstrous head with his free arm. The cat worried his arm, both forearm bones snapping with a sharp crack.

Pain was immediate and excruciating, sickening in its intensity. He went limp, losing consciousness.

* * * *

Theo blinked his eyes. It was morning. He was lying on his back. He sat up, then tried to remember.

The cougar had attacked!

His eyes found his father's crumpled form. Theo crawled over, rolling over the bloodied body. His father was dead, his eyes glazed over, the blood at his ripped out throat still moist in places. His mother was also dead, her throat ripped out, her body partially eaten. Flies were buzzing around the bodies. Maggots had already been born in the wounds and were crawling about eagerly, feasting.

Theo turned and threw up. Then he bit his lip hard, using the pain to make himself move. *He had to get help. He was injured; he'd heard the bone snap... Yet he was bracing his weight on that same arm.*

Theo looked down at his arm, incredulous. While his shirt was rent, half dried blood still covering the flesh, the skin beneath was unbroken.

What the hell?

The crack must have been a branch beneath him, the pain from the sheer jaw pressure of the bite. There was no other rational explanation. What was important now was getting help. The animal had attacked without warning. That meant it was likely rabid. He would need shots very soon, unless he wanted to die.

Theo laid the blood spattered sleeping bags over his father and mother, then grabbed the gun, the few shells left, and his own pack. His father's cell phone was so much smashed plastic. His own was nowhere to be seen.

Theo began staggering back toward the house. He made it to the shore of the lake before collapsing.

* * * *

"Wake up, boy." A boot nudged Theo hard in his side, making him moan.

He blinked his eyes. There was a boy his own age above him, looking down.

"Please help," he said weakly.

"What the hell did you do?" the kid asked. "You've got blood all over you."

Anger flared up inside Theo. He hadn't done anything. The world had once again kicked him in the balls just as everything had been going right. "Do you have a cell phone?"

"Maybe," the kid said. "But I'm not going to let you use it for free."

"Call 911," Theo said. "Please, there's been a murder—"

"I know," the kid said, bringing out a knife. "I saw the bodies."

Theo looked at him, unbelieving. *This couldn't be happening...*

"Give me your wallet," the kid said, brandishing the knife. "I'll put you in the boat, and you can make it back to civilization. That's my one and only offer."

Rage filled Theo. He had lost his father and mother, and this asshole wanted money. He staggered to his feet with a growl of fury, then reached for the kid.

The kid stabbed him without a word, the knife sliding into Theo's side. At the sudden pain, the world went crazy.

Theo roared, his mouth suddenly too full, the sound muffled. He grasped the kid, even as the punk drew his arm back to stab down again.

His hands weren't hands any more. They were paws, huge claws extended.

Those claws raked down, splitting the kid's shirt like butter along with his skin. The scent of blood filled the air. The kid screamed, dropping the knife, pushing away, desperately fighting to live.

With a lunge, Theo buried his teeth in the kid's throat, tearing and pulling. The kid gurgled, struggling weakly, then collapsed. Theo went with him, falling onto the body as he fed.

* * * *

Theo sat up. It was late afternoon. His mouth tasted of blood. Worse, it covered him, and the ruined human body lying right next to him.

It hadn't been a dream.

Theo swallowed his bile, trying to think of what to do.

There was a phone just inside the cabin across the lake. Police could be here within a few minutes, via helicopter. But would they believe his story? *Doubtful.* He'd be carted off to an insane asylum at best.

His father had said a day would come when Theo would have to rely on himself. Here it was. Theo had wished for that day the moment he'd heard his father say the words only a week ago. Now all he wanted was to have his father alive and right here. His father would know how to handle this.

The disgusting evidence was only a few feet away, staring him in the face, the blood on his hands and in his mouth undeniable. Somehow, he, Theo, had become a cougar and killed that kid. It hadn't been a hallucination; it had really happened. But no one would believe that. If they did, they'd put him in a lab and experiment on him.

He had to find a way to cover it all up. But before he left this wilderness, Theo swore to get that thing that had attacked his family and made him a monster. And then, somehow, he had to find a way to get to Casey. She would help him. Together, they could solve this.

* * * *

Theo hid the kid's body in the brush, then used the boat to go back across the lake. He showered off the blood, checking again for bite marks and for a new knife wound. There was none.

"You're a were-cougar," Theo said aloud to his reflection. "Welcome to your new life." He tried to force a smile but couldn't.

Theo called the owner of the house next and asked to reserve it for another week. "Just put the charges on the same card, please."

"Sure," the owner said eagerly. "You and your family having a nice time?"

"The best," Theo managed. "Thanks. Bye."

He ate a large meal, then slept. In the morning, Theo packed some supplies, then headed back out, reaching the scene of his campfire from the night before. The bodies of his parents lay as before. At the sight of them, his rigid façade crumbled. He looked away, then swallowed hard a few times.

You have to be strong. You can only count on yourself now. Stop crying, and do what you came here to do.

Theo sat down near the campfire, laying the gun down, then the pack. "I'm sorry I can't bury you," he whispered softly. "If I do, they'll know I survived. I need them to think that I died, too, at least until I can figure out how to fix this—"

"There's no fixing it," a happy voice said from the tree line. "Trust

34

me, kid."

Theo reached over and clicked the safety off the gun discreetly. "Come in, if you want."

A dirty, naked man slowly ambled in, his expression overjoyed. "I'm so glad to see you," he said, sitting down cross-legged across from Theo. "Tell me your name, please."

Find out all you can. "Theo. Who are you?"

"Professor Ed Staples," the man said, his tone changing slightly, becoming refined. "At least I was once."

"What happened to you?"

"I was out west, doing research on the local populations of elk and mountain lions, studying their reliance on one another. I was attacked by a mountain lion, when I got between her and her cubs. Later that night, when I'd almost made it out of the wilderness, I changed form for the first time." Ed looked up at Theo. "It happened when I was angry, just like the Incredible Hulk. I tore a man to pieces."

Ed laid another log on the fire. "I couldn't go back and risk my wife and kids. So I just disappeared. I buried my clothes and wallet, left everything else and melted back into the wilderness."

Keep him talking. "Why come here?"

"Cougars aren't a protected species," Ed said, a hunted look in his eyes. "I was tracked and hunted, even though I didn't bother any livestock. After getting injured by several bullets, I decided I'd had enough. So I dug up the remains of my wallet, and used the last of my funds to come here. I knew there was enough land to get lost in and hopefully stay lost. Here no one expects to find a cougar. I'm usually laughed off as a large bobcat, when the locals believe that the campers weren't just drunk—"

"Why attack us?" Theo growled. "That doesn't fit with laying low."

"I came here years ago," Ed whispered. "So many years now I've lost count. I see people, and they look strange. I used to be able to follow conversations I overheard. I can't any more—"

He's insane. "You attacked us because you couldn't understand us?"

"No! *You* don't understand!" Ed said plaintively. He reached his arms out to Theo beseechingly. "I couldn't stand being alone any more. There's no one here like me. No one to talk to. I couldn't go on." His tone turned ominous. "And I can't die. Go ahead. Use that gun you've been trying to get into position. You'll see."

Theo grabbed up the gun in a smooth motion, pointing it at Ed. "I planned to."

Before Ed could reply, Theo squeezed the trigger, the recoil knocking the wind out of him even as it blew Ed backwards, the body twisting to fall in a bloody heap.

Theo got up, ejecting a shell as he moved closer. Ed hadn't moved.

Theo fired another shot, this one into Ed's back. Again, Ed jerked. Then he began twitching and shaking, blood pooling beneath his sprawled form.

Taking out a serrated knife, Theo severed Ed's head. To his horror, as soon as he removed the knife, the cut began trying to heal, flesh stretching over the slice, trying to close the wound. Worse, the large hole in Ed's back was also trying to close, even now flesh building in the void before Theo's eyes, the wound becoming smaller and smaller as new flesh appeared at the sides.

Kill him! You hit his heart, and he's still coming back like a damn vampire!

With an inspired cry, Theo sawed at Ed's healing neck, his strength decapitating the man in a few strokes. Standing, he threw Ed's head as far as he could away into the bushes. Then he took off the silver cross his mother had always worn, and put it on Ed's ruined chest, his eyes wide as he settled nearby to wait, his knife at the ready.

Theo kept vigil all night. But Ed did not come back to life. Nor did the silver burn the were-cougar's flesh, or do anything but wink softly in the moonlight shining down from above.

* * * *

The next day, Theo inspected Ed's body. The body had stopped trying to heal and was clearly dead now. The flesh had a bluish cast to it. The blood had dried. The wound was still open, now also drawing flies in the weak morning light. To Theo's sadness, his parent's bodies were also decomposing. As terrible as it was to be a monster, he would have been so much less scared to know his father and mother had joined him in this new life. Angrily, he wiped away tears, telling himself he should be glad that they were dead, that they hadn't become what he had.

Theo buried Ed and his parents. He also buried the kid's body, too, even though he knew it made more sense not to. Now that he'd enacted his vengeance, Theo just wanted it to be finished. When it was done, he said some words over the unmarked graves, then stood a moment, thinking.

The earth here was thick, yet he'd dug the graves in record time, using only a shovel. His strength last night in severing Ed's head had also been extraordinary. In addition to the strength, Theo had gained enhanced hearing and smell. There was a whole host of scents to everything in the world now, the aromas so complex in information that the normal wilderness surrounding him took on a whole new depth. His ears could pick out a number of forest animals roaming the field to his right. A female weasel was in the treeline, her fear overpowering. Belatedly, Theo realized she was afraid of him. Then he noticed his mouth was watering at the thought of warm flesh. Afraid, he packed up his things and jogged back to the lake house.

The rustic setting with its lavish furnishings was surreal. Nothing would be the same from this moment on ever again. Theo's whole world was changing. Yet his mother's sweater was still draped over a chair, her half-finished letter to her best friend on the table. It would never be finished now.

You can't afford to collapse now. You have a lot to do and not much time. Now get busy

The first item on the list of Urgent Things To Handle was food.

Hurrying to the refrigerator, Theo opened the door, the immediate scent of meat irresistible. The steak was raw, yet he couldn't stop himself from gobbling it in great chunks, blood oozing down his chin. When he finished that, he ate a package of hamburgers, then two hot dogs. Sated, he wiped his face, then sat on the couch, his face in his hands.

Second item on the list of Urgent Things to Handle was how to get to Casey.

Theo would inherit all of his parent's money and property, according to their will. Yet with how things were, he would likely be suspected of killing them. He couldn't go back to school. He couldn't go back to his life. That was over, just like Ed had said. He had killed that kid just by getting angry. The cougar within had come out in an instant. He would have to do what Ed had done and stay away from everyone.

But he couldn't lose Casey, not when he'd lost everything else. Besides, he couldn't stay here, even if he wanted to. His parents would be missed, and the police would find the bodies if they looked hard enough. He had to leave. Canada? He'd never been there though. He needed some place he knew well that was remote enough to hide until he figured out a way to get normal again.

Resolute, Theo decided to go back to Heart's Bells. There was enough uninhabited space to hide there. And if there was anyone who could help him now, it was Casey.

* * * *

Theo drove through the next day and night, worried with every cop car he passed that he would see the lights go on as it came after him. His father had carried little cash, only a credit card. Theo had used it at several banks to get cash advances until he reached the card's limit, then left it behind in a truck stop bathroom close to the Canadian border. Someone would either report it or take it to use. Either way, the police wouldn't be on his trail.

He'd had to take his parent's brand new BMW SUV. But he had switched the plates with another totaled SUV at a car repair shop late the next night. It was the best he could do. With all that he had already given up, Theo couldn't risk losing his means of a quick getaway, too.

Luck was with him. He made it to Colorado without mishap or even a close call. He drove up to Heart's Bells and stashed the vehicle in the hidden spot that he and Casey had used so many times before. Taking his pack and remaining money, he got out and looked around.

Now what was he going to do? Wait for Casey to come and find him? He dared not go into the college grounds to find her. Even if he could contact her, he couldn't risk her being around him. But how would he tell her in a phone call what had happened and make her believe it?

Some plan, jerk.

His thoughts black, Theo walked into the hills, the setting sun illuminating the red mountains and setting them ablaze with color.

* * * *

Heart's Bells

The last weeks of August passed quickly for the rest of the world, as students entered dorms for the first time, teachers readied lesson plans, and families had one last party or trip before fall descended. For Theo, the days stretched long and lonely. Worst of all, he was starving.

He had initially tried to change form and found he couldn't. Even at night, with the full moon high above him, he couldn't will a transformation. Fury filled him. Fury at the unfairness of the world, the sheer meanness of it, to have given him everything and taken it away all in the space of a few weeks. In his anger, he began screaming, the human wail of suffering becoming a loud roar that echoed down the mountain. Claws grew in an instant, fur sprouting from his skin, his mouth suddenly full of fangs. Chest heaving, Theo padded down to the amphitheater, turning his round yellow eyes up at the moon above. He sat down with a sigh. Anger fueled the change. Once it started, he couldn't stop it. What hope was there for him and Casey?

He would have to make sure she was safe from him before he went to her. He would have to tame the lion within.

* * * *

As a human, Theo was a decent shot with a scatter-gun. But it was hard to skin the animals with his pocket knife. The ammunition for the gun soon ran out. Starving, Theo forced himself to change to cougar, then used his new body to hunt. At first, he was awful, over leaping the prey every time. He caught a mouse, only to have it bite him. Shocked at the sharp pain, he shook his paw, flinging the creature into the lake. By the time he got there, it had swum to shore and gotten away.

With practice and time, he got better. It wasn't long before he could stalk his food easily, and keep himself fed, even if he was never truly full.

The first week of September, Theo decided he had mastered his beast, at least enough to risk a visit to Casey

* * * *

Theo got up early the next morning, before dawn. Then he walked down to his hidden SUV, determined to seek out Casey and tell her everything.

Instead, Casey was there, asleep inside the SUV.

As Theo made to back up, a branch snapped under his heel. Casey opened her eyes, startled awake, then her jaw dropped as she beheld him. At first, she just stared at him as if he were a ghost. Then Casey threw open the car door and ran to Theo, wrapping her arms around him.

"I thought you were dead! What happened? They found your parents murdered, and this decapitated guy—"

Tell her right now, or you never will.

"—they said it was a mountain lion or wild dogs—"

"It was me," Theo said softly. "I killed that man and cut his head off."

Casey recoiled from him, stepping away. "What?" she asked in disbelief.

"He attacked my parents and me. He did something to me. Now I can change into a cougar. I know it sounds crazy—"

Casey looked scared for a second, then resolute. "I knew it had to be something like that. They'd been looking for that man for years, Theo. His fingerprints were at a ton of murder scenes in that area. They called him the Tupper Lake Killer." She put her hand on his, like she had done years ago on the day they'd first met. "You didn't do anything wrong. You defended yourself." She squeezed his hand. "He had just killed another person that same morning—"

"No," Theo whispered tortured. "I killed that kid, too."

"Then you had a reason," Casey said fast. "I didn't want to say it, but he'd been linked to some break ins at the lake houses near the ones your family rented—"

"I needed his phone," Theo said wearily. "I told him to call 911. He wouldn't. I ripped him to shreds."

"No," Casey comforted. "You couldn't have—"

Theo's desperation turned to panic, then rage. "I did it!" he screamed. "It was me! It wasn't an animal. It was me!"

Casey's eyes went wide, and she backed away. "Your eyes," she choked out. "They're yellow."

Theo shut his eyes, collapsing to the ground, trying to fight the change. "Please," he said aloud. "Please, please stop. Please don't. Please!"

Theo fought his anger, the seconds ticking by into minutes. He breathed deep breaths, the air scents so familiar. Casey's scent was there, too, though it stank of fear and anxiety. Theo pushed it aside, trying to concentrate on staying calm, on keeping his human form.

There was a gentle touch of a hand taking his. "I'm here," Casey said softly. "You're okay, Theo. You're going to be okay."

Theo gathered himself, then opened his eyes, praying they weren't yellow. "I'm not okay," he said. "I'm not ever going to be okay again."

"Yes, you will," Casey said, hugging him hard. "I'm not losing you, not to this, or to anything else. We'll find a way to get through this, just like we did everything else.

"This isn't the same," Theo said, hugging her back gently. "There isn't a cure, Casey."

"Then we'll find a way to live with it," Casey said firmly. "When I said I'd be your wife, that meant for better or worse, for the rest of my life. I'm not going anywhere."

With her in his arms, Theo closed his eyes, daring to believe that might be true.

* * * *

The next week was like old times. Casey would meet Theo at night and bring him takeout food, which he ate ravenously. But when she tried to hug him, Theo kept his distance.

"Are you scared you'll hurt me?" she said finally.

"I'm scared that I'll change you into what I am," Theo admitted, grasping her hand and squeezing. "I don't know why my parents died, and I didn't."

"I don't think kissing me will do the job," Casey joked, hugging him.

Theo let out a sigh, then grabbed her tightly in his arms, hoping he wasn't squeezing too hard. "But sex might."

"Not protected sex," Casey whispered. "I stopped at the store on the way here."

With just the mention of sex, Theo's heart rate doubled, desire for Casey flooding his being. "Are you sure?" he protested feebly.

"I'm sure," Casey said, covering his lips with hers.

* * * *

41

Theo's eyes opened to see Casey smiling up at him. "You wore me out," she said, languidly kissing his nose. "I could get used to this, Theo."

He shifted uncomfortably even as he smiled. He had lasted inordinately long during sex and recovered faster than he ever had. In fact, he wanted Casey as much as he had yesterday, his body throbbing with need. But she was clearly too tired, already dozing in his arms.

Fighting his desires, he closed his eyes. He could fight this if he tried. He had to, for Casey's sake.

* * * *

As fall wound down into winter, tension grew between Casey and Theo. Though they had talked at length of what they should do, they could come to no good solution. Both of them were afraid of taking anyone in the medical field into their confidence. Food was becoming scarce, as Theo had devoured or scared off most of the local game. His own money had run out some time ago. He was depending more and more on Casey, not only for food, but other necessities. Yet with the worsening weather, the seasonal road to Heart's Bells would soon be closed.

"We have to move on," Casey said finally one night, as Theo devoured the burgers she had brought him. "You've been seen by a few people now. There's talk of the local sportsman's group organizing a mountain lion hunt."

"That won't happen," Theo placated, hoping he was right. "No one takes the sightings seriously."

"They've found your tracks," Casey replied, morose.

"That can't be," Theo argued. "I've been careful."

"There's nothing for us here anymore," Casey said, sudden tears in her eyes. "I can't do this, Theo. We need to find someone to help us."

"Who?" Theo retorted, even as his heart sank with a lead weight of despair.

"There must be others like you," Casey said hesitantly. "That man, Ed, said that he'd been infected in Colorado. The were-cougar that infected him had cubs. Even if she's dead, her children must still be here. We could try to find them. You can't be the only one."

42

"Say I'm not the only one," Theo whispered worriedly, taking her hand. "I never believed in the paranormal. But if were-cougars are real, why not werewolves? Vampires? Ghosts? Something tells me if I go looking for others like me, I'm not going to be able to hold onto you."

Casey looked away and didn't answer.

Terrified of the answer, Theo still made himself utter the question. "Are you done with me?"

"I don't know if I can be what you are," Casey whispered. "I need to know that I could be myself. I see a look sometimes in your **eyes**—"

There was a scream of rage from above. Theo and Casey looked up. On the rocks above, a cougar snarled.

It was a female. It had been attracted by his scent and by the meat Casey had brought. The animal's scent was livid, hungry…ready to lunge.

"Run!" Theo shouted, giving Casey a push that instead knocked her sprawling. Then he turned, his eyes already yellowing as the cougar hurled itself into him. Knocking him off his feet, the two rolled over and over, Theo's bellows of anger becoming animal screams as his form twisted and sprouted fur, his claws slashing. The forms landed at the cusp of the outcropping, the cougars wrestling and clawing each other as first one then the other came close to toppling over, then pulled back.

"Help!" Casey screamed. "Help please!"

The cougars were fighting, each one screaming again and again furiously as the other landed blows, ripping open muscle and skin, the scent of blood filling the air.

A shotgun blast ripped the air, silencing the screams in the space of a heartbeat. There was a scream of pain, and the two cougars went over the outcropping, disappearing from sight.

An older hunter ran up. "Knew that I'd get lucky if I stayed here after sunset," he said with glee. "Where did it go?"

"Over the outcrop," Casey stammered. She ran after the man, who was already climbing down the steep embankment to claim his prize.

The crumpled body of the cougar rested at the bottom, a bullet hole in its chest. Casey went to her knees and began to sob.

"Keep back," the man cautioned, pulling her back from the body. "You don't know that it's dead, though my shot was true. Just wait a moment."

Casey continued sobbing, all the stress and frustration of the ordeal pouring out of her in a loud cry of anguish.

* * * *

Theo watched as Casey cried, wanting to go to her, blinking back tears of his own. But there was no other choice. He had to let her go. She could never live his new life with him, unless he turned her like Ed had turned him. More and more, he had been tempted to, knowing if she was a were-cougar too, she wouldn't leave him. And if that cougar hadn't attacked them when it had, he might have done it right then.

He needed to get away from her, far away, where he wouldn't be tempted. Once he was gone, Casey could get on with her life. She had stuck by him when a lot of other girls would have walked away, if not run. The very least she deserved was to be cut loose before he hurt her.

Theo turned and padded away westward. There was a quarry over the rise. A large construction site was nearby. With his new strength, maybe he could get a job there. At the least, he could hide there a few days while he figured out what to do. Ed's disappearance had to be recorded somewhere. He would find out where the scientist had been working and go there, by foot if he had to. Casey was right, there had to be more were-cougars out there. He just had to find them.

Total Eclipse of the Heart

(Also published in the Vampires for Charity Anthology 2013)

"Forever's gonna start tonight…forever's gonna start tonight!" The words rolled off Heather's lips, her joy in each melodic phrase obvious to her audience.

And why not? Heather thought. Tonight might very well be the night she joined her vampire lover in his world of darkness. God knows, he'd kept stringing her along close to a year now. But Dev had promised to turn her, once she was sure being a vampire was what she wanted. The only problem left was convincing her prince of darkness that she was ready to take her rightful place at his side.

She knew that Dev loved to hear her sing. He often told her that it had been her voice he'd noticed first in the bar called Eclipse that warm April night they first met.

"Your longing brought me to you," a seductive voice had whispered in her ear as she stood at the bar after loud applause, triumphantly ordering a drink. When she'd turned with her hand ready to slap the offender, Heather's words had caught in her throat. This wasn't some old letch trying to take liberties. This was a dream man come to life complete with shoulder length shimmering blond hair, wickedly gleaming honey-colored eyes, and a body to die for. He was dressed in jeans and a black T-shirt, but his jacket was butter soft leather of an unusual light grey color.

"Devlin," he'd said in an amused tone, paying for her drink. He handed it to her. "Now tell me your name, so we won't be strangers."

Heather had swallowed back her words. *How had he known I was going to say my mother told me not to talk to strange handsome men?* "Heather."

"Join me for a drink. Heather." Devlin had walked into the crowd without a backward glance.

I followed, just as he was certain I would.

At first, Heather had been too starstruck to say much. Devlin had appeared completely at ease in comparison, asking Heather about her choice of song. "You're a little young to be a Benetar fan."

"That's Taylor, not Benetar," she corrected.

"Very good, Heather. But you didn't answer my question."

"I like power ballads," Heather had answered sheepishly. "My older brother was always listening to music when I was little."

"This is even more interesting," Devlin chuckled. "Your brother liked power ballads?"

"No," Heather laughed, losing some of her unease. "But he had a lot of girlfriends, and a few of them did. I must have heard this song a hundred times the summer it came out."

"I noticed," Devlin said with a touch of appreciation. "Most karaoke singers tend to stumble over lyrics, because they don't know them. The rhythm of the song is lost. But you barely looked at the screen."

"The version that they play as background music rarely matches the song," Heather replied with a frown. "I mean, the song as I listened to it. There are shorter parts with no lyrics, and some lyrics get edited out. So I have to check every now and then to make sure that I'm in the right place."

"I think we're both in the right place," Devlin teased, his implication clear. Then he sang, "I need you now, tonight. And I need you more than ever." He paused, his faint smile more than a little inviting.

Devlin's voice…it's like pure sensation. He's singing my song to me. How romantic is that? Inspired, Heather sang back," If you only hold me tight, we'll be holding on forever."

Devlin burst out laughing.

Embarrassed, a flush colored her cheeks quickly. Grateful of the darkness, Heather moved to get up.

Devlin grabbed her wrist. "Please, don't go." His tone was serious. "I wasn't laughing in jest, but out of surprise."

Heather stood unmoving, still not sure she should trust Devlin. She watched him, expectant yet wary.

"Turn around, Bright Eyes," Devlin sang to her. He released her wrist, then held out his hand to her. "I just am happy to have someone sing to me for a change."

"Are you a professional?" Heather said, shifting from foot to foot, still wondering if she should ditch him.

"I was at one time," Devlin said wearily, his expression becoming pained. "And if you're looking to be a performer, I can assure you it's overrated."

Did he think she was a groupie? "No," Heather said coolly, glad she could prove him wrong. "I'm actually training to be a nurse. I've only got another year of college before I can get my Associate's degree and apply for a job, hopefully one that will reimburse my costs to get a Bachelor's degree. With my GPA, my advisor said I'm a good candidate."

"Commendable," Devlin said with approval. "But I understand how with the pressure you must be under, that every now and then you want to slip away."

Heather nodded. "I'm taking a lot of pre-med courses. I thought that college was supposed to be spring breaks and partying and all these social activities. But all I do is study all the time. I don't have time to socialize much, not if I want to maintain my GPA for my scholarship."

"You must have friends?" Devlin persisted. "Classmates to cut loose with? A boyfriend?"

"Lots of friends," Heather admitted, hoping he wouldn't detect the lie. "But no one special, not since high school."

"I know how lonely that can get," Devlin said softly. His hand closed over hers. Heather was surprised at its coolness. "But you don't have to be alone now, Heather."

Heather drew her hand away. "You're moving a little fast for me."

"My apologies," Devlin said. He stood. "I just meant that I'm usually around, if you want someone to talk to." He offered her a card. "Here's my cell. If you want some company some night, just call."

Heather took it, then drew herself up to face him. "Devlin, you're sexy as hell, but something's off here. Your jacket likely cost more than my textbooks this semester, not to mention that you haven't said one word about yourself." She glared at him, then handed the card back. "Are you married?"

Devlin burst out laughing again. "God, you are just what I needed tonight," he said happily. He took her hand and kissed the top of it gently with cool lips. When his gaze met hers, his eyes that had seemed golden before now had a reddish tint. "No, I'm not married." He stepped closer, his hands resting on her shoulders then sliding down to enfold her. "You have a plan for your life, Heather. I'm not going to hinder that. But I'd like to spend some nights with you, if you'd like my company."

He's offering friends with benefits, Heather thought. There was nothing to consider. All she'd had to do was feel his arms around her once and she wanted him. "When?"

"Tomorrow at dusk," Devlin whispered in her ear. "I'll send a car for you. Write your dorm address on this." He passed her a pen and blank white index card. "That way it won't get lost."

If he wasn't so hot, this would be too weird. Heather did as he asked, then hesitantly gave it back. Devlin pocketed it, then handed her another card with his name on it in silver lettering and his cell number. "Adieu." He kissed her, the sudden sensation making her heart race. Then he was gone, slipping away into the crowd.

* * * *

That next night Heather had been apprehensive as she waited, sure that Dev had been a dream and that no car would show up. But a black SUV truck of some kind was waiting for her as she made her way to her dorm from her last class. She ran inside, dumped her knapsack on a chair, changed clothes, took a few minutes to freshen up, then hurried outside to the SUV. The driver asked her name, and then got out and opened the door for her to get in the backseat. He didn't offer his name, though Heather thought he had an Italian accent. She got in, eager to see

Devlin but also apprehensive. *I've never done anything like this. What if something bad happens?* She pushed the thought away. *Everyone else on this campus probably does risky stuff a lot worse than this every weekend. This is my chance to have an adventure, something just for me.*

The car took her to a Hilton, the fanciest hotel in town. She was shown up to a suite. Devlin opened the door when she was still a few steps away from it, attired in a business suit. "Come in," he said. "Make yourself comfortable.'

Heather set down her purse, then cast her eyes over the room with its couches and chairs, vases of fresh flowers, and several TVs. "Very nice." She flushed immediately at how dumb that sounded. "That's kind of an understatement," she added quickly. "It's gorgeous."

"I wanted privacy for us," Devlin said, locking the door. He strode to the table, shutting the laptop that rested on it with a soft click. "I have something to ask of you, Heather."

Was he going to ask her point blank for sex? This was too weird. "Yes?"

"I want you to be a donor," Devlin said hesitantly. "A blood donor."

Heather stared at him, blinking in incomprehension. "What?"

"I'm a vampire," Devlin said. He smiled at her, pulling back his lips to reveal large canines, both upper and lower.

Heather let out a shriek, then darted for the door. Devlin had hold of her before she had taken a second step. "Stop," he urged, even as she struggled in his grip. "I'm not going to hurt you, Heather. Please trust me. You are in no danger."

Heather sank to the floor, her knees giving out. "I thought…I thought that you wanted me."

"I do want you," Devlin said with desire, crouching before her. He put his hand on her shoulder. "I already have other donors, Heather. But not a one of the current group likes music, not as I do." He scowled. "I want someone to talk to."

"Why?" Heather asked, trying to make sense of the fact that vampires were not only real, they also appreciated music and got lonely.

"Every now and then I get a little bit tired of listening to the sound of my tears," Devlin said bitterly, standing smoothly. He turned away from her. "The words you sang last night moved me, Heather. Do you

49

know what it is to have lived hundreds of years and feel like the best of them is past? To feel old, empty, and irrelevant?"

"You're not irrelevant," Heather murmured. "And you don't look old."

"So many humans worry about looking old when they feel young inside," Devlin said passionately. "But there is no surgery for looking young and feeling ancient." His expression was sardonic. "And even if there were, it likely wouldn't be of any use to me."

Heather went to him, her arms going around his waist. "Do you want me to sing you some Benetar?" she offered, laying her head against his strong back.

"No," Devlin said in a gentle tone. "Sing me something happy." He turned in her arms, sinking to his knees in front of her. "And let me lose myself in you."

Heather ruffled his hair with her fingers, then began singing the same song she'd began at the club. Before she was halfway, Devlin stood, effortlessly picking her up in his arms and carrying her to the bed.

"I thought you wanted to hear me sing?" she teased.

"I adore your voice, but that song is not altogether happy," Devlin said, his sad tone at odds with his lustful smile. "And the truth is I can't wait, Bright Eyes. I want you now more than ever."

He pulled off their clothes, Heather helping him eagerly. Then he pressed his naked body to hers, parting her legs. Heather froze, then pushed him away. "Let me get my purse."

"There is no risk of any condition a condom could prevent," Devlin murmured. Yet he took the proffered packet from her and slipped one on without argument. Then Heather was in his arms, Devlin's kisses inflaming her tingling skin as he again parted her legs. When she felt him try to enter, she froze up.

"You're huge," she said in surprise.

Devlin bent up her left leg at the knee, groaning as he eased inside a few inches. Heather let out a sharp cry as she stretched to accommodate him.

"I'll be gentle," Devlin murmured, pausing to thrust very slowly in and out. "In time you'll let me enter easily." He resumed his kissing, trailing from her cheek to her breasts, each touch making her groan in pleasure, her lust for him building higher with each passing moment. Heather's body's grip on Devlin's manhood slowly loosened. Gently he stroked her clit, teasing and probing. Heather responded at once, arching her back, want and need flooding her senses. Sudden moistness caressed Devlin's erection, spurring him to action. Devlin pushed in further, sliding most of the way inside. Heather again let out a sharp cry at the overly full feeling.

"As soon as I heard your voice I couldn't wait for this," Devlin murmured, kissing her throat, her face, her lips. His left hand cupped her right breast, his right arm bracing his body as he began to thrust in long strokes.

Heather's body loosened again, lubrication allowing Devlin's stiff organ to penetrate deeper. She began moving in tandem with Devlin's thrusts, sweat beading on her naked breasts.

Devlin paused, then rolled onto his back with practiced ease, his body not leaving Heather's. His hands cupped Heather's buttocks, pressing down forcefully. The last inches of his penis slid inside, the sharp pain making Heather cry out yet again.

"I don't care how many lovers you've had before me," Devlin said feverishly, working her hips back and forward on him as he thrust again and again. "I possess every inch of you. You're mine."

Heather panted, her eyes drowning in the sight of him below her, his golden eyes riveted on her, matching her body thrust for thrust. *She was his.* All she was had become one single powerful desire: to climax.

Devlin's breathing became more ragged, his thrusts more rapid, each inward motion deep. Heather wavered, the climax nearing, then ebbing. She chased the teasing sensation, then pushed hard, feeling the beginnings of release wash over her, the cry tearing out of her throat with abandon. Devlin pulled her down into his arms as the orgasm ebbed. Then it blossomed anew as a second orgasm hit her with the penetration of his fangs into her skin, each pull of his mouth bringing fresh waves of pleasure. Too soon it was ending, as Devlin's lips broke free to scream out his own release.

He slumped beneath her, panting hard, then looked up with a lazy smile. "Did I fulfill your expectations?"

"Not yet," Heather lied, her tone wavering with post coital bliss. "But you will before I'm done with you, Devlin."

Devlin smiled, then pulled her down beside him, slipping out of her. "I'll say it again; you're just what I needed." He hugged her. "And call me Dev, please."

Heather curled up beside him. "Do you mind if I rest before we do it again?"

Devlin laughed. "You have a few moments." He kissed her cheek. "But tonight, that's all I'll allow. I've got too much to show you, Bright Eyes. This night will be your revelation."

* * * *

That night with Dev…nothing Heather had shared with her high school boyfriend Carl had come close. It *had* been a revelation, just as her vampire lover had promised. Devlin knew positions she'd never heard of, and had skill she'd only seen the like of in steamy erotic novels. Poor Carl had been bumbling by comparison. But then it really wasn't fair to compare a hundred year old man with a sixteen-year-old boy. In addition, there had also been the blood donation part of their loveplay, something Heather had worried was going to be icky. Instead, the experience had turned out to be exhilarating. Devlin had bitten into Heather's neck a second time later that same evening. She'd orgasmed almost immediately, the sensation surprising Heather as they hadn't been engaged in sex at the time.

"Is it always like this?" she'd asked tentatively afterwards, when she was lying in his arms. "I'd always thought that a woman swooning when being bitten in the movies was bunk."

"No," Devlin said with a half-smile. He kissed her cheek. "You're very sensitive to my bite."

Heather had raised herself up on one arm. "You can do better than that," she chided. "Tell me the real reason."

"Apologies, my nurse in training," Devlin said contritely. "A better answer would be that you're sensitive to the virus that gives me my vampire attributes, specifically to the numbing component in my saliva." He hugged her. "Most women enjoy the embrace and the blood donation doesn't hurt; there's a small pleasure. But some—like you—are very sensitive and feel a heady rush."

"And this virus in you also gives you the ability to heal me after you're done drinking?"

Devlin nodded. "Yes. You'll have not a scratch from our times together." He laughed. "No turtlenecks required."

"But what about exposure?" Heather asked, her brow furrowing. . "You said the magic word: virus. Won't I be vampire eventually?"

Devlin shook his head. "No. I'd have to turn you for that to happen. Small amounts of the virus—such as in my saliva—are not infective." He smiled. "Nor is the amount present in semen."

Heather was intrigued. "Tell me more. How do you turn someone?"

"Don't worry," Devlin said persuasively, stroking her hair. "I won't do it."

Heather lay in his arms, blissful. *But what if I want you to?*

* * * *

Weeks had passed, then months. Heather came to Devlin regularly, always meeting him in the Hilton. The lovemaking was mind-blowing, especially the moment when Devlin took her blood. But Heather was growing more and more obsessed with Devlin. She hated waiting for the two weeks to pass between visits, hated that she never talked to him except on the nights she saw him, hated that she couldn't be with him all the time. She withdrew from her friends, spending more and more of her time alone, fantasizing about Devlin, about what she and he could have if he would turn her.

She was lying on the grass daydreaming about Devlin one late July afternoon when she felt a nudge with a shoe. Startled, her eyes flew open to see a pair of sparking green ones looking down into hers.

"You'd better sleep inside if you're going to moan aloud like that."

"Ulysses!" She pulled her brother down next to her, then shoved him. "Jerk! You scared me."

Ulysses caught her hands in his. "I'm here because you've scared me. What's going on with you? You got an incomplete in one of your classes last semester, and a C in another."

"They were hard," Heather mumbled. "Especially Cell Biology." *And the night before the final was one of Devlin's nights.*

"But you always used to come home over the summer," her brother said, worried.

"I planned to take a summer course to make up the incomplete." *But I couldn't concentrate on it, so I dropped it after the first week.*

"What are you into," Ulysses asked gently. "You can tell your older brother. I only want to help. Is it drugs? Drinking?"

Heather shook her head emphatically. "I'm fine."

Ulysses's eyes narrowed. "You're not fine. Even mom and dad are worried about you—"

Her guilt intensified. "Will you lay off me," Heather said angrily. "I worked my ass off for the last five years. Hell, before that, in high school! I got high honors and did everything I was supposed to! I want to have some fun for a change! Everyone else gets to. It's my turn!"

Ulysses drew back in shock, his expression apologetic. "I'm sorry. I know you've been working hard. I just know how much this meant to you."

Meant was the right word. Heather kept silent, unwilling to share her new doubts about her proposed nursing career.

"I want you to know that there's nothing I wouldn't do for you," Ulysses murmured, laying his hand on her shoulder. "I'm always here if you want to talk, sis. And so is Diana."

Diana, her little sister. "How she doing?"

"Taking the high school drama club by storm. In fact, that's another reason I'm here. She's giving a performance this weekend as Juliet, and she wanted both of us to see her."

Saturday was Devlin's next night. But Heather hadn't seen Diana since she'd left to return to school after Christmas. "I'll come," she said slowly.

* * * *

Heather shifted in the plastic auditorium seat. Only a few more minutes to intermission. Not that Diana hadn't been excellent as Juliet. But she'd also been the only teen with talent in the play; Romeo was sadly lacking in looks as well as talent. Heather was eager to escape her parents' and brother's company to check her messages. Dev had never replied about her cancelling their appointment for later tonight.

Heather made her way outside, then checked. To her delight, there was a new voice message from Devlin. But it was disappointingly short. "Call me when you get this."

Heather clicked to her contacts, calling his cell. Devlin answered right away. "Are you all right?" he said immediately.

The concern in his tone made her warm all over. "I'm fine," she said. "I just had to attend a play."

"When will it be done?" Devlin pressed. "I can send someone for you after, if you like."

There was no question that she wanted to see him. But Heather also liked that he was so eager to see her, and wanted it to last. "I'm not sure. Do you want to come to the theater and wait for me?"

"That's not wise," Devlin said gently. "For either of us. Go back to your dorm, and I'll send a car like usual."

Heather was torn. "I might not be back until dawn," she said. "I'm with my family, and they mentioned something about a late dinner out, then my brother talked about taking Diana out for her first drink—"

"Call," Devlin interrupted, his tone making it an order. "I don't care if it is noon. I do not have to sleep in the daytime, and can afford to face tomorrow night a little sleepy." He laughed, the seductive sound giving Heather a delicious shiver. "We can put those hours to better use, my Bright Eyes. I want to see you." He paused, then sang seductively, "I need you now, tonight."

Whatever resistance remained evaporated. "I will." Heather assured him.

* * * *

Heather didn't get to the Hilton until daybreak. Instead of Devlin opening the door as he usually did, a small man dressed in black answered the door after Heather knocked. His expression was cold, but he opened the door, gesturing for her to come in.

"Come in," Devlin called from inside.

The man in black nodded to her, then closed the door after she was inside. "I'll be outside," he said gruffly, then left, shutting the door behind him.

"I'm in the tub," Devlin called. "Come in and join me, Bright Eyes."

God, all she had to do is hear his voice. Heather moved as if a moth to a flame to the bathroom. Devlin was sitting in the Jacuzzi, smiling wickedly. *And his voice is nothing next to the way he looks at me with those eyes.* She quickly undressed and slipped into the tub. "Who was that?"

"A guard, as its day," Devlin answered, kissing her hand. "It's normal procedure for me in daylight."

"I could have waited till tonight to come," Heather said teasingly, her double meaning clear. "What was so urgent?"

"The truth? That I enjoy our times together," Devlin said easily. "I enjoy your desire for me, Heather. I wasn't going to wait, given a choice." He pulled her close, hugging her on his naked lap. "And I confess to being a little worried, too." He kissed her forehead. "You'd never cancelled before."

"Family stuff," Heather said vaguely, not wanting to tell him about her family's concern for her, or their repeated urging for her to come home for the remainder of the summer to rest. "I hoped you could meet them."

"I think they would frown on our arrangement," Devlin said with a chuckle. "Even if they thought I was mortal and that it was only sex."

Heather didn't answer. *How did Devlin view their relationship? He'd just admitted it was more than sex to him, too.*

"Do you want any breakfast?" Devlin offered. "I can have something sent up from room service."

"I want to go somewhere with you," Heather said softly. "I love being with you, Dev. I want to see you more. I know you said we can't be like this more than every two weeks. But we could do other things—"

"No," Devlin said gently. He kissed her cheek. "You're my favorite donor, Bright Eyes. I'm risking enough by seeing you this much. Most donors I see only once a month at most."

"Why?" Heather asked boldly. "You've never really said why that is."

"You are mortal and I'm vampire," Devlin said patiently. "That will change if I'm not very careful."

Heather sat up and looked at him angrily. "Don't keep me in the dark. Tell me the truth!"

Devlin looked momentarily irritated, then his patient expression resumed. "The vampire virus—for lack of a better label—will eventually cause a sickness in donors who donate too much blood too often. You've heard the vampire legends in stories, such as the death of maidens from repeated nightly vampire visits? They are based on that fact."

Heather moved to get out of bed, but Devlin grabbed her. "No, you wanted to hear it. Hear the ugly truth. Being with me too much will kill you, Heather. You have a good future mapped out, one I don't want to screw with." He leaned in close, lips within a hair's breadth of hers. "Take what I have to give and don't ask for more."

"I'm not afraid of turning into what you are," she said, reaching out for him.

"You should be," Devlin said darkly, getting out of bed. "I think we need to take a break for a while, Heather." He began getting dressed. "I'll walk you downstairs."

Heather gathered her clothes, wiping back tears.

* * * *

Heather shut the door of the car, then stepped back as it pulled away from the curb. Unlike other times, Devlin hadn't kissed her goodbye at his hotel door, or said he'd call.

I should have told him I was in love with him. That it didn't matter what he was or what I would need to become to share his life. Now it was too late.

Heather went to her room, turned her ITunes onto Total Eclipse of the Heart, hit endless repeat, and dissolved into tears.

* * * *

"Wake up."

Heather sat up groggily. "Who?"

"Your brother," Ulysses said angrily. "And I don't want any more lies. Who was that guy you went to see at that hotel?"

Heather opened her mouth to say *my boyfriend*, but shut it. Devlin was not her boyfriend. He was a vampire, and she was just his donor, a thought that made her flush.

Her brother took it for admission. "He's married, isn't he?"

"No," Heather insisted. "We meet there because it's easy when he's here on business."

"Oh really?" Ulysses said mockingly. "What business is he in?"

Heather glared at him, saying nothing. Devlin never talked about where his money came from. He rarely talked about himself at all. They talked about songs and music and movies and current events, sang to one another—sometimes duets—and had sex. Her time with Devlin had been relaxing, a diversion from her schoolwork…until it had eclipsed her life.

"Fine, don't tell me," Ulysses said, furious. "I'll find out on my own."

A shiver of fear went through Heather. Devlin had never hurt her, never so much as yelled at her. Yet he had always set the rules of their relationship, right from the beginning. And the look of the man in black at Dev's hotel room door had spoken volumes about the kind of people Devlin knew. "No. Leave it alone."

"No," Ulysses said wrathfully. "You're my kid sister and he's taking advantage of you."

"It's over, all right?" Heather burst out, blinking furiously to push back her tears. But they spilled out anyway. "We broke up last night. So just leave it alone! Get out!"

Ulysses turned away from her and stormed out.

Heather closed the door after him, shaking. Ulysses was in his first year of college now for computers, after returning from 2 tours abroad with the U.S. Army. He knew how to fight and kill people. But something told her that Dev and his guards had a lot more experience.

* * * *

Heather didn't see Devlin for the next semester. With his absence, most of her old drive to excel returned. She threw herself into her schoolwork, bringing up her grades and ending the semester with solid As. Every time her friends asked her to go and sing karaoke at Eclipse with them, she agreed, desperately hoping Devlin would be there. She always made a point to sing Total Eclipse of the Heart, hoping the words would somehow magically call Dev back to her. But he never appeared.

The phone rang just as she was walking in the door, exhausted from her last final exam.

"Hi Sis," Ulysses said.

Something in his tone said there was trouble. "What is it? Tell me."

"I'm going for another tour," he confessed. "We're leaving in only a day at most. I'm going to miss your graduation. I'm sorry, but—"

"You told me you were done," Heather said, her throat suddenly dry. "You were lucky to come through two tours without a scratch! You can't go back for another one!"

"I don't have a choice," he said defensively. "I need more money for next semester. That job I'd lined up for next year I thought was a sure thing evaporated. This is the easiest way. It's only another year."

"Mom and Dad—"

"They allotted us equal funds for college," Ulysses said lightly. "It's not anyone's fault that you're smarter than me and got those scholarships and I didn't get any. I'll be fine, sis. But I do want you to write me when you can. I'll send an email as soon as I'm settled in—"

"You could get a loan—"

"I made myself promise not to go into debt, not for any reason. I'm not going to break it."

This couldn't be happening. "Don't go, please. I can help pay for your college, as soon as I get a job—"

"In what, like another three years?" he teased, his falsely cheerful tone not quite concealing his sadness. "No, you've got your life on track, sis. Keep going. I can figure this out on my own. Take care, okay?"

"Okay," Heather replied automatically. Then she carefully replaced the receiver, hating the loud dial tone for its cold finality.

* * * *

Heather's next semester was to be her last. She spent hours sending applications applying for internships for the coming summer, and working hard to maintain her GPA. But the day before graduation, Heather stood before the mirror wondering if this was what she really wanted. *How did you ever know for sure what the right path was? Maybe no one ever did.*

The phone rang shrilly, the caller ID identifying her father. Heather knew it had to be serious, as he'd never called her before, only her mother had. "Hello?"

"Heather, Ulysses…he's been hurt. Pretty bad. They're discharging him from the army. He's coming home as soon as he's stable enough to travel—"

Panic seized her. "What happened?"

"Shrapnel of some kind. He'll walk again in time. That's the early prognosis, at least. We can be happy about that—"

Heather sat down, dizzy. *This can't be real.*

"Look, I have to go. Your sister's waiting for me to pick her up at school, and your mother's in no condition to drive—"

"I understand. Keep me posted, Dad," she responded hollowly, then hung up the phone. She sat there for several minutes, her thoughts more and more frantic. Then she called Devlin's cell phone from memory, praying the number was still the same. The same voice mail message that she'd heard close to ten months ago clicked on, asking her to leave a message.

Please let him understand how much I need him. "I need you now. Tonight. More than ever. Please, Dev, I need to see you. I need someone to care."

Heather clicked off the phone, then collapsed onto her bed, sobbing on and off. She cried herself to sleep eventually, succumbing to exhaustion just after midnight.

Heather was roused sometime later by gentle kisses on her face. She opened her eyes to see Devlin lying beside her on her bed. She grabbed him and squeezed herself tight to his broad chest, bursting out in fresh tears as he stroked her hair.

"Shh," he said, holding her. "I'm here. You're not alone."

When she'd calmed down, Heather explained her brother's injury. "I understand you're upset," Devlin said when she'd finished. "But you said he'll walk again. That's much better than the alternative."

"I'm just scared," Heather said, burrowing close. "He could have died, or been blown to bits."

"But he's neither. In point of fact, he's coming home for good," Devlin assured. "You should be celebrating, instead of crying, especially as you're set to graduate soon."

"How did you know?" Heather asked, furrowing her brow in confusion.

"I've paid attention," he said lightly. "I planned to send you a graduation gift, Bright Eyes."

"You haven't seen me in months," she accused harshly. "Not one call."

"Not by choice," Devlin answered, drawing her close. "You were losing yourself in me, Heather. I did what I thought was best for both of us under those circumstances."

Heather didn't soften. "You mean you wanted me to stay human because you can't drink from me if I'm vampire."

"Technically, I can," Devlin admitted. "But that's not half as fun, take it from me."

"I want you," Heather whispered, clutching him. "I want us to be how we were."

"I want that, too," Devlin said lustfully, pressing his hips tightly to hers. "If you'll agree to break things off when they progress to the point they did before."

Heather nodded, then her mouth sought his hungrily.

"No," Devlin said, drawing back. "When I said celebration, I meant it." He stood, then offered his hand, helping her up. "Go get dressed to kill, Bright Eyes. I'll be back with the car in ten for you." He left, tossing her a last wicked smile over his shoulder. Heather dashed for the closet, already planning the perfect outfit.

* * * *

The dinner at the Hilton hotel restaurant was lavish. While Devlin himself didn't eat anything, Heather enjoyed dish after dish, ending with a chocolate cheesecake for dessert. Even the sullen stare of the familiar man in black lurking near the front of the restaurant couldn't take away Heather's joy. Because every woman that came in was looking at Devlin, and casting looks of envy her way. It was as wonderful as she'd fantasized, being out with him and being the center of his attention.

Better yet, when they left the restaurant, Heather and Devlin left together via his SUV, the man in black driving them. "Where are we going?" she asked curiously. "This isn't the way back to my dorm."

"To my home," Devlin answered generously. "It's time you saw it."

A rush of hope rose up within Heather. *He did care about her.* "Why now?"

"Because you had my cell number for months and didn't call, because I said not to." He hugged her close. "I know how much you wanted to, but you trusted me. You didn't try to push for more than I could give. That means I can trust you."

They drove through wide gates, then up a long curving driveway. Devlin helped her out of the car, then up to the main front door. A muscular man opened it—some kind of bodyguard, as he was armed—and Devlin guided her up a flight of stairs to his bedroom. It was more a suite than a room, encompassing a large fireplace, several antique velvet chairs and matching couch, and a huge bed, its wooden headboard carved with an ornate oak tree.

"This is beautiful," she said in awe.

"Thank you," he said cordially. He closed the door, then took her hand. "Come."

Devlin undressed Heather slowly before the fire, then lay her down on the rug. "You're beautiful," he whispered, as he unbuttoned his shirt. "Like a newly hatched butterfly, just spreading its wings for her first flight."

"Help me to fly," Heather whispered hungrily, reaching for him.

* * * *

Afterwards, Devlin held her as they watched the crackling flames slowly die.

"Would you have called me?" Heather said finally. "If I hadn't called you?"

"I'm not sure," Devlin answered. "But you want to know if I wanted to, and the answer to that is yes."

Heather didn't reply.

"You keep taking my absence for not having feelings for you," Devlin continued, irked. "When it's the opposite that is true. I am and remain concerned for you. I didn't want you to get sick, Heather."

"I don't care," Heather said, turning in Devlin's arms. "The truth is I was going to ask you to turn me, if that meant we could be together more often."

Devlin let out a long irritated breath. "I told you, once you turn, what we have is done. Permanently."

Did he only want her for her blood? She couldn't bring herself to ask him. "I just want you in my life," Heather elaborated. "Why not see one another as long as we can, then turn me?"

"You want to be a vampire nurse?" Devlin said, sarcastic.

"You're a vampire," Heather said right back. "There must be ways to hold a job and still—"

There was a crash from downstairs, then a series of shots. A loud siren began to sound.

Devlin jumped out of bed, pulling on his clothes. "Get dressed. Hurry!"

Heather complied. "What is it? A fire?"

"Worse," Devlin said hatefully. "Vampire hunters."

If not for the depth of hate in his tone, she would have laughed. Instead, Heather hurried to dress. Devlin finished and turned to her, grabbing her arm. He sat her on the bed. "Stay here and don't make any noise," he urged. "I'll be back soon."

"Wait!" Heather cried. "You shouldn't go out there! What if they catch you and…stake you?"

Devlin snorted, standing. "I'm in no danger, Heather. But I need to know why they attacked now." He left, shutting the door behind him.

Heather waited what seemed like an eternity. An hour later, she went to the door and opened it tentatively. No one was about. But there was an ominous feeling in the air, as if something evil was lurking in the shadows, holding its breath.

"You can come out," a female voice said in contempt. "If you're done quivering, that is."

Heather looked up and saw a tall woman with long brown hair walking toward her. She was dressed in a simple back dress. There was something odd about it, but Heather couldn't think what. Then she realized the hem was indistinct, as if the woman was not garbed in cloth, but with shadows.

"Where's Devlin?" Heather ventured.

"Interrogating the prisoners," the woman said casually. "He told me to see you got home. If you come with me, I'll have someone drive you home."

"Is he alright?" Heather persisted.

"Once he drains the two hunters, I'm sure his mood will improve," the woman said darkly. "Come now."

Drain? As in kill? Heather followed the woman downstairs to the garage. "Why did they attack?"

"I think it's a test of hunterhood," the woman said with a smirk, gesturing to the SUV. "If you can assail the vampire king's house and live to tell the tale, there's a lot of respect to be gained. Almost no one does." The SUV suddenly started up, startling Heather. A man was already behind the wheel. "Take her home, Vince."

"Vampire king?" Heather said blankly, turning to face the woman.

"Didn't you know who you were fucking?" the woman said in contempt. "Didn't you even ask Dev who he was before you bared your neck?" She shook her head. "Women like you are the reason males continue to rule this world."

"Ease off, Leri," Vince said gruffly, shifting nervously. "I have no problems taking your orders."

"Because you know I'll turn you into a castrated duck if you don't," the woman said sweetly with icy eyes. She turned back to Heather. "Goodbye," she said with an arrogant sniff, then turned and walked elegantly away.

Heather was silent the whole trip back. *Devlin was a king. If he turned her…if she could make him love her…she could be his queen.*

* * * *

In the months that followed, Heather resumed her affair with Devlin. But she was careful this time to hide her desire for him. She made it a point to cancel one of her bi-monthly visits with him that summer, citing her busy intern schedule. The scheme seemed to work. Her bimonthly visits took place every other Friday evening at his home instead of at a hotel.

But one thing still bothered Heather. Devlin refused to talk of turning her. He also wouldn't let her spend entire Saturdays with him, insisting he needed to rest. Heather did what he asked, hoping that by conceding to his wishes she would earn more of his trust. That was the only way into his life permanently, so he couldn't ever shut her out again.

It was the following spring when the illness came. At first, Heather just thought it was a spring cold, a holdover from the fast fading winter. But as she grew more and more lethargic, the symptoms became harder to push away…and impossible to hide.

"You've lost weight," Devlin said one night gently, after making love. "Are you sleeping alright?"

"When I'm here, I sleep fine," Heather answered weakly.

"Tell me the truth," Devlin said, an edge to his words. "How are you feeling?"

"I'm tired more often," Heather admitted. "Sunlight makes me feel sick. So does food sometimes…" she trailed off.

"Except rare meat?" Devlin supplied, his tone distant.

"I'm vegetarian," Heather said evasively.

"Not for much longer," Devlin said hollowly, sitting up. "Unless we take another hiatus."

Fear blossomed in Heather. She couldn't go through another half a year without Dev. "Turn me."

Devlin stared at her, then shook his head. "You don't know what you're asking, Heather." He got up from the bed. "Maybe our break this time should be permanent."

Something told Heather it was now or never. She had only the next few moments to change his mind. "How can you say that to me like it's nothing? Like I'm nothing?"

"Could you be more of an idiot?" Devlin said harshly, his eyes bleeding to red.

Heather, shocked by his casual cruelty, begun hastily gathering her clothes and dressing. All she could feel was hurt, and his next words fell on deaf ears

"It's because I'm fond of you that I don't want to screw up your life. We had good times together, Heather. But we're nearing the end of our story. And unless you want this to be a tragedy instead of a good memory, you and I have to end our relationship." He handed her purse to her. "I'll have my man drive you home."

Heather didn't answer him. When she was in the backseat heading down the long gravel driveway, she burst into tears.

She arrived home to her small apartment, exhausted. Falling into bed, she fell asleep fully dressed. Near midnight, she woke in fear, a hand over her mouth.

"Quiet," a raspy voice said, "Or we'll gag you." Heather kept still as another person began to bind her hands and feet. She watched in fear as several more shadowy figures came into her bedroom, wincing as the light was turned on. There were five people: two women, and three men, the oldest appearing to be the leader.

"This is her?" he stated.

One of the women nodded. "We tracked her coming and going from Hayden three times now. And she's been seen out in the vampire's company more than once in the past year."

"You don't have to bother," Heather murmured. "He's breaking up with me. For good."

The leader grabbed her by the hair, pulling it back sharply so Heather cried out. "Because you're getting sick. Devlin doesn't turn his thralls anymore, not since we began killing his discards."

Heather blinked back tears. "Please don't hurt me. Please."

"Take her to the cabin and set the trap," the leader said. "Then send the note to Devlin to tell him to come alone."

* * * *

Dawn came, but Heather didn't see it. She remained blindfolded in a room as the hours passed. She dozed intermittently, wondering if they would kill her before Devlin could rescue her. *But would he?* He'd always come across as an honorable person, even with his cruel words at their last meeting. He said she'd never be alone again. Now that he was done with her, was any of that still true?

The door opened. A man entered, cursing, then sat beside her on the bed. Heather waited for her blindfold to be removed. Instead, there came a sharp stabbing pain as a blade cut across her left wrist. Heather

66

struggled, blood trickling out steadily to dampen the mattress beneath her.

The door opened. "You do her? He should be here in a few moments."

"Yes," the man said in disgust, getting up. "We could have let her go. We didn't need to kill her."

"She's contaminated. Plus he'll smell the blood and go for her. It's an advantage we need. Now come on."

The man left, the door closing.

Heather struggled to sit up, woozy. With maneuvering, she put pressure on the wound as best she could, pressing down with her other wrist to staunch the blood.

Shots sounded, then a shriek of rage. There was a male scream, then silence.

Heather felt herself drifting. She sagged down on the bed.

The door burst open. Heather felt herself being pulled upwards into a sitting position, the blindfold lifted. To her disappointment, it was not Devlin, but instead the man in black, his expression bitter.

"Can you walk?" he asked, his inflection muddled with an odd hiss.

Heather swayed, then fell backward. The man in black caught her, then lifted her in his arms. Muttering, he carried her quickly from the room as she lapsed into unconsciousness.

* * * *

"Just turn her," a hissing voice said.

"We'll drop her off at the hospital," a dispassionate voice said. "They'll give her a transfusion." It was Devlin's voice. But it was so cold. Heather opened her eyes. She was sitting in the front seat of a SUV. Her slashed wrist had been bandaged, but it was still bleeding slightly.

"Turn her," the man in black said, facing Devlin with a scowl. "She's one of those that's just going to be a pain in the ass until you do."

Devlin's gaze flicked to Heather. "Leave us alone for a few moments, Lash."

The man in black walked away a short distance, muttering under his breath. Then came the touch of Devlin's cool hand in hers as he leaned down beside her. "Where do you want to go?" he asked gently.

"Why don't you want me?" Heather murmured. "I've tried to give you everything you wanted. You've got to know I love you, that I want to be with you. I'd do anything for you."

"You naïve girl," Devlin said with sadness. "I don't want you because I don't want anyone." His expression was bitter. "You see me only from your point of view, that I must have suffered all the loneliness and hurt of the past two centuries only to be waiting for you to come solve all my woes with your love. But that's fantasy, Heather. It always was."

"Don't you want to be happy?" Heather managed, tears trickling down both cheeks.

"I exist for my own reasons," Devlin said coolly. "I don't want your pity. You say you love me, but you have no idea of what I really am, or what horrors I'm capable of. You think forever is a romantic holiday we could spend together if you were a vampire, too. The reality is that this is what you'd have to look forward to: being hunted, alone, and often injured. And that's besides having a liquid diet that never varies."

"Why didn't you let me die?" Heather whispered.

"Because those hunters hurt you because of me. Now do you want to go to the hospital or not?"

"Will I die if I don't?" Heather asked. "Or will I turn?"

"You'll die," Devlin said tiredly. "But I'm done trying to be persuasive. Lash is right about that being of no further use. You want to turn, I'll do it next week." His voice turned cool. "If you want to die, I'll help with that, too, here and now."

His words had a chilling effect, shocking her into awareness. "Hospital," Heather said.

* * * *

Then had come tonight, a week later. With several transfusions, Heather had felt almost as good as new. But after so many delays, she half expected Devlin to back out, or not show. But the vampire was waiting for her, clapping as she sat down at her table.

"Did you change your mind?" he said abruptly.

"No."

"Very well," Devlin said, offering his hand. "Come."

* * * *

The next evening, Heather's eyes popped open. At once, the vivid colors of her surroundings dazzled her. Then she worried that someone was in the room with her, only realizing some moments later that the person she was hearing was out in the hallway. Her hearing and sight had amplified. *What else had changed?*

She stood, checked the time, then headed to the bathroom. When she finished, she washed up and got dressed. Emerging, she checked the clock again and did a double take. She'd done everything in less than a minute flat. Her speed had also increased.

What else?

Lifting the bed was easy, as if it were a bag of groceries. As she set it down, Devlin came in. "How are you feeling?"

Heather rushed to him, hugging him. "I feel fantastic! You didn't tell me how wonderful, how powerful I'd be."

"Because that is relative to humans," Devlin said with contempt. "And you must always be aware of that, because it's going to be very easy to crack bones if you shake someone's hand too hard, or hug a friend. But older vampires like myself will also be much more powerful, Heather. Don't let the power go to your head. You have become a very small fish in a wide and deep ocean."

Heather nodded. "Will you teach me?"

"Tonight, briefly," Devlin said, checking his watch. "Then I have to feed. But I've set you up at the hospital to work the night shift. There are several vampires that work there. I'll introduce you. They'll arrange blood for you as needed, until you make other arrangements."

"Are we robbing the blood bank?" Heather quipped.

Devlin gave her an aloof look. "You'll be working for me, after a fashion. So you won't need to do any thievery, young one."

Anger flared up in her at his sudden condescending attitude. "That's correct, oh Vampire King," Heather said mockingly. "I'm here to serve."

Devlin whipped around, then grasped her by the throat, lifting her off her feet. Heather struggled, but to no avail, fear coursing through her.

"That is wholly correct, that you are to serve me," he said icily. "Remember you wanted it this way, Bright Eyes. You wouldn't take no for an answer, even with all the reasons I gave you."

"Let me go!" Heather hissed, her own eyes bleeding to red.

"I will do with you however I want, if you put one foot out of line," Devlin said darkly. "And bear in mind that my discipline is usually harsh." He shoved her back, making her stumble.

"You bastard," she screeched. "How could you do this to me and walk away?"

"Because I don't suffer fools," Devlin said frostily. "And I can see you are one, in spite of all your learning. I wish you luck in your new life. Adieu." He placed a book on her table, then turned and walked away, followed by Heather's curses.

Heather spent the rest of the night reading the paperback book, which purported to be a vampire handbook. Devlin was listed as one of the authors. Angry as she was, Heather wanted to know her rights.

But dawn had her halfway through and seeing no help. She was not an oathed one—something like a vampire spouse complete with signature jewelry to denote their station—nor was she a Ruler—a vampire that oversaw a territory like a city, state, or country—and vampires aside from those groups seemed to have few rights. The book was more a list of what they were not allowed to do, which was pretty much call attention to themselves in any way.

There was a knock at the door. Heather knew suddenly it was her brother. *She could smell his cologne.* Heading to the window, she slipped out. She couldn't let him know what she'd become.

Heather wandered the night, wondering at how vivid everything looked. Much as she felt wonderful, she also felt empty and alone. *Who could she turn to?* She didn't know any other vampires except Devlin. Maybe the job at the hospital would provide some relief. She would take Devlin's offer, at least for now.

* * * *

While Jason and the other orderlies at the hospital were nice enough, they had all made it clear that Heather was on her own. She'd hoped to learn the vampire ropes from them, but they pretty much worked their shift and went home after. How was that a fun way to spend forever? It felt to Heather like she was back in school, except there would be no reprieve this time. She hadn't finished her nursing schooling, so had to make do with janitorial work and medical technician duties. Even with her new speed, there was no way to finish her degree and work her job in the few hours that night lasted.

That first month Heather went faithfully to her job each night out of fear—the other vampires had told her stories of Devlin, and what it meant for vamps that crossed him. But less than a month after she turned, Heather reached her limit. Friday night she went to Hayden, remaining before the gates until Devlin came out to see her.

"What is it?" he snapped.

"I want you," she whispered.

His eyes narrowed. "We are not oathed, Heather. You can demand nothing of me."

"But you always use sex as part of the turning process," Heather replied. "Jason swore to it. I demand that right, to share that with you as vampire."

Devlin eyed her, then slowly nodded once. "Come in then, and receive your due."

Devlin led her to his bed, removing their clothes. As he always did, he was gentle as he made love to her. But as she climaxed, he bit into her. Instead of orgasmic pleasure, there was only a sudden feeling of terror, then pain.

Heather broke his hold on her, moving away. Devlin watched her, then inclined his head. "You see how it is? That sensitivity you had does not survive the turning, just as I knew it would not." He got up and began to dress.

"Why didn't you tell me?" Heather yelled.

"Would you have believed me?" he scoffed. "No. When you've only had pleasure, you couldn't fathom feeling fear and pain. But vampires have instinctive fear of being drained. It's one of the few ways they can die. So they seldom drink from one another." He finished dressing. "Please get dressed, and one of my men will show you out."

As he left, Heather collapsed into tears.

* * * *

The next week was a blur of days of work, feeding from cold, bagged blood, and studying the damned vampire handbook. But there was no help for Heather in it. She felt cursed and rejected, the seed of anger festering within her until it became full-blown rage. That night after her shift, she followed a teen into a dark alley. When he turned on her with a gun and a grin of surprise, demanding money, she slaughtered him ruthlessly, finding a fleeting relief from her pain in his blood.

Heather killed all that next week, determined that if nothing else it should bring Devlin again to her door. She wanted out of this life, but couldn't bring herself to do it. Instead, Ulysses found her, blood from her fourth victim still staining her hands.

"What happened to you?" he whispered in horror, as she let the corpse drop from her arms.

"A vampire named Devlin Dalcon," she said emptily. Then she was crying in his arms. Yet even as he comforted her, she wanted his blood, the rush of it in his veins deafening. Heather fled that night to her apartment, not answering her brother's pleas through the locked door to let him in.

The next night, Heather left early, avoiding her brother's sleeping form with her newfound stealth. Skipping work, she instead went to stalk a victim. As she was closing down on the woman to snap her neck, the mark turned. Heather recognized a familiar face a split second before the crossbow bolt pierced her heart and she fell, paralyzed. The machete blow descended, severing her head a moment later.

* * * *

"Your nurse is dead," the man in black reported. "The Van Helsing Group sent their usual gross notice. I burned it and scattered the ashes."

Devlin let out a sigh, looking out over his deck into the silent and dark woods of his estate. "I know, Lash. I felt her die through the bloodbond."

"Probably best," Lash answered. "She was killing randomly and I'd have had to put her down this week."

Devlin didn't answer.

"You did what you could," Lash said gruffly. "There's no point feeling bad about women who won't face reality."

"You're right," Devlin said softly. "But I can't help feeling that I corrupted her. She could have done some good with her life."

"Maybe," Lash allowed. "But she probably would have found something else to obsess over."

"You're just trying to make me feel better," Devlin said with a faint smile.

"No, that is what state carnivals are for," Lash said, handing Devlin a ticket. "There's bound to be some song mistresses at this Stones concert. We're going Saturday."

Devlin looked over the ticket, his expression brightening. "This looks great. Thanks."

"Anytime," Lash replied with a grin. "I also wanted to tell you that your new girl Delilah is here. I've got her waiting for you in one of the guest rooms. And I told her that you've recently suffered a loss, and need some serious help to take your mind off it." He winked. "I wouldn't keep her waiting long, if I were you."

Devlin's expression turned to one of lust. "I won't," he said, pocketing the ticket as he strode inside.

* * * *

"Is this her?"

Ulysses nodded stoically, looking down at his sister's disemboweled body. She was at peace now, maybe. But he was going to get the bastard that had done this to her, no matter what it took. "Can I have a moment?"

The coroner nodded, then left.

Ulysses touched Heather's pale hand. "I'm sorry I couldn't save you. I love you." He dropped her hand, then plucked a card out of his pocket, the silver lettering gleaming in the harsh light. "Devlin Dalcon, you're going to pay for this, pay with everything you have. You won't see me coming."

Night Shift

(Previously published in Frightmares anthology 11-2011)

"Pass the scalpel, please."

Becky blinked at the gray haze over her eyes. Why wouldn't they open?

"Is she under? Her eyelids fluttered."

"She's under. It's just a reflex, Doctor. You should know that by now—"

Her surgery. God, she'd woken up in the middle! Frantically, Becky tried to move her limbs, to stretch her lips in a scream.

"Up the anesthesia slightly, anyway, Nurse Jordan. Now."

Becky tensed, fighting, then relaxed, the grey haze becoming black nothingness.

A moment later the black lightened to grey again.

"Only take out three vials."

That was Dr. Miller. Becky opened her eyes a crack.

"She's strong enough for four—"

"No, Jordan. We need her alive."

Jordan leaned over her, empty vial in hand. "We can't survive on just ten vials a piece—"

"And I can't have another of my patients die," Dr. Miller hissed, baring fangs. "You're going to blow our cover here—"

Nurse Jordan snarled, his own fangs bone white. "Some patients die in surgery. It's routine—"

74

Becky managed a squeak, her panicked eyes darting madly. Both vampires looked down at her.

"She saw us," Jordan said, smiling wickedly. He connected the vial. "Now we have to."

Please don't, God, please, please, Becky thought wildly, her heart beating like a trip hammer as she watched the vial fill.

"You're right, Jordan. She won't remember anything, anyway," Dr. Miller assured, tapping a syringe. He slid it into Becky's arm, then depressed the plunger.

Their leering faces dissolved back into grey black night. Then the night lightened steadily, becoming grayish-white.

Becky blinked and then moaned softly.

"She's coming out of it, Doctor."

Becky opened her eyes wide, then struggled to sit up. "It's over?" she asked weakly.

"Yes," Dr. Miller said, patting her arm. "You did fine. We got the tumor out, but you did lose a lot of blood."

Becky squeezed his hand gratefully, her face breaking into a relieved smile. "Thank you, Doctor. Thank you so much."

"You're welcome," he replied, then turned to his nurse standing nearby. "Nurse Heather, please see she gets a transfusion as soon as possible."

Nurse Heather nodded. "Of course. We'll take care of it right away."

As Dr. Miller watched her wheel Becky away, Nurse Jordan came up to him. "You're needed in emergency surgery, Doctor, stat."

Dr. Miller took the proffered chart, walking quickly toward emergency. "Brief me, please."

"Accident victim, male, mid-twenties. Severe neck injuries. Emergency personnel had to cut him out of the wreck."

"Is his family here?"

Nurse Jordan smiled. "They were all in the car, sadly. All DOA."

"Is he conscious?" Dr. Miller asked, his eyes glimmering as he began to walk faster.

Nurse Jordan shook his head. "No. And it's just you and me for this surgery, Doctor. Everyone else is busy with other emergency patients tonight."

"Then my prognosis is he won't wake," Dr. Miller said, the tips of his fangs showing in his smile. "Let's go to work."

Just Business

Angelica sauntered down the sterile hallway, wrinkling her nose as the strong disinfectant smell permeating the air. *Why did hospitals always have to smell so awful? God, let me not die in a hospital...*

"Can I help you?" a passing nurse said, stopping in mid-stride to block her way.

Angelica gave the nurse a once over, as she did every woman she met. *Plain blonde pageboy, non-descript mud-brown eyes, at least five pounds overweight.* The nurse's nametag had her name with no prefix at all. *Not any threat. But don't waste the smile. It'll be lost on this one.* "I'm looking for Nurse Jordan. I think that's his name? He's an EMT."

The woman smiled, but her eyes were still cool as she looked at the buxom blue-eyed temptress in the formfitting simple black dress. "I'll tell him you're here. He's likely with a patient. Please go back and wait in the visitor's lounge."

Angelica resisted her urge to tell the woman she needed a better concealer, as well as clothes that weren't from Wal-Mart. "Of course."

Angelica headed back to the lounge, irritated but also glad she wasn't going to have to go looking for Jordan in her 2" heels. It was much better for him to come to her. *If she crossed her legs just as he approached, he'd be putty in her hands.*

She paused as she passed a ladies room, then hurried inside. It had been raining hard outside. Her hair could use a quick fluff with some hairspray.

After primping for a few minutes, Angelica emerged. As she turned to head for the lounge, she caught site of a familiar waxen face walking down the hall. *Jordan!* Eagerly she hobbled after him, slipping slightly on the tile floor. "Jordan! Hey, wait!"

Jordan didn't seem to hear her as he continued to wheel the sheet-draped gurney towards two double doors. Angelica followed him, still calling.

It took a distance of a hundred yards and Angelica taking off her shoes to be able to run, but she finally caught up to Jordan at the elevator. He was nearly through the elevator door when Angelica's hand shot out to grab hold of the gurney. "Hey!"

Jordan turned, his expression one of surprise. "Angelica! What are you doing back here? This area is off limits to patients." He looked down and laughed. "At least the living ones."

"I'm not a patient, I'm a visitor," Angelica said with coy deliberateness, stepping onto the elevator and slipping her heels back on. "And I wanted to see you. You broke our date for tonight."

Jordan looked uncomfortable, then pressed the button for the basement. "Because I can't be what you want me to be. We've been over this, Angel."

Angelica's beautiful blue eyes narrowed angrily. "You mean you still won't make me a vampire."

The door opened with a metallic bing. Jordan wheeled the body out into a basement hallway, Angelica following. As he tried to leave, she grabbed hold of the gurney again.

"Answer me, Jordan!"

"Believe me, it's no fun being a vampire," Jordan said tiredly, even as his gaze flicked back and forth, watching anxiously in opposite directions. "Count yourself lucky you can still eat butterscotch crumpets." His expression turned wistful. "It is stuff like that I miss the most."

Jordan always gave me this speech, ever since the first time I asked him to turn me. Sure, that he couldn't make vampires was believable. He didn't have the right Old World charm to be an influential vampire. But someone made him. And I want an introduction to that someone, no matter what I have to do. "You said the more powerful vampires had donors. Can't you take me to the one who turned you? I could offer myself as a donor."

Jordan shook his head. "They don't bother with vampires like me, as long as I keep my head down." He gave her a smile. "And as much as I enjoyed your warm skin that night we spent together, I'm not changing that for you." He headed away with the dead body without a backward look.

"You bastard!" Angelica yelled after him, stamping her foot. Then she grimaced, taking off her shoe to see a large new nick in the heel. "Stupid concrete floor."

Angelica reluctantly pressed the elevator for the first floor. But when the doors opened, there was another vampire there waiting, his expression tired and grumpy. "Are you lost?" he asked gruffly. "You're not supposed to be here."

"Yes," Angelica stammered, taken aback. "Um, I mean no, I'm not lost. But I meant to go to the first floor and came down here instead—"

The vampire pushed her into the elevator, then hit the 1st floor button.

"Thank you, um—?"

The vampire didn't reply, just gave her a pitying look as the elevator doors whispered shut.

Angelica's resolve weakened, then promptly solidified into steel. *I'll go back down to the ground floor and wait.* There was a little cul-de-sac to the side of the elevators near a drinking fountain. Sooner or later that other vampire would have to come back through, so he could go back up wherever the hell he'd come from. And when he did, she'd follow him.

* * * *

Angelica's alarm on her watch went off, startling her. She straightened, then looked at her wrist in disbelief. It was six in the morning! She'd waited all night and the vampire hadn't come back...and she'd given in to exhaustion and fallen asleep.

Cursing aloud, Angelica straightened her now dirty dress and staggered to the elevator. She was going to be late for work. Tony didn't like that, or to have her look anything but perfect.

"Who said working for a mobster was easy?" she muttered, stabbing the button for the first floor.

* * * *

"You know better," Tony sneered into the phone. "So don't be making that mistake again, Richard. Or you're fired."

"You're really going to fire him?" Thane said darkly, glaring at Tony over the rim of his scotch glass.

"Yes," Tony answered, smoothing the lapels of his expensive Brooks Brothers suit. "Then he's going to have an accident. Dumb man can't choose if he should leave his wife or leave his mistress. You've seen both of them with him. There's no contest."

Thane smirked slightly. "Richard never understood his blessing in Anita."

Tony frowned at him. "That's his wife, right?"

"I'm sorry I'm late, Tony," Angelica said, opening the door slightly to peek inside the office. "I overslept." She watched her two bosses carefully as they studied her, hoping they hadn't had a stressful morning. If they had, she'd might be looking for a new job. But both were in clean expensive suits, their dark hair freshly combed, clean shaven, looking as if they just came into work. That was a good sign.

Thane had his scotch glass filled, but Angelica knew better than to think he was drinking this early. The whiskey was an affectation. Thane truly believed he should look the part of a movie perfect Italian Mafioso at all times. Just why that was important she'd never understood, only that Thane's odd quirk didn't make him any less dangerous.

"That's a new one," Thane said harshly, yet his smile was in his black eyes as he beheld her. "Are you sure it wasn't a new love?"

"No," Angelica stammered, flushing. "I mean, yes, I'm sure."

Thane chuckled.

Tony had picked the phone up again and dialed another number. "Get me Dalcon. Yes, I know it is late morning, Lash, but I need to speak with him, please."

Tony never said please to anyone. Get out, quick, before you hear something you shouldn't! Angelica hurriedly looked away. "Excuse me, Tony. I didn't know you were on the phone—"

"Please leave, Angel," Tony said, his tone also kind, but clear that he expected obedience.

Angelica shut the door, then went back to her desk. She opened her compact to look at her face, then tossed it aside. *What was the point? I look like hell.*

At least I still have a job. Most runaways that were 15 years old got sent right back to their parents. At best, they could hope for foster care. Angelica had been blessed by her strict father's religious upbringing to always be a lady. Her politeness when she'd come to his door asking for work had impressed Tony, along with his appreciation for her leggy fragile beauty. Not that he'd ever taken advantage, because he hadn't. But if she'd been ugly as a dog, she probably wouldn't be sitting here at this desk no matter how polite she'd been.

Tony paid for her furnished apartment and gave her a small check for expenses every two weeks. He'd arranged for a fake ID for her to say she was eighteen. He'd even given her a small compact car, too. While he made it clear, he expected her utter loyalty in return for his benefaction, Angelica was happy to give it. She didn't have expensive tastes. *Not that she wouldn't mind developing some…*

Angelica turned on her computer and logged on, checking out various internet sites. There was no point fantasizing about "someday" with a man who only saw her as a child.

While there wasn't much to do on a daily basis as Tony's secretary, part of Angelica's job was researching various organizations and people that Tony left for her in a daily list on her desk. It wasn't usually exciting, but at least it wasn't hard. Angelica didn't pretend that Tony wanted the information just out of curiosity. Some places were obviously ones he intended to shakedown for profit or favors. Others…they obviously had pissed him off for some reason. Tony had several gunmen working for him. The one in charge of office security—and Tony's personal safety—was Geo. With the amount that man was paid per week, he had to be doing a lot more than standing around an office all day with a holstered gun.

I just do my job and keep my mouth shut and hopefully I don't ever see anyone's name I know on one of Tony's lists…or open my apartment door to find Geo waiting for me…

There was a sound of commotion outside the office doors, then three men came in. All of them had on long coats. As one, they headed toward her with purpose.

Silent alarm time. Angelica felt under the desk, and pressed the small button that meant there was someone with a gun in the main office. It would alert Tony within his private headquarters, as well as his various men in other parts of the building. *Please let Geo be close!* Then she pasted a smile on her face, trying hard to keep it from wavering. "Can I help you?"

"Yeah," one man said, drawing a Beretta. "Get your boss out here."

Angelica picked up the phone, and dialed Tony as slowly as she dared. "There are three men out here to see you."

"Are they armed?" he replied quietly. There was the sound of guns being cocked in the background.

"I think they want you to come talk to them," Angelica stated. "I'm not sure what it's about."

Tony hung up.

"I think you warned him, Princess," the frontman said with slitted eyes. "So maybe we need to do something else, since you and your boss are so close!" The man yanked her forward, grabbing her hand. Angelica struggled, then let out a terrified scream. Another ragged cry followed on its heels as the man placed her hand at the end of the desk and slammed the desk door on it, the crack of her breaking finger loud in the silence.

"Get out here, Tony, or we'll hurt her bad," the man called. "We just want to talk to you—"

Shots emitted from the stairwell to her left. Angelica's attacker sagged to the side, a hole blossoming in his forehead. The other two men panicked, firing wildly into the direction of the stairwell as Angelica ducked behind her desk. Both were hit with return fire and fell to the floor, groaning.

A robust light-skinned man with pale grey eyes darted in, scanning the room. Five more men followed him. Geo shot both wounded men again where they lay, killing them. "You can come out, Tony."

Angelica gripped the desk with her good hand and pulled herself to a standing position. Her hand throbbed, but more than that, she was in shock. There had been close calls before, but no one gunning for Tony had ever hurt her before. "Thank God, Geo."

The mercenary turned mob gunman smiled back at her. "Don't you mean 'thank Geo'?"

"Andre Mencini," Tony said angrily, emerging from his office. "Go see him today, Geo. That upstart doesn't know how to handle things the new way, like gentlemen. We can't have a mess like this on our home turf, not without getting noticed." His eyes glittered with something dark and primitive. "So take care of it the old way, since that's all that fuck understands. Capice?"

Geo nodded. "I'll take care of it."

Angelica swayed, close to fainting. *Oh God. I'm going to be next after Mencini. I can't pretend I didn't hear that!*

"Angelica, are you hurt?" Thane said, steadying the bloodied woman with his free hand.

"They broke my hand," she whimpered.

"We'll have a guy take you to the hospital," Thane said gently, guiding her to the door. "Take the rest of the day off. Geo, drop her off on your way. The rest of you take care of this mess."

Geo gestured with his hand for Angelica to follow him. Reluctantly, she did, the sounds of dead bodies being dragged away behind her loud in her ears.

* * * *

After Geo dropped Angelica off at the entrance to the ER—much to her relief—she spent the next three hours in the ER waiting for someone to set her hand. She was splinted, taped, and processed. After waiting another hour for Geo to return for her, she reluctantly decided she'd have to find her own way home.

Any normal woman would have a girlfriend to come and rescue them. Or at least a family member. I don't have either. But that's the price of independence...and true beauty. Angelica sighed dramatically aloud, then reluctantly dialed a cab company. She settled into her chair to wait. A few moments later, a drunk man came in, bleeding from a gash over one eye, his hands clenched into fists.

"I'll fucking kill that dumb bitch! See if I don't!" he roared.

Glancing up in his direction in worry, Angelica glimpsed the other vampire from last night. He wasn't headed downstairs this time, though. This time, he went into one of the ER rooms, a large bag in his left hand.

Angelica discreetly followed, curious. She tiptoed up to the ER room and peeked behind the curtain. There was the strange vampire, and Jordan, too. A guy with a mutilated right side and a missing cheek lay there on the gurney, breathing shallowly, his limbs jerking slightly. Jordan was monitoring his vitals. The other vampire was taking out his blood via IV inserted in his jugular. As she watched, the man spasmed again, the movement filling up the IV bag halfway. The vampire quickly disconnected it, then put a new one onto fill. There was a grunt from the table, a muffled sound of pain mixed with panic that drew Angelica's horrified gaze.

The man on the table spasming was watching them kill him, his one good eye rolling wildly in his socket!

"Argh! Angelica yelled. Jordan looked up, aghast. The strange vampire started toward her, then stopped.

"Say nothing," he whispered. "Or it will be you on this table, woman."

Angelica ran, slipping and sliding, yelling for help. She ran straight past the emergency main desk and out towards the main entrance…and into the arms of a very startled Geo.

He caught her, even as she struggled, flailing. "Whoa, Angel! What's a matter? I'm sorry I'm late picking you up—"

Right now I don't care if you did just come from killing someone. "Please Geo, take me to Tony."

"Why?" Geo said, suspicious.

"Because someone just threatened to kill me," Angelica said truthfully. "And I need his protection."

* * * *

Jordan and Jonas stood shoulder to shoulder in a brightly lit room, doing their best to look calm. A blond haired man stood before them, furious. Behind him stood a red-skinned demon with short black hair and small horns, dressed in plainclothes, his expression solemn.

"Morgues are bright, aren't they?" the vampire said in a melodious tone. "Much brighter than the two of you put together."

"Sire, we did our best to put her off," Jordan said weakly.

"When you sleep with a woman and take her blood, she usually wants more than a 'see you later' for her trouble," the blond vampire replied. "And I have a name and title. Use it."

Jordan and Jonas looked at one another, shifting uneasily in their terror.

"Lord Devlin Dalcon," the demon supplied in a bored tone.

Devlin opened his mouth to correct his demon Titus, then thought better of it. *Such as these will make no distinction between Vampire Ruler and Vampire Lord. I'm not sure I see the distinction clearly myself anymore.*

"Lord Dalcon," Jonas said respectfully. "I did my best to contain the situation. But this woman, Angelica, kept returning to the hospital! Without killing her, there was no way to keep her away. And now she's threatening to go to the police."

"We could not take action against her," Jordan added. "Your law forbids it."

How could Garrett have let these two become vampires? No wonder Heather went on a killing spree. "Yes, but why didn't you take the matter to Garrett?" Lord Dalcon said searchingly. "He could have easily given permission…or else handled the matter himself."

"I called the emergency number in the handbook I was provided when I turned," Jonas replied cautiously. "I'm sorry, lord, but he never replied."

"He didn't get back to you?" Devlin was incredulous.

"Nothing," Jonas said. "I tried him twice last week, and nothing. I was sorry to bother you, but—"

"But you had to," Devlin said with an angry grimace. "Very well. Jonas, can you arrange for this Angelica to meet with you?"

"Yes," Jonas said. "Jordan said she wanted to be a vampire, that she was interested in becoming a donor—"

Well, I always can use another of those. It's probably too much to hope for that she enjoys music. "How old is she?"

Jordan looked uncomfortable. "Eighteen."

Devlin's golden eyes reddened. "Don't lie to me. *How old is she?*"

"Just sixteen," Jordan admitted.

Too young for one of my donors, regrettably. "Too young," Devlin stated. "Donors must be of age to legally consent, Jordan. What in the hell possessed you to approach an underage girl for feeding, much less couple with her? Because I can tell by your fear that you did."

Jordan fell to his knees. "She had an ID that said she was eighteen! I didn't know!"

"Spare me the dramatics," Devlin said. "None of that matters now except containing the situation. I need to see this Angelica. Are you sure she'll come to you, Jordan? Jonas admits he threatened her."

"If she doesn't, I can tell you where she works," Jordan said in a pleading tone. He named an address.

Devlin closed his eyes, his rage rising. *Just what I didn't need, complications with Tony and Thane.* "Get out of my sight! Both of you!"

* * * *

Angelica filed her nails nervously, watching the door. *What if Jordan shows up here? Don't be stupid, it's daytime. He can't be outside in the daytime… .*

The door opened. To Angelica's utter horror, it was a vampire she'd never seen before, followed by a short man in black that looked Mexican. Angelica let out a screech and jabbed her silent alarm.

Geo came out of Tony's office, guns drawn…to stop cold, staring at the man in black who'd smoothly stepped in front of the vampire.

"Put them away," the man in black said in a lisping voice.

Geo put away his guns, missing the left hand holster in his haste. Angelica shrank back in her chair, ready to bolt. *The man in black hadn't even drawn his own gun.*

"We're here to see Tony and Thane," the vampire said politely. "We're expected."

"Sorry," Geo said contritely. "We're on edge. There was an attack yesterday and now Angelica's been threatened—"

"That was a misunderstanding entirely," the vampire said. "Would you let Tony know we're here? Devlin Dalcon, to see him."

Geo nodded, then went back into Tony's office. The vampire's attention turned to Angelica, who made herself even smaller under that inspective gaze.

86

"And you are?"

"Angelica."

Devlin stared at the black haired beauty, drinking in her large blue eyes. Suddenly a solution to the entire problem of what to do about Garrett, Jordan, and the young woman before him fell into place. *Danial. He can fix everything...if properly maneuvered. And the girl's terrified. That will take a deft hand, also...and immediate action.*

"Good to meet you," Devlin said pleasantly, striding over to her. Angelica opened her mouth to scream...then left it open as Devlin gently took her hand in his, then bent slightly at the waist to brush it with his lips. He let her hand fall, then straightened. "I understand that you've had the misfortune to only acquaint yourself with the clods of my kind. Please know you have nothing to fear from me."

Angelica closed her mouth, then swallowed, wariness not leaving her expression. "Thank you."

"Come in, Devlin," Tony said from his office doorway.

Devlin gave Angelica a respectful incline of his head, then went into Tony's office, the man in black following. The door closed behind him.

Angelica sat in her chair, still afraid but also excited. *That Devlin had to be one of the powerful vampires, the kind of vampire I'd wanted to meet!* But would he let her become a donor in exchange for turning her into a vampire?

* * * *

"Shall we get right to business?" Tony said gruffly, sitting down behind his desk.

"Why didn't we meet at Thane's place?" the man in black asked.

"Because I wanted Devlin to meet Angelica," Tony said meaningfully, looking at Devlin. "Once he did, he'd know she was just a mixed up kid, not someone who was a threat."

"I already know the lacking nature of those two brothers at the hospital," Devlin said with a dismissive wave of his hand. "And they will both be dealt with. But threatening exposure is serious, Tony. You know that."

"I know," Tony agreed. "This is why I called Garrett as soon as I knew that Angelica wasn't making up the wild story at the hospital. I thought he might be able to put some fear into Jonas and Jordan, so they wouldn't bother her anymore. But he hasn't gotten back to me." He leaned back in his chair, hands behind his head. "Just why you let so many local vampires work there, I don't know, Devlin. With that much blood disappearing, it's a wonder no one had discovered them already."

Devlin's mind worked furiously. *I thought there were only three vampires working there. But he makes it sound like closer to twenty.*

"It's not your place to question," the man in black warned. "So shut the fuck up."

"We are all here to find a peaceful solution, Lash," Thane said firmly, casting a look. "Tony and I don't want trouble. But Angelica's a good kid, Devlin. We don't want her killed just because she's got a teenage thing for vampires."

"But I also can't have her exposing us, or following us," Devlin retorted. "She obviously recognized what I was here in your office before I said a word, which is already too much knowledge for her to remain out of the game." He looked at Tony. "She's way too young to turn, and she can't be one of my donors, either." He paused. "I propose a third solution: replacing Garrett with an old acquaintance, Danial Racklan."

"Can he be trusted?" Tony asked. "Other than that, I've got no issues. This isn't the first time I've had a vampire-related problem and Garrett's been unavailable."

"I know, I know," Devlin said, holding up his palm. "I will deal with it, Tony." He looked at Thane. "What about you?"

"I've heard of him, that he runs a detective business out west somewhere," Thane mused. "The associate who used him spoke highly of him." He paused. "But will he be amenable to doing a little work for us? You know I trust coworkers more who play well with me and mine. Garrett never did."

"Danial will need donors, and I know for a fact that Angelica will please him," Devlin assured. "He will also be respectful of her, until she reaches the age of consent to turn. He also does not have that power, so he'll have to come to me when that future day comes."

"Good, Angelica needs a little kindness," Tony said, relieved.

"Tony has a soft spot for the girl," Thane said coldly. "I just want things to go smoothly, Devlin. Will Danial be a team player or not?"

"I'll see that he does," Devlin stated. "If you supply him with donors, he'll stay out of your way. And he'll also do a little side work for you as part of the deal, provided you make sure anyone you want him to eliminate is evil to the core. He has an overdeveloped sense of decency, I'm afraid."

"That can be arranged," Tony said with a nod.

"No one asked me about Danny Boy," Lash hissed, baring one snake fang. "I think he's an asshole and I hate his guts. But sure, have him come on back to the north, Dev. Just don't be surprised if he and I get into it."

"But you think he can do the job?" Tony asked Lash.

"He can do the job," Lash assented. "But he's a prick to women. Be warned. Don't be surprised if he breaks your sweet little Angelica's heart."

Devlin shot Lash a look to kill. "Danial will not be romantic with Angelica, Lash. He never is with donors. But when she is of age, if she chooses to pursue a relationship with him beyond the donor relationship…that's his business and hers."

"But it's then also your business, right?" Tony said darkly, staring at Devlin. "I heard that you tend to kill those women Danial loves."

"Seduce them," Devlin corrected. He held up one finger, the nail grown to an inch long talon. "I have never killed any of Danial's loves. But Angelica must follow the rules, *especially if she turns*. If that happens, she'll be provided with a copy of the handbook, and she must adhere to it. I make no assurance for her safety if she does not. That must be clear utterly, Tony. Once someone becomes a vampire, they answer to me for all their actions. Angelica will not get special treatment if she betrays my rules as a vampire…or even as a donor."

Tony let out a long breath. "Agreed. Angelica's a good girl, Devlin. She's always done good for me. She'll do good for you, too."

"Then let us hope she does the same for Danial," Devlin said, standing. "Can you arrange for her to be sent to my house in a few weeks' time? I'll want her to meet Danial and also have him meet her, so we can see if it's going to work."

"Of course," Tony said, holding out his hand.

Devlin shook it. "Good seeing you, Tony."

Thane also offered his hand. "I'll look into additional donors for Danial, Devlin."

"Thank you," Devlin said, shaking his hand. "It's a pleasure to work with you both."

Lash and Devlin walked out. Angelica was not at her desk.

"Think she ran off because of me?" Lash asked with evil hilarity as they headed out the door. He snickered.

"We're ready for pickup, Titus," Devlin said into his cell phone. He hung up and looked over at Lash. "I wouldn't be surprised if she did, Lash. But Danial can finesse her."

"You really think that this is going to work?" Lash said sarcastically. "Bringing Danial back here? You'll be at each other's throats. And why would he go along with any of this?"

"He has his reasons," Devlin said cryptically. "This is just business to all of us. And let's hope it does work out. Or you'll have more work than you know what to do with."

Lash shook his head, then smiled. "Fair enough."

Partners

(This is an extended version of the tale previously published in Midnight Thirsts 2)

A tall, dark-haired man crouched in the cab of a parked crane. The light of the full moon illuminated the many stacks of plywood and two-by-fours that surrounded the machine, casting long steady shadows. Far to the left, a mansion-in-progress stood, its bare wood bones already bleached slightly by the hot summer sun. Close by, to the right, a rough building stood dark, with a port-a-john next to it. No sound stirred the unnatural quiet of the deserted construction site.

Someone or something was causing that stillness, Danial thought to himself, shifting slightly to check his left view from his vantage point. Construction workers rarely were the neatest employees, especially in midsummer. At the very least, the resident rodents should've been fighting over the remnants of discarded sandwich ends or the lone left-behind Cheeto.

From beside the port-a-john came the sudden rustle of cloth. A moment later, one of the garbage can lids was lifted.

That was no hungry rat. That was what he'd been hired for. Danial slipped out on the opposite side of the cab, balancing his weight on the crane's large treads.

The noises stopped. Danial froze, waiting.

There was a stealthy footstep toward him, then another. Danial tensed, his hand going to his semiautomatic at his waist as he prepared show himself.

Here we go…

A loud ring shattered the quiet.

A metallic bang rang out, then a trashcan flew through the air towards him. Danial ducked, the can sailing over his head to smash into the building's side, showering the smelly contents all over him. Cursing, he stood and fired blindly toward the sound of rapidly retreating footsteps. After squeezing off two rounds, he threw down his gun in disgust.

"Goddamn it!"

His cell phone continued to ring, the signature tone telling him exactly who'd ruined his well-planned trap.

Danial wiped the garbage off his face as best he could with his handkerchief, and then wiped his hands, grimacing at remaining smears of rotten meat. Gingerly, he plucked his phone from his cell pocket and answered it.

"This better be good, Dev."

"It's not Dev," a hissing, self-satisfied voice said. "And it's not good either, Vampire."

Danial grated his teeth together, trying to control his fangs from growing in his anger. "What do you want, Lash?"

"It's not what I want. It's what your brother wants, Danny—"

Danial hung up, then picked up his gun from the ground. Wiping it off, he holstered it, and strode back to his car, thinking.

There was one thief involved so far: amateur level, to have run without a fight. The throw could have been a diversion by a startled male; the industrial metal was much too heavy to be thrown at that velocity and height by a female, even a non-human one. There had been an odd scent around, possibly some type of werecreature. After four hundred years, he trusted his nose more than his eyes.

He might as well get to his campsite. Dawn was only a few hours away.

* * * *

Blearily, Danial awakened. Daylight could be seen as a dim glow through the dense fabric of the tent.

The damn phone was ringing again. Worse, it was the same tone.

He pushed dark hair out of his eyes, wincing at the still present smell of stale nachos, and answered it.

"What?"

"Danial," a smooth masculine voice purred. "Are you enjoying your little excursion in the great outdoors?"

"I was until you called. What is it you want, Dev?"

"I've got a problem that could use your expertise."

"Then why have Lash call? You know I hate him."

"Then you should've bought your own camping equipment and not borrowed his. He only lent that to you as a favor to me. The least you could do is be civil to him—"

If only there was some other scent that covered the smell of vampire better than weresnake and was just as off-putting to nonhumans. Alas, that five star protection came at a high price. "I'm always polite to him, when it doesn't mean risking my life. Now get to the point."

Dev sighed dramatically. "It's the usual problem with young adults. There was a girl dating one of the newly turned; you know, one of the groupies who think it's all everlasting love and romance. She knew what he was and wanted that for herself. He knew I'd kill him if he gave her what she wanted, so he broke it off like a good little vampire."

"So what's the trouble? Your minion was towing the line."

"The girl," Dev retorted, exasperated. "She was upset and went looking for another vampire, hoping to make him jealous." He paused. "She found Jonas."

Someone was rapidly approaching the tent's location. Danial transferred the phone to his other ear as he hurriedly pulled on his shoes and socks. "So what's the problem? Didn't he dispose of her? He was never squeamish about who he drank from."

"No, Idiot," Dev griped. "I said she found him, not that he found her. She sprained her finger and went to the ER that afternoon—"

The footsteps were almost inside the clearing where Danial's tent was. Danial finished tying his shoes, shrugged on a hooded sweatshirt, then pulled on gloves. There was nothing more to be done to cover up, damn it; he hadn't brought a ski mask. "Will you get to the point?"

"The twit caught Jonas and a friend working over a newly dead car accident casualty."

Not surprising. Jonas worked in the morgue more for the blood than the paycheck. "Why are you bothering me for this? Send her ex to bring her to you. You can convince her to keep quiet, or Lash can dispose of the body. It's a simple solution either way."

"Can't. Jonas took too long covering up. By the time he had, she'd blabbed to her friends. They don't believe her, of course, but that could change if she disappears—"

The footsteps went to the door of the tent, then suddenly veered off, moving past it.

Danial sagged in relief. Thank God. If he'd had to kill someone, it'd be hell getting their body out of here unnoticed, not to mention the shot might be overheard. Any shot outside hunting season would provoke interest, especially inside a public park.

"—Jonas is worried she'll come back with the police—"

"More likely she'll demand he turn her in return for her silence," Danial mused. "That would be the easiest all around, Dev. You could always kill her if she doesn't behave once she's under your rule."

"Much as that's tempting, no," Dev said firmly. "She's only sixteen. The age laws are one of the few I strictly enforce." His tone became sarcastic. "That's where Solutions, Inc. comes in. Find me a solution."

There wasn't another easy one that came to mind. "If I find you a solution, what's my payment? Money isn't enough."

"You wanted to be closer to a city," Devlin said enticingly. "What about trading the rural West for the hustle and bustle of the East?"

Danial did a double take. Dev couldn't mean it, not after what had happened last time. "You're offering me my own state?"

"I'm offering you a shot at New York with my blessing," Dev corrected. "Garrett is not even a fourth of your age. You can win easily if you fight him."

Danial snorted. "That means he's going to fight fang and talon to keep it. I've been there before, Dev. Not enough. Besides, I've grown accustomed to the freedom of not having a territory to rule—"

"Then what about some steady lucrative work?" Dev offered. "As you're aware, I'm in a position of power and I have allies. You've always wanted to expand your business. Here's your chance. Take the position and I'll throw in the work as incentive."

This was the perfect offer, which meant there was something dark and oily unseen underneath. "What do you get out of this?" Danial said suspiciously. "You want this much more than you're telling. If Garrett's young, he's no threat to you."

"I have my reasons," Dev said cryptically. "But make your own choice. Let me know at your earliest convenience. In person." Click.

Rain pattered lightly on the tent roof, then pounded as if buckets were being dumped on the fabric. A crack of thunder sounded.

Danial put down the phone, blinked at the display, then groaned. It was late afternoon. There was no way to fit more sleep in before he left for his stakeout tonight.

There was a frantic rubbing at the tent door fabric. "Excuse me? Can I come in?"

Shit. Danial leaned back out of daylight range of the door. "Who is it?"

A young woman unzipped the tent door and then stumbled inside, her muddy clothing soaked. "Cami. Thanks. It's pouring and I can't find the trail markers—"

"Sure, come in and dry off," Danial offered with a sexy smile, moving backwards into the darkness as he pulled off his gloves. "Just please zip the door after you. I don't want to get wet."

* * * *

As soon as it was dusk, Danial packed up his tent and gear and left the campsite. By that time, Cami was awake and showing no ill effects of the half pint of blood she'd lost. He dropped her off near her car, pale and swooning goodbyes as if he'd saved her from marauding pirates instead of a little rainstorm.

He had overdone it a bit with the poetry, perhaps. Still, Cami had saved him a lot of time and discomfort, not to mention her fresh blood had been much more satisfying than the packaged blood he'd brought with him. A little romance was the least he could do in return.

* * * *

An hour later, Danial resumed his vigil at the construction site, this time from a new position behind a stack of fresh lumber. There was no sign of anyone yet. To keep his mind sharp, he began going over all he knew.

An unidentified person had been seen lurking after dark by several employees. Some building materials had been stolen, chiefly the easier ones to resell, like the portable power tools and the mobile generators. There were no cameras except those within the central trailer the foreman used as an office, so there was no witness to the theft. The tools had been stored in a locked portable building that showed no signs of breaking and entering. The foreman had questioned all employees and exonerated them, blaming the unidentified stranger for the theft.

It seemed a straight case of embezzlement done from inside in Danial's estimation. Either way, he'd find out soon enough.

As had happened the previous night, there came the sound of a trashcan lid being lifted slowly, then some plastic began rustling. Danial left his hiding spot, this time ghosting along the far side of the building silently until he'd come up behind the searching figure, his pistol aimed and cocked.

"Don't move or I'll shoot—!"

The figure whirled, the lid slamming into Danial like an oversize Frisbee. He grunted, but didn't drop the gun. His shot aimed for the figure's torso instead hit its neck. With a yelp, it crumpled.

Danial moved closer to the gasping figure. The skinny blond man in his early twenties clutched his neck. Surprisingly there wasn't much blood. "Who are you and what's your business here?"

The figure coughed, spitting out blood. "My name's Theo. I was just trying to scrounge a little food. Why the hell did you shoot me?"

"You moved. Now tell me where and to whom you're reselling the tools."

Theo sat cross-legged, rubbing his neck. "That's not me, smartshit. The supervisor's the one stealing. He's got a helper, too, but I don't know his name."

Danial nodded. "I suspected as much. How do you fit into this?"

Theo sneered. "I don't. Like I said, I just wanted food." He got to his feet, then faced Danial. "And that gun isn't going to be much use against me."

Theo's neck wound was healed, new skin showing through the drying blood.

Danial holstered his gun. "You're a were of some kind. What?"

"Cougar," Theo grated out. "Are we done?"

Sounds of feet approaching came suddenly.

"Hide," Danial said, ducking down. Theo also crouched, the both of them watching the building.

Three men came into sight, all carrying drawn guns. "I heard a shot," one said, gesturing with his gun. "Go find out who's here and get rid of them. I'll get the stuff."

The leader headed into the building. The other two men spread out and began searching, heading directly toward Danial and Theo.

Danial turned to Theo. "Do you want to help or leave?"

Theo nodded. "I'll help."

"Wait for my signal."

The men crept closer as Danial and Theo waited silently. As the first passed Danial, he shoved hard, knocking the man off his feet, the gun clattering into the shadows. Theo punched the other, who went flying ten feet.

Danial glared over at Theo as they tied up the men with some bungee cords from Danial's pocket. "Why'd you hit him so hard? You not only broke his jaw, you also knocked him unconscious."

"Their stealing made my life harder and it was already bad," Theo growled.

"Watch these two," Danial replied, exasperated. "I'll be back with the last one."

He ran off quickly, slipping into the building after the leader. Danial found him transferring power tools from metal shelving into several boxes. With a light push, Danial knocked him sprawling.

"Your boss is going to be surprised," Danial said with a smile, handcuffing the disoriented man to the shelves. "He swore you could be trusted." He got out his phone and began dialing.

"Let me go," the man groaned, his eyes panicked. "I can't go back to prison—"

"Sit tight," Danial replied coolly, hanging up the phone and leaving. "You won't be alone long."

* * * *

An hour before dawn, Danial returned to the construction site. After a few minutes, Theo appeared.

"It went fine, in case you're curious," Danial said, irritated. "We could've used your statement, though. It was my word against theirs."

"Then I'd have to explain what I was doing here," Theo shot back. "Why were they stealing?"

"Just in it for the money," Danial said, studying Theo. "What were you doing here?"

"Nothing," Theo said bleakly, turning away. "Just go away and leave me alone."

There was potential opportunity here, no question, Danial thought. "You helped me. I'd like to treat you to a shower and some food in appreciation."

Theo turned around, sarcastic. "Who are you? How did I get blessed to have a benevolent vampire as my guardian angel?"

"I'm Danial. I do detective work, mainly."

"Crimes?"

"Mysteries, usually. Sometimes they're tame. About six months ago I took a case where a family's two cats went missing."

"Who calls a detective for a missing cat?"

"They called me in when they found a white bone of a front paw sticking up in their flower bed like a plea for help."

Theo grimaced. "What was the mystery?"

"Strange, actually. A neighbor boy was interested in the girl. He'd tried to kidnap the cat so he could return it and be a hero. Instead, it had dashed away from him as he'd chased it and gotten hit. He buried it out of respect, not because he was trying to scare anyone. He felt terrible."

"And the other cat?"

"He was several houses over, locked in a neighbor's shed by accident." Danial smiled. "One of the happy endings."

"That's the tame end of the spectrum. Give me an example of the other end."

"Last year I spent a month shadowing a killer who was going after blonde has-been cheerleaders at high school reunions—"

"Serial killers frequent high school reunions?"

"Frequently. Where else do people trust a name card to identify a person they can't recognize?"

Theo shrugged. "You've got a point. Do you only do murders?"

Danial laughed. "I do anything I'm interested in. If you partner with me, I'll give you a say in what cases you handle, at least some of them."

"Are they always humans?"

"Mostly other than human, actually. I just took the cat one because I have a soft spot for cats." Danial opened his wallet, took out some money and offered it to Theo. "For your help tonight. No strings."

Theo took it. "Thanks."

Danial walked away. "Take care of yourself, Theo."

"Wait."

Danial stopped. "Yes?"

"Are there any cases you've committed to already nearby?" Theo said slowly.

Danial nodded. "There's an amusement park that's supposedly haunted that's next on my calendar. If there's anything to the story, it won't be a tame one. Interested?"

Theo's eyebrows shot up. "You're shitting me."

Danial laughed for the first time in ages. "I'm due there in two days. You want to meet me or not?"

Theo nodded. "I'll be there."

* * * *

Theo was waiting when a showered and rested Danial pulled up in front of the rusted gates of Fantasy Land a night later.

"I couldn't believe this was the place," Theo said, walking over. "It looks like it's out of business."

"That's because it is," Danial said, checking his gun. "The new owners want to tear the place down and build a new mall."

"What happened?"

"A teenage couple crept in here to have sex. They were found the next morning dead in each other's arms. The media frenzy has panicked the investors. Two have already backed out of the project. The owners need this solved fast before the rest pull their funding."

"Why a media frenzy? They might have had a suicide pact, or—"

"They had cuts all over their body, so many they were almost completely exsanguinated of blood. There was no weapon found."

Theo made a face. "I'm guessing you ruled out vampires already. Any other ideas?"

Danial rummaged in the back seat. "No. I favor a human killer who was jealous as the culprit. That's the usual motive in a crime like this."

Theo leaned against the truck, incredulous. "What do you do if the cause isn't human? Do you have access to magic?"

Danial chuckled, slipping a vial into his pocket. "Yes, to a small extent. Come on, the night is wasting."

Opening the locked gate with a key, Danial and Theo entered the park. The night was balmy, the dry air cool on their faces. They wandered down one path, then another, passing rides, empty concession stands, and vacant game booths, a few dusty faded prizes still hanging from hooks.

"Sense anything?" Danial asked. "I don't."

"I smell stale popcorn faintly," Theo replied. "But nothing supernatural. Where did the murders take place?"

"The bodies were found in the House of Mirrors," Danial said. "In the center room." He pointed. "There."

The attraction wasn't very big, no more than an acre. The outside was painted dull black with no ornamentation other than the word Mirror Maze above the door. Each huge letter was itself formed out of mirrors, their reflective surfaces shining in the moonlight.

"I smell blood now," Theo said uneasily. "And something else I can't identify. It's sickening, whatever it is."

"That's sulphur," Danial said darkly. "That usually means a demon—"

Theo turned to Danial. "How do you know that? How did you get called for this job?"

"I have a lot of experience," Danial replied, moving past him towards the building. "This particular job came from the sister of one of my donors. It was her best friend that was killed."

Theo blinked. "What's a donor?"

"Someone who contracts to donate blood to me."

"Don't you hunt for blood in nightclubs or something?"

Danial gave Theo a dour look. "Very funny. Come on."

Danial pushed inside the open door, Theo right behind him. Once their eyes adapted to the lack of light, they followed the police markers to the center. A large pool of dried blood was there, many smears and tracks from police shoes at the edges. Danial crouched near the blood, studying the floor.

Theo shrugged. "I can't smell anything but blood and that sulphur—"

All the mirrors cracked abruptly, shards shooting out to bury themselves in Danial and Theo. Theo dropped, screaming and writhing, his body a pincushion of glass razors. Danial fell forward into the blood, his back and neck a mass of blood and silica.

Theo jerked, keening in pain. Danial was still.

An apparition formed slowly, the features of a young boy scowling. He ghosted closer, peering down at Theo.

"I'm not leaving," the thing whispered longingly. "You can't make me leave—"

Danial reared back suddenly, throwing a cloud of power at the ghost. The specter screamed, burning holes appearing, the flames eating it in a shower of white glowing fire. It flailed, falling to its knees, then disappeared.

Danial got to his feet gingerly, then helped Theo up. "Brace yourself on the mirror frame and hold on." He began to pull out the shards, Theo's skin healing up as the glass came free.

"Son of a bitch," Theo snarled. "What the hell was all that?"

"A demon masquerading as a child," Danial said, still working efficiently. "That white fire burnt up his physical form. He's back in Hell now."

"Ouch," Theo growled as Danial yanked a large chunk out. "Why not just use some holy water or something?"

"I'm agnostic. You need faith for that to work, not just a Bible." Danial plucked out the last piece. "Turn and I'll get the front."

Theo turned, grimacing. "That white fire was magic."

Danial nodded. "A witch friend makes it for me. It's white magic."

Theo stretched, pulling out the last few shards on his arms. "You don't do dark magic?"

Danial laughed, but the sound was resigned rather than exuberant. "I do whatever it takes, Theo. Don't sugarcoat me. I get enough of that from my donors." He turned away. "Do my back, please."

Theo pulled out the shards, Danial flinching and hissing in pain. "Is one of the reasons you offered me a job because I can take wounds like this and not die?"

Danial nodded. "I'd be lying if I said otherwise. Regeneration is an asset in my business. But I offered you a job because when I gave you the choice of helping or running, you chose to help." He faced Theo. "I need someone who can be trusted to make not only a quick decision, but also the right one. Are you in?"

Theo nodded. "Yes."

"Good," Danial said, pleased. "Now let's get out of here."

They retraced their steps, their gait slow and stiff from their weakened state. As they left the building, the lights all around them came on, the rides suddenly coming to life as carnival music blared tinny from the loudspeakers.

Theo turned to Danial. "I hope you've got more of that powder."

"Fresh out," Danial muttered, his eyes scanning in all directions.

Unnatural shadows gathered growing larger and darker as the music swelled. Eyes appeared in the inky blackness, red-orange pupils staring.

"What are you?" Danial shouted. "What do you want?"

"They want your blood," an old voice creaked from behind them. "So do I."

Theo and Danial whipped around. A bloated clown floated there, his painted face skeletal, his eyes dark holes, his mouth a twisted misshapen slash that opened revealing pointed teeth like a shark.

"Any ideas?" Theo whispered.

"Yes…run!"

Danial and Theo turned, only to find the clown behind them. It kicked Theo with his left boot, the solid blow sending him crashing through a rusty fence into the bumper car rink. Driverless, they converged at once on his prone form, ramming him hard from all sides as he cried out in pain.

"You're no man," Danial said, dodging as the clown reached for him. "Show your real form, demon!"

The clown grinned, his outline morphing fluidly. "What do you wish, Danial? There are so many horrors from your past I'd love to become—"

The thing knew his name. What else did it know? Danial gritted his teeth, fighting his sudden fear. "What do you want?"

"To make you suffer," the clown lisped, leering. It lunged for him, ripping his shirt.

Danial drew his gun and emptied it into the phantom. The bullets passed through harmlessly, thudding into the side of the building.

Suddenly the outline morphed, the clown's body becoming masculine and blond as an elegant face formed, its golden eyes gleaming.

"No," Danial breathed.

"Yes," the figure purred, beckoning with two taloned fingers. "Come to Dev."

Danial drew a knife from his boot. "Come and get me."

"You're just like me," Dev said lovingly, moving closer. "You become more like me every year—"

"No!" Danial shouted, backing away.

Dev advanced, long fangs smeared with blood. "You could've killed me long ago, but you didn't. Don't you rue that day, Danial? How many lives could you have saved? Thousands? Millions?"

"That's not true—!"

"I've drunk an ocean of blood and I have you to thank." Dev laughed wildly. "Without your deeds, I'd never have come to America. It was you who killed Annabelle—"

"No," Danial said weakly, going to his knees. "It wasn't my fault."

Dev stood over him, gloating as an ax formed in his white hands. "It was. Your paltry good deeds of the last century can't atone for all the evil you've done." Dev raised the ax. "You deserve to die—"

Water hit Dev in the back, the force of it propelling him over Danial. The creature landed hard on its side, momentarily stunned, its clown's form reappearing for an instant before Dev's features reformed. Danial threw himself at it, his knife coming down in a deadly arc. The figure screamed and shifted, Dev's features melting into a tiger's ravening jaws that lunged up for Danial's throat. Danial snapped with his own fangs, latching onto the beast's shoulder as it buried its fangs in his forearm, his arm driving the knife deeper into the monster's chest, twisting it.

The thing shuddered once, then sickening black smoke wafted up from the body as it fell in, crumbling.

Danial climbed to his feet shakily, then walked to where Theo sat, his bloody hands still clutching the fire hose.

"You okay?" Danial asked.

"Broken ribs," Theo answered, wincing. "Are we done?"

"For tonight," Danial said, putting Theo's arm over his shoulder. "Let's get out of here."

"Walk slow," Theo said weakly as Danial helped him to his car. "I can't walk well, much less fight. I wasn't sure what to use as a weapon—"

Why hadn't Theo changed form in the fight, Danial wondered. Not only would it have speeded the healing ribs, but a cougar's powerful form would have withstood the blows better than Theo's human form. In fact, Theo had not even partially shifted at all, which was behavior Danial had never seen from any were in a fight. His aversion to change was something to keep in mind, as it could prove a potential weakness.

"—thank God that fire hose was nearby."

"Thank God for you, you mean." Danial rubbed his eyes.

"Who was that?" Theo asked. "That person the demon became? It was someone you knew."

"A vampire I know," Danial lied uneasily. "A bad one." He managed a smile. "You did good, Theo."

"Thanks," Theo said awkwardly. "Do you need blood? You look like hell."

104

"Yes, but not yours," Danial said, taking out his phone. "That's what donors are for. Do you prefer beef or chicken?"

"Chicken," Theo replied. "After we eat, what's the plan?"

"We take a few days to rest and heal up at my house. Then we'll head to the next case. I have a small job in New York, if you're interested."

Theo grinned. "Looks like there's never a dull moment with you around."

Danial smiled widely, baring fangs. "That's right. You sure you want to do this?"

Theo bared his own cougar fangs in a smile. "Yes, partner. Let's go."

* * * *

Later that week, Danial and Theo disembarked from the plane in Syracuse, New York.

"Be on your guard," Danial cautioned, getting into the truck. "Devlin is a fiend, as I've told you. Lash, his henchman, is no better."

"Why you'd consider moving here closer to them is beyond me," Theo said bluntly. "You could've shipped back the equipment you borrowed."

"I need to know what Devlin really wants with me," Danial said darkly. "It's time to face him and find out."

* * * *

An hour later, Theo and Danial were standing in Devlin's home, the tall striking blonde man dressed in gold and black regarding them intently, his interest no longer on the poetry he'd been writing.

"Danial," Devlin purred from his ornate chair, his golden eyes shining, "What an unexpected surprise."

"Not really, when you all but summoned me for an audience," Danial said. "Pass on my thanks to Lash, please."

Theo put down the tent and other camping gear on the floor.

Devlin nodded. "Unfortunately Lash is not here to accept right now. He's out west himself, tending to a personal errand."

Danial tensed. "Where?"

"Not sure, really," Devlin said with a dismissive gesture. "And you don't care anyway, so let's get to business. Are you coming back east or not?"

"Spell out directly the lucrative work you mentioned; who it's for, what it entails, and how long it's expected to last," Danial countered.

"Or?" Devlin asked, picking up a pencil and twirling it.

"Or my new partner and I will be on our way."

"Partner," Devlin said deliciously, studying Theo with new interest. "This is unprecedented." He dropped the pen and steepled his fingers. "The work is hits for the mob, it entails killing degenerates, and it will last as long as you and I will, Danial."

"Murder?" Theo asked, repulsed. "I didn't sign on for murder."

"I don't kill innocents for pay," Danial added. "That's assassin's work."

"Don't pretend you're Sherlock Holmes with me," Devlin hissed, his eyes reddening. "You're old enough to know the only true innocents are children. None of those will be on your list."

"No," Theo said staunchly. "We're not interested."

"You don't matter," Devlin retorted coldly, snapping the pencil in two. His hardness eased as he addressed his brother. "Danial, you have been playing detective for years now. You're known in Colorado, but nowhere else. That is how it will stay unless you take the next step. To do that, you need cash."

"Blood money," Danial replied evenly.

"It isn't the first you've been offered," Devlin said meaningfully. "It wouldn't be the first you've taken."

"Danial, you can't seriously be considering this," Theo said.

Danial didn't reply.

"Of course he's considering it," Devlin said gleefully. "His business is the most important thing to him." He bared his fangs at Theo in a wide grin. "Something you would do well to remember, Cat."

"Don't call him that," Danial said mildly. "There will be no insults, Dev. That's one of my first terms. Make sure your snake henchman agrees."

Devlin nodded. "Of course. What else?"

"I want freedom to do what I wish, without your interference—"

Devlin nodded. "As long as you give me the necessary respect at formal events."

"—I want all my employees and friends, such as Theo, given freedom from persecution—"

"As long as they obey the vampire laws."

"—I want a loan and your backing to get Solution's Inc. on track to a global business—"

"Name your price. The references will not be a problem. You are a master sleuth."

"—my business will take me all over the world if I succeed. I want you to secure me safe passage. I have enemies here and abroad—"

Devlin nodded. "Expected. Done."

"—lastly, I want to know the real reason you want me here," Danial finished, his eyes locked on Devlin's. "The truth."

Devlin eyed him, then smiled. "There has been too much between us to have you believe that I want you back for old time's sake."

Danial stared back, unsmiling.

Devlin nodded slightly. "I want Garrett removed. He's becoming unstable. He is one of my turns, Danial, so if I do it I must admit to the error of making him. If you do it, I'm spared that embarrassment."

"That's it?" Danial said skeptically.

"Pretty much," Danial said persuasively. "My home is here in New York. Garrett is not doing his job, and I'm tired of putting out fires like the one I called you about a few days ago. I need someone who can handle a state. I know you can."

Danial let out a breath, then nodded once. "I'll accept, but I need a month or so to make arrangements and move."

Devlin beamed. "And my problem?"

Danial smiled back, fangs bared. "Take me to her and I'll solve it."

* * * *

"Jonas told me if I met you here you'd make me a vampire."

If only I had that power, Danial thought. "No, Angelica," he said enticingly. "I'm here to make you another offer, one I believe you'll welcome."

The beautiful young girl gazed at him, her blue eyes suspicious. "What?"

"Become my donor," Danial said seductively, taking her in his arms. He kissed her throat, then pricked it lightly with his fangs.

Angelica sighed happily. "You'll bite me?"

Pity; all that beauty and no brains. "Yes, and drink your blood. I'll also pay you a stipend."

The suspicious look was back. "What else are you expecting?"

Like you wouldn't give me sex if I asked, Danial thought. "The stipend is for your promise to save your blood just for me. It's the normal arrangement."

"But you won't turn me," she said plaintively.

"If I did, I couldn't drink from you anymore," Danial lied. "This way I can over and over, Angel. Besides, there's that rule about turning someone so young. It's all right if I call you Angel, isn't it?"

Angelica was excited, but still reserved. "Yes, of course. Will you turn me when I'm older?"

"You can turn at twenty-one if it's approved," Danial replied carefully. "Until then you have to agree to keep me and our arrangement secret. Will you do that?"

Angelica stared at him, then kissed him. "Yes, please. Will you bite me now?"

Problem solved. Danial grinned. "Come to me, my darling."

* * * *

After solidifying arrangements with Angelica for next month, Danial boarded the aircraft to find Theo waiting.

"How can you consider Devlin's offer?" Theo asked incredulously. "Or were you just playing him?"

Danial shook his head, taking his seat. "The price was right, Theo. I've wanted this for a long time. A few human deaths are of no consequence, especially if they're vermin."

Theo sat down a seat away. "You aren't who I thought you were."

Danial whipped around to face Theo, his eyes blood red. "I am who I've always been. You're like the rest, glutted on tales of benevolent vampires. This is the real world. I do what I can. That's all I can do."

"You didn't even introduce me."

"That was on purpose," Danial replied evenly. "Devlin rules the United States, if you haven't already guessed. You know what would happen if he knew your name and you don't sign on with me? You'll be killed. I was giving you a way out."

Theo didn't reply. The silence stretched.

"Did you kill that girl?" Theo finally said.

"Of course not," Danial replied. "She wants the thrill of being with a vampire. As she ages, she'll outgrow it. By being my donor, she can have both. It's a simple solution."

"What are you really offering me?" Theo asked.

Danial's expression softened slightly. "Friendship as well as partnership. A fifty-fifty split on all profits above the needs of the business. Protection, to an extent. Your life doesn't have to be like it was." He paused. "What happened to you?"

"I'd rather not talk about it," Theo said stiffly.

"That's fine," Danial said hurriedly. "But I need to know now if you'll be my partner or not."

"No," Theo said softly.

Danial got to his feet, livid. "You ungrateful ass. I offer you the chance of a lifetime and you throw it away to go back to scrounging in garbage for scraps?"

"I can't murder people—"

"Who asked you to?" Danial snarled. "I can take care of the killing myself."

"I'm sure. You shot at me just because I startled you."

"I didn't know you were there."

"Yes, you did," Theo replied.

Solution's Inc. wouldn't grow without someone Danial could trust to help him. He needed Theo.

"Yes, I did," Danial sighed, swiftly switching tactics. "Dev has become a monster. Every year I see more and more pain and suffering and too little good. The line between evil and good is growing indistinct. I'm starting not to care and it terrifies me."

"You're nothing like him."

You don't know he's my brother. "I need hope. I need someone to help me find the line again." Danial held out his hand. "I need a partner."

Theo stared at Danial's hand, then reluctantly shook it. "You're right. I've nothing to go back to. I can do good as part of your company. Partners."

Thank God, Danial thought happily. "Partners."

State of Grace

(Previously published in Dark Moon's Vampires Anthology 2011)

The broken-down factory loomed from a hundred yards away in the pale moonlight, its broken windows like still, jagged teeth. No light beckoned, nor did any sound break the silence.

An old van paused for a second at the driveway before driving up quickly past the broken chain-link gate. Ten minutes later a furtive figure darted in. As it crept toward the factory, another form exploded from the shadows.

Jackie turned smoothly, her gun in her hand. "Get out of my way, Rod."

"Get out of here!" Rodney urged frantically, his eyes flicking from Jackie's face to the empty road. "Kale's going to come down that road any minute with his buddies. If they find you here, you're dead."

"I have to try," Jackie replied, pushing him away resolutely. "You know what's going on in there. I can't let it happen and do nothing—"

"What's going on in there's been going on since before there were vampires," Rodney hissed back, his blue eyes reddening. "One human isn't going to stop it, especially not you alone—"

"It's easy to see your soul's dead," Jackie threw back with a sneer as she headed towards the factory. "Someone has to do something. Just run away, Rod. Leave."

Leave you to die, you mean? Rodney thought, watching her walk away. Jackie would be no match for what waited through those doors. He was a vampire and even he wasn't.

If there was ever a time she'd needed him, it was now. Warily, he followed.

He'd only gone a few steps when Jackie screamed. The sound squeezed his heart like a vise, galvanizing him into action. He dashed around the corner to find her on her back, a tall, lithe vampire above her holding her down, fangs already sliding into her soft flesh.

"Get off her, Kale," Rodney hissed, drawing a survival knife. "Now."

Kale laughed, fangs gleaming wickedly. "Make me, coward." He bit down. Jackie struggled and cried out in pain.

Rodney plunged the knife into his back. Before Kale could recover, Rodney kicked him off Jackie's prone form, the vampire flying back to smash into a low concrete wall. As Kale struggled to get up, Rodney began hacking at his neck.

"Stop, Rod," Kale hissed, pushing weakly against Rodney. "You can't win this. Nathan will kill you—"

Kale's words were cut off as Rodney bore down with all his inhuman strength. The flesh of Kale's neck parted completely as his spine rent, blood and fluid leaking out. Kale's body slumped, his arms falling limply at his sides.

"He's dead," Jackie whispered.

God, I hope so, Rodney thought desperately. "You hurt?"

"He bit into my shoulder muscle. It's nothing some Neosporin won't fix." She got to her feet, wiping at her mud-spattered jeans. "He was guarding this entry." She switched on a flashlight and gestured to a yawning door, concrete steps leading down. "That's our way in."

Rodney turned to face her. "No. You can't save them, not any of them. They'll just find others to kill—"

His words fell into emptiness. Jackie was already down the steps. The light of her flashlight dimmed, then disappeared.

"Damn it." Rodney wiped his blade on Kale's clothes and went after her. His eyes adjusted quickly to the darkness, making out a dark concrete tunnel ahead. He started walking as fast as he dared.

How had it come to this? He had been a senior close to graduation, with parents who loved him and big plans for the future. Instead, he'd gotten bitten late one night as he walked home from the bus stop. His maker had been half-dead already from some run in with a foe; half of his face missing. Rodney had fainted dead away when the creature had burst out. He'd come to with the thing lying dead across him, blood in his mouth along with a newly grown set of fangs.

A sudden noise startled him, his hand clutching the knife hard. Damn it, he was going to get killed walking down memory lane. Face reality, Rod, he thought grimly; you're probably going to get killed anyway. You might as well make your peace.

Peace. When was the last time he'd had peace? After the first shock, his parents had been understanding, and said they'd find a cure together. They had contacted some of the best doctors involved in blood diseases the next day. Almost instantly, others of his afflicted brethren had discovered their wayward lamb. His mother, father and younger brother had been killed, their home torched. Then Kale had come for him.

He'd tortured Rod badly, telling him this was his only warning. "This isn't nightclubs and teen sex," Kale had said harshly. "We have rules. You follow them or you die." He'd paused then cut another slice into Rod's abdomen, bringing a scream. "The first is you keep your head down. Don't interfere in the human world; don't kill; don't make friends and don't call attention to yourself." He'd sliced Rodney again, this one deep enough to make some pink intestine peep out along with a louder scream. "You were born in this state without Nathan's permission, Rod. He's the boss here in Tennessee. I'm his enforcer. That means if he sends me for you again, you're dead." Kale had grinned, baring fangs. "You'll think your family got off lightly. Be smart and do the right thing."

Kale had left Rodney in a pool of blood, his regenerative powers weak. It had taken him a week to heal. Since then, Rodney had kept himself hidden, his hope extinguished just like his future had been.

The noise sounded again. Up ahead, a door opened. Rodney clutched his knife, ghosting closer, but didn't dare peer around the corner.

"Put him in there with the rest," a cold voice said. "He's a loser. Hurry up."

There was an animal snarl, then a curse and the door slammed, metal rasping and clinking.

Rodney waited until the footsteps receded, then turned the corner and ran up to the padlocked door. Pressing his ear to the metal, he listened. There were five heartbeats, two of those uneven and weak.

Damn it, where was Jackie? This is what she'd been after. She'd gone right past them.

It wasn't the first time her compassion had led her into danger. That was how they'd met. She'd been feeding semi-feral cats at an abandoned farm, the same one where he'd been hiding out. She'd glimpsed him watching from the shadows, screamed then run. The next day she'd returned undeterred with more cat food, a few Have-a-Heart traps, and a shotgun loaded for bear. After feeding the cats, she'd set the traps to the side and come looking for him.

"What are you doing here?" she'd demanded, leveling the gun at him.

"I live here," he told her.

She gaped at him, then took in his dirty appearance and his ragged clothes. The next day, she brought him some worn but clean clothes and a box of moist wipes.

They'd gotten to be good friends this past summer. That lasted until the first day of fall, when she'd come early one day and caught him feeding on one of the cats.

The shotgun blast had knocked him off his feet, the cat screeching away in ball of claws and puffed fur. He'd come to with Jackie peering at him from a safe distance, her gold cross in her hand brandished like a sword.

"What are you?"

Rodney had smiled for the first time in a decade. "You already know, or you wouldn't be hanging onto your cross for bravado." He brushed himself off, fingering the bloodstained hole over his newly healed chest. "I don't suppose you brought any clothes with you?"

Jackie shook her head, tears welling in her eyes. "How can you feed off them? They're defenseless."

"It doesn't hurt the cats," Rodney said, his eyes sliding away from hers. "I heal them afterwards. I never kill any, and I feed from different ones each day—"

"That doesn't make it okay—"

"I have to live," he'd hissed back at her, ashamed of how pitiful he sounded. "I don't have another way. You don't know how it is—"

"There's always another way," Jackie had replied evenly. "You just need to find it." She paused, and then said grimly, "I'm a vet. Part of the job is euthanasia. In short, I can get you some animal blood that isn't in use anymore. Will you stop if I do?"

"Yes," Rodney agreed, knowing she'd shoot him again if she didn't.

From that night on, Jackie brought him animal blood in plastic containers whenever she came. It wasn't a feast, but it was enough to keep from starving: much more than he'd dared take from the cats. In the last month, they'd even talked a little…

Footsteps approached. Rodney tensed, slowly moving back his arm for a slashing blow. Another young vampire walked in, his red eyes scanning intently. As soon as he got within reach, Rodney swung his knife, separating the head from the body in one clean blow. The body fell jerking to the floor as the head rolled down the hallway, slowly coming to rest.

How many more would he have to kill? He'd never killed any of his kind before.

There was a sudden shriek then footsteps pounding toward him. Jackie ran into view, another older vampire hot on her heels. She slipped into the pool of blood and went sprawling, the pursuing vampire stopping with a deft maneuver.

"I'd thought to only get animal's blood tonight," the vampire said, salivating. "You're going to be so good going down—"

Rodney tackled him, the knife going in to the hilt as both went down in the blood. Thrashing in the gore, Rodney and the vampire fought, their fangs rending muscle as Rodney tried in vain to get his blade free.

There was a sudden blast. The vampire's head exploded into bloody chunks. Rodney leaned back and looked up at Jackie, her handgun an inch away from his face.

"Is he dead?" she whispered.

"He's got no brain," Rodney replied, cleaning off his hands and knife on the body. "Separate the brain and the body, and the stories say vampires die. I'm glad you brought a weapon—"

Jackie lowered her gun, defeated. "I've looked all over, Rod. I can't find them—"

"They're in here," Rodney said, going to the door. "I think there are five or so—"

Immediately, Jackie straightened, her head snapping up as she holstered her gun. "Can you break the door down?"

Someone heard the shot. More vampires would be down here in a minute, maybe two. "Not fast enough. Check for keys, quick."

A ten-second search of the two headless bodies produced a key on a skull chain. Jackie quickly stuck it in the door and twisted.

"Brace yourself," Rodney whispered. "It's likely bad."

Jackie swung the door open wide. Two growls issued forth from the darkness.

Rodney hit the wall switch. The stark light from the bare bulb above revealed five dogs post dogfight, fresh wounds oozing blood.

"The back two are dead from their wounds already," Rodney said, looking uneasily down the corridor. "Which one do you want me to grab? We've got to go—"

"We have to take them all," Jackie said resolutely, kneeling. She tried to touch the closest dog, a small brown-and-black mutt. It recoiled, whimpering. "I can fix them up; the wounds are mostly superficial—"

"We can't take all three," Rodney retorted. "That black pit-bull isn't going to make it, anyway." He went for the nearest dog, a bloodied white pit-bull mix. It lunged at him but he evaded it, slipping a noose around its neck. He turned back to Jackie, offering her the leash. "Here, take—"

Jackie was on her knees, the wounded mutt in her arms. She was trying to prod the black dog to rise. "Come on, please—"

Footsteps approached. These were the kind Rod had dreaded: unhurried. What if it were Nathan himself? Fear engulfed Rodney. "You have to leave him or we're both going to die—"

Jackie turned to him, tears in her eyes. "I can't. Please, Rod, please help—"

They were going to die and she had never looked so beautiful.

Thrusting the leash into her hands, Rodney grabbed the black dog. It let out a growl, then a painful moan. "Run!"

Jackie and Rodney ran back down the tunnel the way they'd come, the injured dogs heavy in their arms, slowing them down. The footsteps gained behind them, still methodical and deliberate.

They weren't going to make it.

They burst free into the cool air. Rodney slowed. "Keep going, Jackie. Get to your van."

Jackie stopped, shifting the dog in her arms. "Not without you."

"Since when do I matter?" Rodney said lightly. "Get them out. I'll take this one and try to draw off the scent."

"No, you can't—"

"It's almost day up there," Rodney interrupted. "Go where you'll be safe. I'll hide in the factory."

"But the dog—"

"I'll heal the worst of his wounds," Rod replied, hoping because that had always worked with the cats it would work with a dog, too. "He'll make it."

"I'm not leaving without you—"

Rodney grasped her hand. "Get to your van and leave. If I can delay them until dawn, they'll be stuck here." He squeezed. "I can't follow, but neither can they."

Jackie stared at him for a moment, and then leaned over swiftly, brushing her lips with his. "I'll leave, but I'll wait a hundred yards down the road until dawn. You get there, understand?"

"Yes, Ma'am," Rodney drawled, then kissed her one last time. "Now go!"

Jackie flashed him one last smile, then ran.

Rodney watched her go, counted to ten, then hurriedly skirted the building, and then ducked through a broken window. Kicking debris out of his way, he found a basement access door and headed back into blackness.

He waited several minutes, watching his pursuers search. As soon as they'd moved out of hearing, Rod headed to the surface. When he finally burst free into the rapidly lightening night, it was too late: the dog in his arms was dead.

He lay it down carefully under a nearby poplar tree. "I'm sorry," he whispered. He bolted for the road, casting an anxious glance at the crimson rose sky.

Jackie was waiting there in her van. She'd treated the wounded dogs and sedated them. She got out and beckoned to him, smiling, telling him to hurry. She…

The fantasy dissolved into bright light, blinding him. Rodney cringed backward instinctively, waiting to burn in the sun's rays. The chains that bound him to the chair clinked.

"Stop cowering," a voice growled. "We aren't going to hurt you just yet."

Rodney blinked his eyes in the floodlight's glare, taking in the tall man before him. "Kale."

Kale nodded, flashing a toothy smile. "Who'd you expect?"

Rodney lunged for Kale, who quickly stepped out of reach. "I killed you!"

"You did," Kale replied, his tone slightly grudging. "But you didn't separate the head far enough. Minimum distance of five feet, my man. Your loss." He stepped closer. "All I want to know is where's the girl?"

Rodney snarled at Kale and struggled, even as tears crept into his eyes. "What girl?"

"Sit tight," Kale said, walking away and shutting the door. "It's not like you have anything else to do, hero. I'm sure you'll remember right before dawn."

Rodney listened to the retreating footsteps then slumped, remembering.

There had been no last minute reprieve. There would be no reunion up above, either. Jackie would wait most of the morning for someone that would never come.

They parted with a kiss. Rod followed her into the yard, ducking into a shed to wait out the day. Thirty seconds later, three vampires emerged, then stood still, listening.

"Anything?" one said. "I smell nothing but grass and wood rot."

"I don't hear anyone—" another started.

The dog in Rodney's arms whimpered faintly.

"Shh," the last hissed. "I heard something."

"It's nothing," the first vampire said. "I don't know why we're here anyway. We already know Rod and his girlfriend took them—"

Rodney muffled the dog's mouth and nose with his hand as quietly as he could, utterly terrified, his eyes fixed on the vampires.

"Move it," the last vampire ordered. "We've got just another half hour before dawn."

As soon as his pursuers were out of sight, Rod laid the dog down gently, then bit into his own wrist, praying he wasn't making a big mistake. They knew his name and they'd track him back to Jackie. When they did, she'd die, along with the dogs they'd risked their lives to save. But there was another choice, if he was brave enough to see it through.

Rodney smeared his blood on the dog's wounds, biting again and again to keep the wrist wound open. By the time he'd delivered his brand of poultice, he was woozy with blood loss.

After a few moments, the black dog opened its eyes then quickly rolled onto its feet, covered in vampire blood and completely healed. Rodney put out a hand. The dog ventured nearer, unafraid, then sniffed, wagging its tail once.

"Run while you can," Rodney whispered. "Take care of her. I'll buy you guys some time."

The dog gave him an almost human look then tore off toward the road after Jackie.

Rodney slumped back to the shed floor, too weak to stand. A few minutes later, he was found. The three vampires dragged him here to the blood-spattered dog fighting ring and chained him up, informing him with evil smiles that traitors had a special way of dying.

Each moment Rodney was counting down the minutes, hoping morning would come.

Jackie was smart. She wouldn't wait once the sun came up.

The door opened, admitting an African American vampire dressed in an expensive suit. Kale followed him, sullen. The vampire came to stand before Rodney. "I'm Nathan, Ruler of this state. Where is she?"

"Who?" Rodney said angrily. "Let me go. You have no reason to hold me—"

"Don't I?" Nathan purred, his dark eyes like ebony. "You killed some of my men, and stole a few of my dogs—"

"You were going to let your men drain them anyway—"

"That's my right," Nathan retorted. "They're mine. Everything in my territory is mine, including you, Rod. Now tell me about the girl you brought with you."

"Kale saw her," Rodney stalled. "I don't know much about her other than that."

"She was cute and she had a gun," Kale said, shaking his head. "My memory isn't clear. But she was definitely human, not vampire."

"That's what happens when you let yourself get decapitated," Nathan said sharply. "You're lucky someone came along when they did."

Kale went to his knees, groveling. "I'm very grateful—"

"Good," Nathan said coldly. He turned back to Rodney. "Be warned, young one: I was snapping necks like matchsticks only two centuries ago, and that was before I was turned. One last time, who is she?"

"What are you offering me?" Rodney asked. "Will you set me free?"

Nathan looked at Rodney, then gave a peal of rich laughter. "Alas, for you all of eternity will be these next few hours. My offer is for you to die a little more peacefully than you will if you don't tell me what I want to know."

"I followed her here hoping for an easy meal," Rodney lied.

"You lie so badly it's almost entertaining. Almost. One last chance, Rodney. Where is the girl? Where are my dogs?"

"You're going to kill me anyway," Rodney replied with a smirk. "Go to hell."

"We'll see how much you smirk after we roast you," Nathan replied. "Kale, go to work."

* * * *

It was near dawn, the faint light just touching the horizon. Rodney watched it in a fog, his pain throbbing relentlessly.

Kale had burned him with fire, cut him with razors, and beat him with chains for most of the next day and night. Just when he'd begun to lose consciousness, Nathan had come back bearing a cup of blood. That had been the worse torment. In Rod's weakened state, he hadn't been able to regenerate, growing steadily weaker with each new torture. Nathan had held it just out of reach, promising to give it to Rod in return for information on Jackie and the dogs. The smell had been intoxicating, causing Rod to drool slightly.

But Rodney hadn't given in. In fury, Nathan had Kale stake him to the wooden cross on top of the factory, adding the last steel spike through his chest.

"You should be honored," Nathan said appreciatively, watching with interest. "You've renewed my taste for suffering, Rod. I haven't had this much fun in ages." He came to stand near Rodney, Kale at his shoulder. "They say in your last minutes you rethink your life," he mused, gazing up at Rodney. "Are you? Or are you wishing you gave her up and saved yourself the pain?"

Rodney's good eye moved slowly to focus on the blur that was Nathan, his head bobbing slightly.

"You transformed her, didn't you?" Nathan said resignedly. "Somehow you got the power and you turned her. You lost a lot of blood somewhere. That's the only logical conclusion."

Rodney slowly smiled, his fangs now broken shards under his split lips.

"Too bad your entire family's dead," Nathan continued. "I would have liked to leave you with the promise of your sister becoming one of my cows." He shrugged. "Be comforted that your gal won't have to live long alone in her new life. All Kale has to do is look for is a newbie who doesn't know what she's doing. Your get will be easy to find."

"I'll make sure she doesn't die unfulfilled, either," Kale added with a leer.

Rodney didn't speak or give any sign he heard, the smile fixed on his lips. The sun crept higher, illuminating the edge of the roof.

"Come, Kale," Nathan said, eyeing the dawn. "We're done here. The sun will take care of the mess."

Kale nodded, then looked back at Rodney. "Why is he smiling like that? He's got to be in agony, even if he really didn't give a shit about that girl."

"They call it a state of grace," Nathan replied, walking away. "When you're about to die, you stop feeling pain and make your peace with the world, or so it's said." He paused. "His heart just stopped."

"He was tough," Kale said grudgingly.

"He'll be ashes in a moment and so will you, if you don't hurry your ass," Nathan said sharply, ducking in the door. "Go get some sleep. By the end of tomorrow night, I want that newbie girl dead. Understand?"

"Sure, Boss." Kale hurried inside, the door locking behind them.

Sunlight flooded the roof, bathing Rodney in warm white light. Smoke billowed up quickly, then his broken, forlorn form burst into flame. Within a few moments, nothing was left except the cross with its embedded metal stakes and a few curling wisps of smoke.

Sonata

It began as most dares began between Nate and I. The enjoyment of a shared bottle of wine after the latest grueling Gathering of all the State Vampire Rulers was a welcome and familiar release for both of us. And if Nate looked to curry a little favor, I was amenable to that. Friends were hard to find in my world. There was much that was evil about Nate, but he was an ally that had always had my back in the past. After a hundred years, that was a rarity for me. When you are master of a country, friendship must often give way to the necessities of control.

The Gathering had been like usual: stultifying. I had—as always—to reiterate my warnings to those who dared to involve themselves in the human world to the point of discovery. The subject of werecreature rights had also come up, and also that of other supernaturals. In that regard, I admit that Nate was often on the list of those that had to be disciplined, even if I counted him friend. That he was annoyed at this was also a usual occurrence.

"I do not like being called to task for things you yourself have often done to excess," he grumbled as he poured us both a second glass of wine. His resentful brown eyes caught mine across the oak table.

"You give me no choice but to make an example of you," I said mildly, taking the proffered glass from him. "What you do in your state I leave to you, within reason. But it's not wise to attract attention with too many murders." I took a sip. "And this is not the first time I've had to address this issue with you, Nate."

"I take only those that come to me," Nate said defensively. "I have never sought out any human and taken them against their will. You have always done the same. Have we not told each other enough tales over the years of being the pursued, rather than the pursuers?" He smiled, baring just the tips of his fangs. "And have we not always agreed that pursuing was always the more delightful role?"

I grinned back, baring my fangs completely. "Yes. But as the years pass, the more we must watch our steps. My chiding this year was not human related, but vampire related. If you must dispense justice to those turned illegally, you must also make sure they are aware of all the rules before declaring them guilty of breaking said rules."

"I acted within my rights to protect my business."

"I know what happened on that rooftop," I said, my tone edging to anger. "Your business was never in any real danger."

"You have often said that one vampire more or less is not an issue. Rodney was—"

"He was a child in every important sense of the word," I grated out, my eyes bleeding to full red. "Make examples of those that deserve it, Nate. That neither one of us are saints does not mean that we can't show mercy to those few that actually deserve leniency."

Nate wrinkled his nose. "As you will. But be advised that if I have to check with you about all my judgments that you may be in Tennessee more often than you are at Hayden."

"That would not be so bad," I said darkly. "In spite of my harsh words just now, I enjoy our talks." I offered him a faint smile. "I do not want to hear that you are dead, friend. I have lost too many I knew to gluttony and the hunter's stake. We cannot be the monster gloating outside the window, obvious to all."

"Too true," Nate agreed, sipping his wine. "Though I have you to credit for that, my friend. I was just a brash unlearned boy when we first met. It was you who helped me become the cunning chameleon, able to hide my nature in plain sight. You who gave me the taste for culture and the direction to shape my life into something extraordinary." He smiled, spreading his hands to indicate the fine restaurant we were in, his well-tailored clothes, and the cream of society that surrounded us. "Do I not look every inch the successful businessman, instead of a bloodsucking brute?"

"Something we all must strive for as the decades pass," I said with reluctance. "There is too much at risk. The humans are fresh from triumph over yet another perceived evil on a distant shore. They would eagerly seek to stamp us out if we were suddenly revealed in their midst. We must remain the paramour of fiction stories, never stepping off the page."

"I know, I know," Nate said, rolling his eyes as he sat back in his chair, surveying the room. "I will do as you bid, as I have always done."

"Good," I said, pleased. "I value your friendship, Nate. And my desire for fairness does not mean we cannot enjoy our usual adventures."

Nate smiled wickedly. "Exactly what I'd hoped you say." He took a long swallow, then replaced his wineglass on the table. "And what adventure do you propose this year?"

"Seduction, of course!" I said, laughing. "First one to lay the girl wins."

"And the mark?" he asked eagerly.

"Alas, Danial Racklan has no loved one to try for this year," I said, thinking of my brother's loneliness with glee. "We shall have to try for someone else who is attached."

"How about a virgin?" Nate suggested. "We have done married women to death, Dev."

"Passé," I scoffed. "And in that regard I must also adhere to my guidelines of legal consent, Nate. No virgins under 18."

"My sister was taken against her will at 14," Nate said angrily, his dark skin flushed with fury. "Mal Jenkins did not care she was a child, only that she was his chattel to do with what he pleased."

Nate had never truly come to terms with his human past, the agony of once having been a slave. "Your sister has been avenged," I soothed. "There your methods of punishment were richly deserved. And your sister is safe now from all who would abuse her, with her brother as her protector. Colette lives as a queen."

Nate took a long breath, then let it out. "Some hatreds die hard, Dev. Let us not speak of it further. Your point was that it is too easy in these immoral times to seduce a young virgin, and I assent." He paused for a long moment, then held out his glass with a winning smile, as if to toast me. "I think I have a challenge for you, if you're up for it. The mark is legally of age."

"Go on," I encouraged, intrigued.

"There is a successful woman I have pursued," Nate stated. "She has not fallen to my advances, as she cares nothing for wealth."

"If they were made in your usual rough manner, I shouldn't wonder," I teased.

"I sent flowers and gifts of jewelry," Nate retorted, peeved. "All were returned. If you can persuade her to accept your touch—"

He smiled.

"—and mine as well—"

His smile widened.

"—then I will owe you a favor, which you may collect at your convenience or need."

"Any favor?" Nate was unquestioningly an ally. He had always been one, since our first contest of wills years ago. But he was also a highly competitive businessman, the hard circumstances of his youth leading him to always do what was most advantageous for himself and his sister at the expense of most everything else. His allegiance was not without cost. In short, I could always use a future favor that I would not have to pay for with some concession of my own.

He offered his empty palm face up with fingers splayed. "Anything."

"What is the catch?" I asked drolly. "Is she a nun?"

Nate laughed. "A religious woman to be sure, but currently belonging to no other man or to God."

This was too easy. "She must like females."

"By observation, no," Nate assured. "She likes men. She just will not entertain my suit, as I'm a man of dark skin, and not of her social class."

Being white and a former aristocrat myself, this conquest he suggested sounded like no trouble. "I accept."

"Shall we say a week?" Nate offered.

I nodded. "I'm surprised that you give me such an easy challenge."

Sonata

"There is one simple request, however," Nate said gleefully. "You cannot use your voice, Dev. You must gain her acceptance—and mine—without uttering one word of your own."

My spirits sank. "What about written words?"

Nate smiled. "No more than one or two sentences at one time…and only five such sentences in the entire pursuit!"

In terms of courtship, my skill with words was unequalled, and my voice in song one of my most powerful persuasive tools. Without either, any seduction would be an incredible challenge, even with my looks and money. But my blood was up now. "Agreed."

* * * *

The next night found me at the address that Nate had specified. Like a contemporary Dracula, I stood outside the mark's first floor window and looked in, hoping to get an idea of inspiration in how to proceed. The woman herself was not at home. The room in view seemed to be a living room, with a couch, a coffee table, some lamps, and some plain paintings of seascapes.

She likes the water. That's something to go on, at least.

Finally, there was the sound of car in the drive, a small Subaru SUV. A woman with short brown curly hair emerged, then entered her home. After turning on lights, she poured herself some wine, sat down on the couch, and began to work on her laptop computer. From her intent expression, I concluded she was working hard at something, rather than just chatting online with friends or bidding on various internet auction items.

I watched for a solid two hours, but the woman did nothing exciting, just kept typing on her keyboard. Even her wine was ignored, after the first sip. I was about to leave when she finally shut the lid of the computer, put it aside, and went to bed.

I lingered outside until I was sure she was asleep, then crawled in the basement window. While I could have asked Lash to procure her laptop—or even for Titus to simply teleport me inside her home to look at it—my old instincts of hunter were re-emerging. I wanted to experience the thrill of stalking my prey, not just the inevitable triumph at the end.

127

I walked over to the table quietly, secure in the fact that even if the woman were to awaken, I would be able to move fast enough to avoid being seen.

I opened the laptop, scrolling through her desktop files. There were spreadsheets of grades, lecture notes, and two papers in final stages of completion, rendering up a lot of useless facts and figures, along with that most coveted of info, my quarry's profession and name. She was a professor of English Literature at Southwest Tennessee Community College. Her name was Mary Ann Bridges. I committed the name to memory, then kept looking through files, hoping for something to leap out at me.

Mary Ann had tried to be a poet, though she was an amateur from the verse I discovered. But her papers—in my opinion—were excellently written, all the points clear and concise, with well-drawn supporting arguments. This was a woman with intelligence who had an appreciation for the poetical arts, but was not gifted herself in them. *Interesting.*

A phone rang shrilly, startling me. I looked over with alarm at the cell phone on the end table, then heard Mary Ann stirring in her bedroom. The phone shrilled again.

I shut the lid of the computer, darting into the darkness of a shadowed doorway. Mary Ann emerged rumpled, trudging sleepily to the phone. "Yes?"

I couldn't make out what the caller said, only that the tinny voice was male and insistent. Mary Ann was equally forceful. "I don't want to hear your excuses, Mike. This is the second time you cancelled on me for dinner at the last minute."

Mike said something to his defense. I took it for a poor excuse, the way Mary Ann's face twisted in annoyance.

"We're supposed to be engaged," she snapped, her resentful voice rising in volume. "No one who loves a woman treats her like this, Mike."

Mike began to give some explanation, but Mary Ann hung up on him. After turning her phone off with a vengeful push of a button, she trudged back into her bedroom.

She was bound to be vulnerable on the rebound, especially with her fiancé's behavior. Something to consider. I just had to find way to communicate with her without words…

Then the answer leapt out at me. Music. I would serenade her using the voice of another to communicate my pining…No! Nate might say later I had cheated, if the song had lyrics. I would write my own classical composition, something to call her to me with its pure beauty and longing. That was the answer.

* * * *

I shifted again in my chair at Hayden, rubbing my left upper fang against the lower one. I had been sitting there in my study the better part of the last hour, a blank sheet of paper in front of me, pen in hand. The solution that had seemed so easy mere hours ago now appeared insurmountable.

What is wrong with me, that I'm not inspired to write one single note?

I'd never been big on my own compositions while travelling as a bard centuries ago, tending to be more comfortable giving perfection to popular songs with my voice than in bringing my own stories to life in song. But in my many years as vampire, I had always been able to write poetry, when the situation called, even if my stanzas were not exactly in Lord Byron's exquisite class. Yet each time I had brought my pen to paper this evening, I stopped, the beginning of the proposed unwritten "new" melody revealed to be just another song I was remembering from my past. While any of those old songs might have been suitable for this situation, it bothered me that I could not write my own song, something new and bursting with not only beauty, but also life.

After another hour of false starts and more than a few muttered oaths, I gave up and went for a walk, trying to recall what a fellow vampire David Helm had once told me about song writing. Something about pieces of his soul being written into his lyrics, so that they wouldn't just sound beautiful, they would cascade into a powerful living thing capable of moving the listener to ardent emotion. I could not remember his exact words, but the passion in his tone as he'd spoken had been more than memorable, the stirring inflection of his voice coming to mind instantly. That passion was what I needed now.

I chuckled aloud. *Maybe my soul was too old and ragged to have any pieces left to spare for a song.*

Be that as it may, I had only six days left before I lost my bet with Nate. There was no time to try to rediscover my own passion. It was time to pay a visit to David, and call in some vampiric help.

* * * *

"You want a nocturne," David said blithely, as he sat at his electric piano, working on a small melody.

I watched the handsome former rock star from a short distance, wondering why he'd chosen an electric version of one of our shared favorite instruments instead of the real thing. Yes, he had once used that same model keyboard in his mortal life, but as a student of music, he had to know that the truest form of notes could only come from a grand piano, or at the very least, an upright. Electric keyboards played only recorded music at the touch of a button.

This is not the time to critique, when you have come seeking help. And he's probably still clinging to the vestiges of his mortal life.

"I want a song of the night, yes," I agreed, pacing back and forth. "Something to call to her, to evoke her interest. I can take it from there. But I need something to initiate first contact."

"I'm glad you're doing this," he said, changing the scale of the instrument. He hit a few keys, testing the sound.

The new tones were too high-pitched, grating on my already frayed nerves. "What do you mean?"

"That I've never known you to have someone you really cared about, not since I've met you," David replied absently, still tweaking his instrument.

"What makes you think I care for her?" I said scornfully. "This is not about love, David. It's about seduction. There's an abject difference."

David dropped his gaze, but not quick enough that I didn't see his disapproval.

"You object?" I said dangerously, moving closer to him.

"I do," he said very quietly.

I stared at him for a long moment, trying to overcome my shock. David had always been loyal since the night I'd saved him from himself and made him vampire. He had never refused anything I asked of him. He certainly had never dared to sit in judgment on any of my actions.

"This won't make you happy, seducing this woman you don't even know," he continued. Although soft, his voice had doggedness. "You don't want her. Why pretend you do, or that claiming her will change anything about your life?"

"Who said I wanted anything about my life changed?" I growled at him.

"You didn't pick the word abject on accident," he replied. "Think about what you really want. That is worth writing music for. You need to consider that your lack of creativity may be due to lack of passion—"

"You know nothing," I said wrathfully, glaring at him with red eyes. "Come to me in two days with a composition, David. And it had better be the best song you have ever written."

"I will not," he said quietly. "You can command anything else of me, my Lord. But not this."

I sputtered my words, so livid I could barely talk. "How dare you—"

"Songs must come from the heart," he said, talking over me. "Lies ring false, their dissonance magnified a hundred times. Anything I make you will be garbage, do you understand?"

He advanced on me. "Tell me her favorite things, how her kisses would make you feel, how you long to make love to her! Tell me her dreams, what you wish your future would be like with her. Tell me you love her and mean it!" He slammed his hand down on the keys, striking discordant notes. "This is all that I can write for you, without that. Do you understand, Devlin Dalcon, Lord of Vampires?"

I struck him then, barely restraining my taloned hand so it didn't take his head off in one swift blow. David was thrown backward into his keyboard, both of them falling to the floor with a crash. I stood over him threateningly, wanting to kill him.

"Go ahead," he said, spitting out some blood. "Beat me. You will only hate yourself more than you already do." He looked up at me, his expression not so much angry, but instead sad. "It will not change anything about what you are."

I left the room rather than tear him to pieces, knowing I'd regret it later. After teleporting home to Hayden, I stormed into the ballroom, then slammed the wooden doors and locked them. Sitting at the grand piano, I launched into the Moonlight Sonata, doing my best to make it sound as mournful as possible. I didn't want light and love, happiness and life. I wanted anger and somberness, hopelessness and death. Because I was only those things, just as he'd accused. They were all I had been now, for hundreds of years.

I felt tears on my cheeks, and hated them. I hated myself. I hadn't wanted this! Not any of it!

I wanted Anna. I wanted to be loved. I wanted all of the horror of the last two hundred years to be washed away in music and the slate set clean. Why hadn't the years blurred some of the terrible times, or mellowed the anguish over her loss? Why couldn't I remember our love as clearly as I remembered her death? I wanted to feel hope again. I wanted to feel warmth again. I wanted to unthaw from the dead thing I'd become and live again.

The sound of clapping startled me. I struck a discordant note, then turned to see one of my werebear guards, Nick, behind me. "That was beautiful," he said, looking apologetic. "I'm sorry to interrupt, but you have a call from Nate on line one. He—"

I resisted the sudden urge to rise from my seat and tear his hands off. "Tell him I'll call him back tomorrow," I said sharply, turning back to the piano. "And don't disturb me again tonight, please."

As the door closed, I was already losing myself again in my emotion, hearing the new haunting and plaintive music pouring out of me. I stopped briefly to set up some recording equipment to capture it, then resumed. Over and over I put all my anger, all my hate, all my hope and all my despair over my lost love into musical verse that swelled and grew greater and deeper, encompassing me in oblivion where only I existed in its void of true singular passion.

By daybreak, I had a breath-taking melody, one filled not only with anguish but also fresh yearning. Carefully, I closed the piano keyboard and burned a compact disc of the music, titling it "Yearning."

I sent one of my guards to leave my composition on her doorstep with a quick note that said only, "For you. Please meet me at seven if you would be so kind." I named a public restaurant, one within walking distance for her. I, of course, would teleport in via my demon, Titus.

Excited but exhausted, I headed to my bedroom for a good day's sleep, congratulating myself on reawakening my thirst for adventure. My wellspring of passion was flowing once more. "Yearning" was one of my best efforts. I would soon discover whether it would be enough to ensnare Mary Ann.

* * * *

Waiting at the restaurant that night, I wasn't sure if she would show. I had been proud and satisfied with my efforts in the wee hours. But in the dusk of evening, now rested and refreshed, I worried that my song wasn't good enough. I was out of practice, after all. *What if she didn't like "Yearning"? What if she stood me up? I was going to be mortified. I'd have to pretend to Nate that some crisis had come up elsewhere that had needed my attention, so I'd never have to admit what happened...*

To my abject relief, Mary Ann walked in that very moment, scanning the crowd anxiously. Catching her eye, I beckoned to her. She came over, drinking me in with her eyes, and sat down.

"You wrote the song?" she said in disbelief. Her tone was heavy with ill-concealed lust.

I nodded, pleased that she was clearly enraptured.

"It was beautiful."

I smiled.

She looked at me oddly, clearly wondering why I hadn't said the expected thank you for her accolades.

Nate would never know. And this is still my first sentence, technically. "I'm glad you liked it, Mary Ann."

"Your voice is beautiful," she said, enraptured. "But what's your name? How do you know me? Have we met before?"

Answering just her questions would lose me the bet easily. I had one chance. "Then would you like a private serenade?" I said meaningfully, standing and offering my hand.

At first, I was sure she was going to refuse me. He eyes narrowed slightly, obviously thinking that I had done this merely for sex. Then she put her hand in mine, and rose from her chair.

"Yes."

* * * *

Mary Ann was not an easy conquest. While I told her only my name, she gave me a long speech as she drove us to my home about how she was not the kind of woman who usually did things like this, that she was engaged, etc. etc. I nodded and squeezed her hand where appropriate, but otherwise said nothing. I was sorely tempted to ease her mind, to tell her that she owed her dolt of a fiancé nothing, that no one would know of her dalliance with me save Nate, unless she wished it otherwise. But my silence seemed to oddly be more of a comfort to her than any words would have been.

That night, I loved her. But while her flesh yielded its own pleasures, I found greater ones in playing for her, in hearing both the song I had written and also others flow through my fingers and into the piano. Her enthusiasm for my art—and my body—was nothing short of exhausting. When she finally slept, I wearily rose from the guest bed where we'd frittered away most of the night and made a call to Nate, telling him that one half of the bet had been completed.

He, of course, would not believe me without seeing her with his own eyes.

A few minutes later, with a little demon assistance, Nate was staring enviously down at Mary Ann's sleeping, satiated form. "You son of a devil," he said darkly. He looked up at me. "You must have gone over the word limit."

"Only two sentences written, and two spoken," I said proudly with a satisfied smirk.

"But how do you propose to complete your success?" he challenged. "You have only one more sentence worth of words, Dev."

I had no idea. Actually, I was somewhat surprised I had gotten this far. "In good time, my friend. Come. She may wake if we stay here."

I led him to the ballroom, then played him my composition. "You should have written her poetry instead of giving her the standard gifts." I smirked at him again. "I needed only a song and an invitation to snare her, plus my name." I laughed. "All women are not seduced the same way, my friend. You must tailor the lure to the woman."

Nathan grimaced at me. "Point taken. Now how do you propose to get her to agree to be my lover as well as yours?"

134

"I suggest that you meet us at a social outing," I said, thinking quickly. "I can introduce you as a friend, then quickly excuse myself. She likes the arts, so give her an example of your talents. You aren't bound by your own rules, so you can take all night discussing—"

Nate looked disgruntled. "I have none, Dev. My expertise is in business dealings only." Old pain and rage flashed across his features. "You know that slaves of the original America did not often enjoy free time to learn the luxuries of life, only the basest toils."

"I know that you've had close to a century and a half to accommodate yourself with the luxuries of life, as you call them," I countered. "Yes, most everyone you deal with in today's world remembers you for your ruthlessness alone. But what about Colette? Do you not show your sister another side, when you two are alone together? That of the doting brother who never raises his voice, who buys her every new book of poetry her heart desires? You must have talked to her at length about her interests—"

"But I have never composed something myself!" Nate said stridently, a trace of panic etching itself momentarily on his features.

"There must be something you can come up with," I persisted. "Some instrument you have familiarity with, some form of creative enterprise you could exploit—"

Nathan snorted. "I know how to play the harmonica, and the knowledge of several bawdy songs the other slaves used to work to. And I have not played in close to eighty years."

I gave him a baleful look. "That is not going to do it, Nate. This woman is genteel. She will not appreciate crudeness in any form."

Nate grumbled something, then sat down beside me on the piano stool.

"Why is it you want her?" I asked softly. "Knowing the both of you, I'd say you were an ill match, no offense meant."

Nathan slumped slightly. "Because she refused me for the exact reason you mention," he admitted. "She said I was crude, that I couldn't buy her. And that just made me want her more."

You don't want her. Why pretend you do, or that claiming her will change anything about your life? David's words were not only true for me, but also for Nate. Both of us wanted to unmake the past, an impossibility for us. That feat was only more so for a human woman to attempt, even if she wanted the task anyway, which was unlikely. But I didn't give voice to my convictions. Nate and I were much alike; his reaction would be just as furious as mine had been with David, if I were to say those words to him and ask him to let Mary Ann alone. No, a more nimble touch was called for here.

"If you want her just to have her, the easiest way now is to take a potion to take on my physical form," I suggested. "She'll accept your lovemaking when she wakes without reservation."

"That is not her accepting me," Nate said testily. "That is just her accepting you."

I grated my fangs together slightly, my mind sifting through suggestions, trying to think of what would be honest and also cause the least hurt in my friend. "You want Mary Ann to admit that she was wrong about you," I said delicately, after some minutes. "To get her to do that, you're going to have to show her the gallant side of yourself, the one you show Colette alone. You have to give her a reason to care for you." I made my tone sterner. "And you must admit right now, this bet was somewhat of a lie, on your part. Mary Ann's refusal of you was never about the differing color of your skins, Nate. This was about your difference of propensities and aptitudes."

Nate glared at me, his face flushing angrily. "The truth here is that you want her for yourself, Dev. So fine, keep her! The bet's off!" He stood, shot me a last glare, then stalked out.

I let him go, knowing that in his mood, there was no sense going after him. I was already tired from the events of the last few days. I didn't need to heal up bullet wounds as an additional measure. Nathan was never without at least one gun, and he would not hesitate to use it, in the mood he was in.

I absently plinked a few piano keys, wondering what to do next. *I could ask Mary Ann to become a donor. She was sure to accept, at least for the coming year, if I threw in sex and serenading as part of the deal. It would be nice to have a fan as part of my donor base. Nathan was right in that aspect, that I wanted her for myself. But I'd have been willing to share, if he hadn't been such an ass...*

"Devlin?"

I looked over my shoulder. Mary Ann was at the door, dressed in her date clothes of last night, her expression embarrassed.

"Good morning," I said politely, rising and closing the keyboard. "Would you like some breakfast? I can have one of my servants make you something."

"That would be nice," she replied, her tone subdued.

I took her hand, leading her to the kitchen. Hopefully one of the female werebears was around, or I'd have to call on my sorceress Leri to create something edible. Since we needed to walk a few moments to our destination, I gave her a short tour of the house. In spite of my efforts to engage her, Mary Ann remained quiet.

"Morning regrets?" I asked, as we entered the kitchen.

Mary Ann stopped still, then turned to me. "Yes," she said, biting her lip. "It's not that I didn't enjoy last night. But I shouldn't have done it. Mike is a good guy. He—"

I let her go on for a few more seconds, then interrupted. "Mary Ann, you don't have to make any excuse to me. I enjoyed our time together, but I'm not looking for a permanent arrangement."

She had the gall to look pissed off and also like I'd broken her heart. "Then why did you write that song for me?" Her tone changed to anger. "Or was it even for me?"

I was tired, and in no mood to argue. "I know you have a fiancé," I said tactfully. "I don't want to get in the way of that. But you did inspire that song, and I wanted to share that with you, and what happened last night." I brought her hand to my lips and kissed it, then released it carefully, so the action didn't appear insensitive. "But we don't have to continue seeing one another, if you'd rather not. And it goes without saying that I will not reveal our tryst to anyone, least of all your fiancé."

All the fight went out of Mary Ann as I spoke. By the time I'd finished, it was her who held my hand in hers, caressing it. "I'm sorry," she whispered. "I'm just not sure how to act this morning. Part of me is scared Mike will know."

Odds are he has his own little dalliance on the sly he is hoping you will not discover. "He will not know, Mary Ann, unless you tell him."

"What was this to you?" she asked bluntly.

"Just what I said," I replied, trying not to yawn.

Mary Ann looked at me, then away. "I can't see you again. Please show me the way out."

While I was in secret relieved—and impressed that her strength of character was so remarkable to stop our relationship cold turkey—I was the picture of regret and politeness on the surface.

"Very well," I replied dolefully. "Thank you for your gift of last night." I led her to the door of the garage, then opened it, revealing her car parked just outside in the harsh light of day. "Adieu."

Mary Ann walked off without a word, got in her car, and drove off. I shut the garage door, then walked back inside and up to my bedroom, thinking I was glad everything was over.

* * * *

My normal life resumed of various meetings, donor visits, hours on the computer, and days spent in well-deserved-if-solitary sleep. In short, things were back to normal, except for one thing: my urge to create had been reawakened. Yet as before, my muse that had been so recently found seemed to have abandoned me.

In normal times, I would have taken my concerns to my best friend—and long-time bodyguard and companion—Lash. But he was off on a string of freelance jobs, which meant our conversations were mostly him touching base about various aspects of my estate Hayden's defenses, and making sure that when I needed him for appointments, he was available to teleport in. I could have persisted, sure. Even if he'd have bitched about listening to my inspiration worries, he would have made time for me if I asked him. But Lash was cut from a similar cloth to Nate's, having no interest himself in any creative enterprises. In summary, I wasn't sure that he would even understand my artistic angst, much less be able to give me any pointers on how to overcome it.

I worked hard to overcome my imaginative block, even going so far as to purchase some additional instruments, and procure training in them, thinking that some new endeavor might spark some artistic fervor. Instead, I was frustrated, and ended up discarding most of them, those I didn't destroy in my fits of pique.

So it was that when Mary Ann called me three months after our night together and asked that I accompany her to an overnight masque ball on Halloween, I readily agreed. I was in dire need of inspiration. That was worth a little risk, even if I was regretfully skipping my dear brother's first efforts at a Hallow's party of his own to celebrate his ascension to the throne of New York.

* * * *

I met Mary Ann at her house on a night in early fall. As she had specified, I was wearing full evening dress circa 1860s, complete with top hat, gloves, watch chain, boots, and cane with a carved bear's head in silver. Mary Ann was also decked out beautifully in a fancy blue satin and lace dress. While its design was not traditionally correct, it did regale me with a lovely view of the tops of her breasts, something I was very willing to put aside historical accurateness for.

We took a limo to the address of the party, which was some lonely looking mansion. When we were dropped off at the wrought iron gates, an old-fashioned horse-drawn carriage picked us up. While we crept at a careful walk up the long hickory lined driveway, I read the hand-lettered invitation that Mary Ann had received. A list of events was on the thick vellum, along with a timeline.

6:00 Orientation
6:30 Tour of Mansion
7:30 Dinner
8:45 Dancing
12:00 Stroke of Midnight

"We're just going to make the tour." I turned the card over, but there was nothing on the back. "Who is giving this party?" I asked. "And why were you invited?"

"A benefactor of the college," Mary Ann explained. "He's big into history, especially funding several chairs, as well as three graduate programs. The entire history department was invited, as well as professors in music, romance languages, and literature." She smiled. "I was only one of five people selected in my department."

I took her hand, trying to soften my words. "Why did you invite me and not your fiancé?"

139

"Because he's no longer my fiancé," she said, swallowing hard. Her eyes were already tearing up.

Thanking my presence of mind to include a handkerchief in this evening's outfit, I took the small cloth from my breast pocket and handed it to her. She dabbed at her eyes.

"What happened?" I inquired, knowing it was expected.

"He asked for his ring back," she said, clutching the hanky. "He had someone else. Bastard waited until right before the wedding practically. I lost all my deposits."

Her swearing surprised me, but then I recalled that she and I hadn't exactly spoken that much in our previous time together. "Why were you paying for the wedding, if you don't mind my asking?"

"I had the better job," she said, flushing slightly. "But I'd rather not talk about it, if you don't mind, Dev. I want to be happy tonight."

"Of course," I said. "Your dress is beautiful, Mary Ann. It sets off your eyes perfectly."

"Thank you," she said, a smile returning to her lips. "And thank you for coming. I wasn't sure you'd say yes."

"I never miss a chance to role-play," I said, giving the words a double entendre. Then I kissed her full on the lips, enjoying the way she gave herself over to my desire. When I moved to set her astride me, she stopped me with a shocked admonishment. "Dev, we can't!"

"Why not?" I said gleefully, opening my pants to let my member spring free. I gave her a wicked look, enjoying her slack-jawed look of riveted lust as she stared at my slightly bobbing organ. "No one will see anything, with your long skirt. And we have minutes yet before we reach the mansion. Why not truly enjoy the ride?"

Mary Ann hesitated, then moved onto me. Settling her skirts over us, she began to move. Our twin sighs filled the small carriage as it clopped slowly up the long drive to the mansion.

* * * *

We enjoyed ourselves thoroughly, but didn't lose ourselves completely. As the carriage pulled up, we were again sitting side by side, clothes in place, our boisterous post-coital laughter filling the air.

"Think everyone enjoyed their ride as much as we?" I quipped as we stepped down. Mary Ann flushed, then took my arm and pulled me toward the large oak door. Queerly, there was a knocker with a label above it in engraved bronze plate which said "For Old Friends" and also a normal modern electric doorbell button.

"Which shall I push?" Mary Ann said.

"The one for old friends, of course," I chuckled.

Mary Ann lifted the knocker and rapped hard twice. The door opened into a hall, where a coat man took her coat and my cape.

The house was intimidating. A butler showed us into a large parlor, where at least a hundred guests were mingling and eating h'ordoerves. Everyone was in historical dress, though it was all different, from Roman togas to medieval armor to peasant garb to ladies in waiting. Most of it was also inaccurate and over the top, a garish modern version of what had once been. This comforted me. That might sound odd, but I did not want to deal with any vampires or other long-lived supernatural beings tonight. I was in the mood for a little human fun of the light-spirited variety. My one thought as we waited was that we might somehow chance on meeting Mike, so I could not only tell him he was a complete loser, but also deck him for good measure.

"Attention!" a man called loudly from one side of the room. He was dressed as I was, in top hat, gloves, cape, and a black suit. "Thank you all for coming."

Conversation ceased as the costumed crowd turned to face him.

"The tours are about to begin," the announcer called. "Please let me have all the 1200 and previous years historically dressed people over here for the first group."

Mary Ann and I moved aside to let several other people pass by in gladiator costume. One was a woman, which briefly took all my attention.

"She must think she's Leia in Return of the Jedi," Mary Ann said mockingly, taking my arm and leading me away.

An apt description of the woman's voluptuousness, though I would not say it aloud. "Do you want anything to nibble?"

"No," she responded. "You?"

There was no one nearby, and I was in front of a cordoned off doorway which had to lead somewhere that we'd have a little more privacy. Now was a good a time as any, because when we parted ways tonight, I did want to see Mary Ann again. "Actually, yes." I led her through the curtains, then shut them after us. I turned to her, then took her hands in mine, trying to make my expression earnest. "I'm a vampire."

Mary Ann, blinked at me, then her expression changed into burgeoning realization. "Of course. That explains your cool skin...and why you weren't starving that night we skipped dinner, like I was."

"You should have said something," I said quickly, slightly embarrassed that I hadn't thought of her physical needs. "I could have ordered in some takeout, at the very least—"

"Never mind that," she said impatiently. "Are you going to drink my blood or not?"

Maybe she was a vampirephile? God, that would be incredible luck. "Would you like me to?"

"Only if it's like it is in the movies," Mary Ann said with a look of distaste. "I don't like the sight of blood, especially my own." She kissed me, stroking my cheek lightly. "I've seen some movies where the woman almost orgasms as she's bitten, because it feels so good. Does it really feel like that?"

It will for me. "Why don't we try it?" I offered. "Just a little bite here, to see what you think? If you don't like it, then we'll consider the matter closed."

Mary Ann didn't reply, but she took a step back and opened her arms. I went to her immediately. I shivered a bit in anticipation as I put my mouth to her neck. Kissing her skin once, I bared my fangs, ready to bite.

"Excuse me!"

Startled, I bit my lip, then turned with a snarl. The announcer stood in the doorway, looking at us with a stern expression. "The last tour is leaving," he said stiffly, clearly irked. "You can't stay in this area anyway, as it's off limits to guests."

"Why not?" I said belligerently. "We don't need a chaperone."

142

"Please come with me," he said, making it an order. "Or I'll have to call security."

I would have thrown the man out the nearby window, if Mary Ann hadn't taken my arm, murmuring that there would be time later for us "to experiment."

We followed the man out to a small group of similarly dressed people. One couple was clearly some colleagues of Mary Ann, as she said hello to them and introduced me, something I was not keen about. But when she added I was only a friend, I relaxed a bit. Another man strode in as we were exiting the now empty reception room. He was both anxious and also clearly angry about something, though he stayed silent. I surmised his date had stood him up, then promptly ignored him.

The tour commenced, and lasted about a half hour. It consisted of most of the upper floors of the house, save the attic and master bedroom, and did not include the basement or kitchen either. Most of the rooms were done in antique furniture, and the dressings were authentic, so much so that the smallness of the beds made my back ache again, remembering how for years I'd had to sleep on my side to avoid my heels being off most beds. I had been a tall vampire in a time when not very many men were tall, and furniture was much smaller than its current modern gigantic proportions.

The two women exclaimed about everything, and took many pictures with their phones. The two men with us seemed as bored as I was, though that did not prompt us to converse.

At last, it was over. On our way back to the others in the reception room, I glimpsed servants carefully laying out the china for the dinner to come next, and knew I did not have the patience to last another hour in silence, let alone polite conversation. I wanted the blood I'd been denied, if not also a quickie in one of the upstairs rooms.

"Let's slip away," I whispered in Mary Ann's ear.

"No," she replied. "I'm hungry. I need to eat something. Besides, all my colleagues are here, Dev. They'd want to know where I was if I disappeared. I'd have to answer questions later."

"Let them wonder," I teased, kissing her neck. "Come on. I want you—"

"Don't you ever want to do anything but have sex?" she accused sharply. The couple who was just within earshot stiffened and turned, staring at us, before they hurried into the reception room.

Not now, I don't. "Go have dinner," I said grumpily. "I'll meet you at the dance." Without a word more, I left her there, and snuck back upstairs, avoiding servants.

The master bedroom wasn't hard to find. I took off some of my trappings like my gloves, hat and jacket, then set them aside, stretching out happily on the modern bed which could accommodate all of me with plenty of room to spare.

The silence stretched while I thought about the night and how to salvage it so I ended up between Mary Ann's thighs again, and not on the end of a slap. At this point, the latter was looking very possible, and the former close to impossible.

Why are you in such a mood? Because that man stopped you from feeding? You could have fed before you came. Why is it such a big deal to have her blood here tonight?

Because I wanted to do it, and now I have to wait. I was never good at waiting, especially when I'm so bored.

But what did you expect? This is how humans have fun, by dressing up and pretending they are great lords and ladies. They don't know how it was, that half the time the clothes were too hot or too cold, that with no lawful rights there was the constant threat of being out of favor and having lands and title stripped away, that just the base necessities like enough clean water or unspoilt food were usually not met, that disease was so terrible with no vaccines or modern medicine. They think of the good only. The ugly truth is consigned to history books...and your memories.

I know. I just....I wanted...

What?

"Something different," I said aloud in the stillness. "Something new and intoxicating, something to make me feel alive."

Why? Mary Ann is fun, but she's the same as so many before her. There is nothing new. There is nothing left you haven't done. There is nothing left, period. Just drinking blood and meetings and sleeping alone and thinking stupid thoughts like these in empty bedrooms.

I had no response to that except melancholy.

Why not end it?

Because then that would be the end, I thought, afraid to give voice to the words. *Then there is no hope of anything new. There can never be, because there are no options left.*

What do you have to live for?

I felt myself clawing against the sides of a steep decline, sliding further and further into despair. *While there is life, there is hope. I have to hold to that. I let that go and it's over.*

There was a sudden bang on the door, as a figure barged in. "What are you doing here?"

I blinked and sat up, shocked to see Nate, his costume that of a pirate complete with a huge hat and a feather. I'd have laughed, if his expression wasn't so angry and I wasn't feeling so desolate. "Contemplating suicide," I said with a false smile. "Care to join me?"

"No," he said, grabbing my arm and yanking me to my feet. "Get up and stop being a jackass."

"Why the hell are you here?" I said, latching onto my own anger as I pulled away from him. "Are you haunting my footsteps?"

"I'm the one funding this damned party," he said angrily. "Where's Mary Ann? You came with her, didn't you?" He scented the air. "I smell her scent on your skin."

Thank goodness for that stupid tour or he would have smelled more than that. "She asked me to come. Her fiancé is history." I put my jacket, gloves, and hat back on, then studied him. "Did you have something to do with that?"

"No, but I'm glad to hear it," Nate said as we exited the room. "Now I won't have to kill him."

"Why don't you leave her alone?" I said incredulously. "This ridiculous pursuit is not helping her to love you."

"That's my business," Nate countered. "You're in my home state, remember? I can do anything I please here, as long as it's within vampire law."

"All of America is my territory," I said dangerously, redness bleeding into my gold eyes. "I don't answer to you, Nate. You answer to me. Now why are you doing this?"

He expelled a breath in frustration. "Why can't you just butt out, Dev? This isn't your concern."

I took a breath to yell again, then stopped, watching my friend standing there. An odd scent was in the air. "You're in love with her," I said taking in a long breath. The scent was unmistakable: lust, hope, happiness, satisfaction, and just a touch of fear.

Nate didn't answer.

Fury filled me, hot on the heels of knowledge. "Why in the hell would you ask me to seduce a woman you love!" I shouted at him. "You had to know it would come between us!"

"You weren't supposed to like her!" Nate shouted back at me. "You were supposed to seduce her!"

"And then what?"

"I don't know," Nate admitted, rubbing his eyes. "I just didn't want to feel this way anymore, that there was something I couldn't have, no matter how much I wanted it. I was tired of being angry and tired of trying and getting nowhere."

"You didn't think I'd seduce her," I said slowly. "You thought I'd fail. That was why you set me those ground rules of not using my voice. You wanted me to fail because you knew I'd be furious if I did."

Nate didn't reply.

"What did you want me to do, in my fury?" I purred, circling him and seething with my anger. "To lash out and kill her, to drain her dry? To do myself what I'd forbidden you to do to anyone else?"

"No!" Nate shouted. "I just wanted her!"

"Wanted who?" a female voice inquired.

I looked over slowly, terrified that it would be Mary Ann standing here. But it was instead Colette, Nathan's sister.

She advanced to me slowly, her slow pace from an old injury she'd sustained at an overseer's hands before being turned vampire. Her dress was that of a Victorian lady, with plenty of ruffles and almost none of her beautiful dark skin showing. But Nate had always dressed her fancily since the day I'd turned her for him, years ago. He had always sheltered her, too, keeping her far from me and all other vampires except when it was absolutely necessary. *Had he been afraid I'd seduce her?*

146

"Colette," I said happily. "It's wonderful to see you. You look well—"

"Wanted who?" she repeated, not dissuaded in the least.

"Your brother is in love," I said lightly, making sure to stand beyond Nate's reach. "Though he has an odd way of showing that emotion."

"A human woman?" she said to Nate, clearly surprised. "That one you were watching earlier?"

"Yes," he admitted. "Her name is Mary Ann—"

Colette shook her head lightly, then turned and went back the way she'd come. Nate followed, and I went after him.

Colette strode down several flights of stairs, then moved through the reception area to the dance floor. Greeting several of her guests, I saw her make a beeline for Mary Ann, who was sitting talking to an older gentleman in a corner of the room. For close to ten minutes they talked. Mary Ann glanced over us at a few times, her expression ranging from angry to curious then back to irritated.

"What are they saying?" Nathan asked me.

"How should I know?" I retorted, as I watched them talk. "There is too much noise in here to hear properly."

Colette finished talking to Mary Ann, then came back to us. "That is settled," she announced. She turned to me. "I'd like to dance."

I offered her my hand. Nathan made to stop us. Colette turned on him. "I am your elder sister, not your younger one," she said with maliciousness. "And I am tired of your wasting your time on this matter. Now stay here and be silent."

I moved away with her in my arms, awed by her treatment of him. Nathan was as fearsome as myself, and she had practically emasculated him.

"Cat got your tongue?" she said finally.

"I'm afraid you will," I teased.

She blushed prettily. "I would not dare such, Lord," she said demurely. "In fact, I must apologize for this entire situation. Nathan should not have let this get so out of hand."

"How so?"

"Because it was I who led Mary Ann to meet Nate," she said with a sigh. "I thought that it was good they knew one another, with my interest in history and patronage of the history program at the college. I never guessed he'd gotten infatuated with her."

"And now?"

"Mary Ann had no idea he liked her, only that some secret admirer was sending her gifts. She did not feel she could accept them, and so returned them. I also understand there was a human she was seeing at the time that is now no longer part of the equation."

"So she does she like him, then," I asked, slightly jealous.

Colette nodded happily. "Look. They are dancing even now."

To my surprise, Nate did indeed have Mary Ann in his arms. He was positively beaming as he swept her around the dance floor. She didn't have the worship in her eyes for him that she'd had for me—which pleased me more than slightly—but she was talking to him with an excited expression, clearly happy.

"You may have to do another turning before the year is out," Colette said with a smile. "My brother is smitten, like I haven't seen since his mortal days."

"Would you welcome that," I asked curiously. "Having Mary Ann as part of the family?"

"Of course," Colette said evenly, without missing a beat. "I enjoy the girl's work very much."

That wasn't really an answer. But looking into her solemn brown eyes, I could see that was the best I was going to get.

* * * *

At the stroke of midnight, there were many kisses out on the dance floor. Sadly, I did not participate myself. But Nathan and Mary Ann did share a chaste first kiss. After he escorted her to his limousine, as Colette and I followed at a distance.

"You needn't worry," she said, offering her hand for a farewell kiss. "I'll make sure he treats her correctly. Nathan has a great deal to learn about women." She laughed. "And I have great things in store for Mary Ann. She seems a smart capable woman who knows opportunity when she sees it."

While I was pleased to know that Mary Ann would not come to some gruesome end, I was still sad to lose her. "Please keep me informed, if you would. I would be happy to turn her, if that is the choice she makes."

"Good," Colette smiled broadly. "I'll also see that my brother honors his side of the bet with you, Dev."

"How did you know about that?" I asked, staring at her.

A knowing expression I'd never seen graced her lovely features. "Mary Ann heard your talk, that night you came in with Nate to see her sleeping. She knew about the bet, Dev. That's why she left that morning, because she was upset over what you had done, what she had let you do. She felt used."

Another hundred years could pass and I probably still would not understand the female sex completely. "Then why did she ask me to come with her here?" *Much less have sex in the carriage several times?*

"Because she knew Nate was throwing the party," Colette said. "She knew appearing with you here would make him jealous. She smiled. "She did not show the invitation to you, with his name at the top, did she? She hoped you would come to blows. She felt it served you both right."

The woman had deceived me. I made a face, Mary Ann's actions during the carriage ride suddenly attributed not to my sexiness, but her own motives of revenge. "It worked."

"You should not underestimate women, Dev," Colette said over her shoulder, as she walked to the limousine. "Most of them want more than a sonata and sex in exchange for their hearts."

"Then what do they want?" I called back jokingly.

"That is not a secret for any woman to tell you, of all people," she said with a wink. Then she got into the limousine, disappearing from sight.

As I watched them drive away, I chuckled. *At least I know one secret. Next time I have trouble finding my way into a woman's heart, I'll ask another woman for advice.*

I turned, almost running into another pretty young woman dressed as a peasant behind me. I gave her a smile, then a curious look. Her expression was mournful.

"What is it?" I asked.

"I think it's terrible what they did to you tonight," the woman said hesitantly. "That woman helping her brother spirit away your date. I just wanted to say I was sorry."

"It's all right," I said, seeing my limousine pull up the drive. "He really likes her and she likes him. I don't want to stand in the way of that."

"You're very understanding."

No, I'm not. But I am a realist. I took her hand and kissed it. "What's your name?"

"Jessica," she said shyly.

She was beautiful. Better than that, she likely was intelligent and had a better than average chance of knowing some history, with her choice of dress. Odds were she would also accept if I asked her to be a donor. "Do you like music?"

Jessica nodded.

"Then get in, my dear," I said kissing her hand. "I'm a musician. And I'd love to play you a song or three."

Night Music

(Previously Published in Midnight Thirsts 2)

Krys walked slowly toward the low stone wall, the roaring of the falls capturing all her attention as she rested her hands on the cold rock slabs. The view was as magnificent as ever; the towering waterfall spanning the wide river, the trails beside it framed with stone and concrete walls more than fifty feet below. The early spring afternoon felt more like late summer, the air balmy and comfortable, even in her T-shirt and jeans.

Letchworth State Park. The place was exactly the same, but everything was different. Her parents were gone, and now her brother was, too. They'd come here as a foursome every summer and stayed for a week, renting a rough built cabin. It had been bare bones, lacking heat, water, or even a private outhouse. But it had always been a good time to her and Bill: fishing, hiking, playing games, and encountering the wildlife. Each summer, her parents always treated Krys and her brother to one special adventure. For Krys, that had been the whitewater rafting outfit that operated below the lower falls. For her brother, Bill, that had been either horseback riding or a ride over the river via hot air balloon.

They'd had such good times here...

Pretending to brush back her hair, Krys brushed away a tear, conscious of the many tourists still snapping pictures of the falls. *Why had she come here? What had she hoped to find?*

151

"Excuse me," an old woman said, tapping her elbow. "But we'd like to get a picture together. Would you take one of us, please?"

Krys nodded, then snapped a few pictures as the couple posed in front of the falls. Handing back the camera, she hurried inside the Glen Iris Inn, calling herself an idiot. Ringing the bell, she waited.

A desk clerk came in quickly. "Can I help you?"

"Krys Markman," she said. "I'm checking in. I'm staying in Caroline's Cottage."

"Please fill this out." The woman handed her a form. "And I need a credit card to make an imprint."

Krys handed over her credit card, then took it back a few minutes later, handing in the filled out form.

"Staying with us all week?"

And probably going to rue it, Krys thought miserably. "Yes."

"Have you stayed with us before?"

"Yes," Krys said quickly. "I'll just need one key."

The woman began reciting the checkout times and other rules, all of which Krys knew by heart. She fidgeted, then grabbed the key, not replying to the startled clerk as she ran outside. A couple jumped back as she nearly banged in to them.

"Hey!" the man said, throwing an arm in front of his wife to shield her. "Watch where you're going—"

"Sorry," Krys stammered, flushing.

The couple gave her another dirty look, then walked upstairs hand in hand. Krys sat down in an empty wrought iron chair, rubbing her eyes.

Enough already. This was her vacation, a long break to recoup before embarking on a new chapter in her life. Relaxing was the first step. Walking was out; the lamps scattered around the Glen Iris Inn were coming on. So it would have to be alcohol instead.

* * * *

Krys sipped her wine flight, while looking around at her setting, marveling that so much was still the same, and still so beautiful. She'd been in these same surroundings so many times, yet they were still magical to her, even as their familiarity soothed her…

"Will you want dinner?" her waiter asked delicately. "Or would you like to try one of the wines you sampled?"

Where had the time gone? Krys had finished all three samples already. While another flight and more reminiscing sounded wonderful, it was better not to tempt fate, not when she had a hell of a climb in the dark to reach her rented house. "Yes." She chose an entrée at random from the menu, then one of the wines she'd sampled.

As the waiter walked away, Krys noticed a tall man sitting by himself off in the corner. He was writing something by the light of the table candle. What was compelling was he was doing it in longhand in a small paper book instead of via electronic device. The act was so uncommon that she stared at him. Within a few seconds, the man raised his eyes and caught her staring, his dark eyes meeting hers. Krys immediately looked down, flushing. By the time she gathered enough courage to look up again, the man was gone, his seat empty.

The waiter came back, her wine on a tray. "We're all out of the salmon, Ma'am," he said apologetically. "Would you like to choose something else?"

The only craving Krys had was to find out who that handsome man had been. Food could wait. "There was a man sitting out here. Do you know who he was?"

The waiter shifted uneasily. "We're not allowed to give out information on guests, Ma'am. Sorry."

"So he is staying here?" Krys said hopefully. "Will he be here a few more days?"

The waited leaned down slightly, his expression secretive. "Aren't you staying for a few days in Caroline's Cottage?"

"Yes," she answered conspiratorially.

"Then I'd advise you to get to know your neighbor during your stay," the waiter said meaningfully.

Krys looked at him in puzzlement. "What?"

The waiter straightened, then set down her glass of wine. "Will you have another entrée, Ma'am?"

Comprehension dawned. "No," Krys said, hastily grabbing her purse. "Put my drinks on my bill."

* * * *

The steep climb was long and wearying; mostly from lack of light and that her decade old memory had identified it as being much more fun. Or maybe it was just doing it alone, without sharing the striving and complaining with someone else.

It seemed like ever since her parents had died everything had gone wrong, cumulating with Bill's death a few months ago. She'd made one mistake after another, like Adam and…

"Don't think about him," she murmured aloud angrily, rubbing her left shoulder blade. She cracked a smile. "You've got more important things to consider, like are you going to make it to the crest of this hill?"

Taking a few deep breaths, Krys continued on for another thirty minutes, her shoulders relaxing with relief when she reached the top. Turning down the side road, she headed toward her cottage, her eyes drawn to the expected but unfamiliar sight of the Chalet, hoping to see the man from the patio. Yet the entire place was dark, except the lowest level, where bright lights shone.

Who in the hell would live in the cellar with a wraparound balcony on both the second and third floors? The mysterious stranger was certainly hot, but he was also weird. What was he doing down there all by himself?

Maybe he's not by himself, like you are, Krys thought. *Even if he is, it's not your concern. You're here to focus on what comes next for you, not another flash-in-the-pan romance that won't last.*

Annoyed at herself, Krys grabbed her bags from the car, then hurried inside, exhausted from her climb. The door opened with a hard push of her shoulder, the lock squealing protest. Krys locked the door behind her, dropped the bags, and then flipped on the lights.

"This is nice," she said aloud, her eyes roaming the cozy living room and stereo, the bright kitchen and the white bathroom. Stairs led upward on the far wall. Krys grabbed her clothes bag, and went upstairs, her shoes silent on the carpet.

There were three bedrooms. One faced the falls, but just had a view of the forest. The opposite one viewed the maintenance area. The third was the center room with one double window. Krys chose that one, hanging up some of her clothes. Taking out her book and cell phone, she laid them on the nightstand. Unlocking the old-fashioned clasp, she swung wide the windows, letting in the night air, the moonlight streaming down. She stopped still for a second, sure she'd heard something. But there was nothing but the sound of crickets and the wind through the trees.

Krys ran her hands through her long brown hair. *What had she thought she would hear? What was she doing here, anyway? Trying to relive the good old days?*

She crossed to her phone and turned it off. It made sense to save the battery. *And why not?* There was no one who would be calling her tonight. The divorce had been final for three weeks now.

Krys sat down on the edge of the bed, looking at her phone. She'd met Adam the afternoon she'd purchased it. Her first practice picture with it had been one of him. Six months later, Adam and Krys were married, her pregnancy already showing.

Then Bill had been diagnosed with cancer. With her parents gone, she was the only family he'd had to turn to. Krys had taken care of him tirelessly, pushing herself hard. Too hard, it turned out; she miscarried the baby just shy of six months.

Adam had been devastated, especially to know that with the complications Krys had suffered, they would never have children. He withdrew from her, even as Bill got steadily worse. Adam had served her with papers a few days before her brother had died.

Ironic, Krys thought bitterly. *My phone contract lasted longer than my marriage.*

Angrily, she lay down in bed, and turned off the light. There was no use hashing over the past, or going over all the roads she'd regretted taking. What she chose to do tomorrow and after were the decisions that would shape the rest of her life. Those were the ones she had to focus on.

* * * *

Krys jolted awake, blinking her eyes, her hand moving for the light switch. But before she could turn it on, strains of an unearthly song washed over her, freezing her motionless. Captivated, she listened, the forlorn notes breaking over her, their beauty and pain as one with hers, bringing up her repressed feelings as tears slipped down her cheeks. Krys began crying in racking sobs, huddled on the bed. When she quieted many minutes later, the music had gone. Exhausted, she fell into a dreamless sleep.

* * * *

The next morning, Krys lay in bed, pondering the music she'd heard. It had been a violin, or some other string instrument. That hadn't been a dream, either; it had been real enough to move her to tears. The creator had to be her mysterious neighbor.

As much as she hadn't wanted to cry, an unseen weight had run out with her tears. Instead of thinking on the past this morning, she was eager to explore. She also wanted to talk to the man about his music, to tell him how it had moved her last night. Intrigued, Krys decided that she would do her best to accidentally meet him today. Pushing back the covers, she got moving.

That morning she visited some of her family's favorite spots at the park, like Inspiration Point, the Tea Tables, and St. Helena. In whole, Krys walked more than seven miles that first day. Evening saw her sitting on the porch reading her book, the sunset through the tops of the trees nearby, a light rain pattering down.

Curiously, Krys peered over the top of her book. She'd read less than a page in the thirty minutes she'd been out here, hoping to catch sight of the neighbor. His vehicle, a brand new GM truck, sat in the driveway of the Chalet, testament that the man was home. Also, as dark had come on, the same basement lights had also.

It was clear that the man wasn't going to come out for an evening stroll after another thirty minutes had passed. Krys had moved past waiting for providence, and was now working up her courage to walk over there and introduce herself. The most he could say was that he wanted to be left alone.

The longer she waited, the more anxious she became. Finally, closing her book with a snap, she tossed it on the table and walked determinedly across the lawn to the huge house. Should she go to the back door on the deck, or around to the front? He was likely more able to hear her at the front door, if he really was in the basement.

Krys took a deep breath and climbed the steps. She knocked on the door, wincing at how loud the knocks were, then stepped back, waiting. Minutes passed, but no one came to the door.

He had to have heard her. Irritated, Krys banged louder on the door, then stepped back, listening for footfalls. There were none, the seconds again stretching into minutes.

Fuming, Krys stomped down the steps and headed back to her house, then switched her course, instead heading up the road for another walk. She was too angry to read now.

The night was quiet, the only sounds crickets, and the occasional passing car. It was so different from how it had been in the summers, with so many campers and visitors around all the time. She'd originally thought to visit in July, but hadn't been able to face seeing so many families like hers had once been, here together having fun…

With a startled gasp, Krys stopped dead, her gaze looking into the Letchworth family's cemetery. There was her mystery man, standing near a grave. He was in jeans and a shirt, his dark blond hair unkempt, his eyes on the gravestone.

"There you are," she accused aloud, then clapped her hand to her mouth, mortified.

The man looked up. He was handsome, but not in a pretty way, his features more friendly that proud. "Yes. Who are you?"

"Your neighbor," Krys said, coming closer hesitantly. "I think I heard you playing music last night."

"I'm sorry," the man said immediately. "I had the stereo turned loud. It won't happen again—"

"No, I liked it," Krys said quickly. She stopped walking, hands in her pockets. "I liked it very much, actually. It…um, affected me."

The man didn't answer, staring at her.

He must think she was addled. "I'm sorry if I disturbed you," Krys said stiffly. "Have a good night."

She continued up the road, grumpily going over the exchange again and again, visualizing herself saying anything but what she had. Why hadn't she been cooler about the whole thing? Why hadn't she invited him to meet her on the Inn's patio for a drink?

157

Spying a picnic table near the large fishing pond, Krys sat down and considered her options. She was paid up through the rest of the week, so she might as well make use of it. Maybe it wasn't too late to schedule a horseback ride or something...

"May I join you?" a hesitant voice asked.

Krys looked up, startled. It was the stranger. She hadn't heard him approach. "Sure, sit down."

The man sat down, then extended his hand. "My name is David. And you are?"

"Krys," she answered, extending hers.

"For Krystin?" he asked, kissing her hand.

Krys nodded, smiling. "But no one ever calls me that."

"I'd like to, if you don't mind," David said pleasantly. "Please call me David. I much prefer it over Dave."

He certainly did have charm. "Good to meet you, David."

"And I, you, Krystin," he replied. "But why are you out so late alone?"

"I thought you were ignoring me," Krys said, smiling and shrugging. "Turns out you weren't home. Were you making gravestone rubbings, or something?"

"Paying respects to a descendent," David answered vaguely, rubbing his eyes. "But we were talking about you."

He must have meant ancestor and misspoke. "What about me?"

"That I should escort you home," David said, standing up. "This park is likely safe, especially where we are. But you shouldn't tempt fate and walk around unescorted."

He obviously wanted to be by himself out here and wanted her back in her cottage out of the way. Irked, Krys stood up, her tone icy. "I'll head back myself. Thanks for your concern."

As she began walking. David fell into step beside her. "You're angry with me?"

"No," she admitted with a sigh, shaking her head. "I'm just lonely, really. I came here for a vacation and didn't think it through."

"How so?"

"I used to come here with my parents and brother. They're gone now. I'm alone."

"I understand," David said, nodding, slipping his hands into his pockets. "I'm also alone. My sister died some years ago. She was the last of my family."

"I'm sorry."

David walked Krys to her door. She faced him awkwardly, not sure if she should invite him in. She didn't want the evening to end, yet also didn't want him to think that she was inviting a sleepover.

David looked at her, then reached out, pushing the door wide. "You didn't lock your door," he said patronizingly. "Wait here." He went inside and began looking around.

"Hey," Krys called irately, romantic thoughts forgotten as she went after him. "What do you think you're doing?"

"Being chivalrous," David retorted. He checked the three bedrooms, then descended the stairs. "Please lock up after I leave."

He went out, then headed across the yard without so much as a goodbye. Angry, Krys slammed the door and locked it, then stomped into the kitchen and opened the bottle of wine she'd purchased that day.

There was a law against bringing alcohol into the park. But that was fine. If anyone came looking tomorrow, they wouldn't find any left.

* * * *

Someone was playing music. Groggily, Krys opened her eyes, and sat up in bed. Though her head was pounding and her eyes felt like sandpaper, her senses were awash in that same unearthly music. Yet this was a subtly different tune, more longing, more hopeful somehow than the other had been. Odder, it came from no violin; this was some kind of piano, or electric keyboard.

It had to be David.

Suddenly struck with a plan, Krys grabbed her cell phone, turning it on.

* * * *

The next evening, Krys was ready and in position when dark fell. Soon after the sun disappeared, David appeared, again walking up the road toward the forest. She hurried to intercept him.

"I heard you playing again last night," she said, stepping in front of him.

159

He looked at her innocently. "I'm sure you're mistaken—"

Krys clicked playback on her phone. The melodious tune broke the silent night, drifting on the night air.

"That's not on any radio," Krys said. "It's too original, for one thing." She clicked off the recording. "What I don't understand is why someone so talented doesn't want to take credit for his work. You wrote that, didn't you?"

"What do you want from me?" David said pointedly, folding his arms across his chest. "Sheet music to sell, or my autograph?"

"Just the truth. Who are you?" Krys asked. "Are you a famous musician?"

"I was once," David said sadly, letting out a breath. "I was a lot of things once. But I'm not anymore."

There was so much loss in his dark blue eyes. Krys stared into them, riveted.

"I need to be by myself now," David said. "But if you would welcome my company later, I'll come to your cottage."

Krys gaped at him. *Was he asking to sleep with her?* Even though the prospect was tempting, how could she morally just agree without being sure that was what he meant?

"I'll visit with you on your porch, is what I meant to say," David amended, smiling slightly. "Will that be all right?"

"Yes," Krys said, returning the smile. "How late?"

"An hour to two," David replied. "I'll be as fast as I can." He walked away, up the same road towards the cemetery.

Krys watched his shadow merge with the forest, then walked toward her cottage, impatient for the minutes to pass.

* * * *

David showed up as he'd promised. Walking up the stairs, he settled in the other wicker chair, then turned toward her expectantly. "Ask away, Krystin."

"Who are you?"

"My name is David Helm. I used to go by another name when I worked in the music industry. I was well liked by the crowd, to the point

I put out an album. After that, I had money, and a little fame. Then I made some bad decisions, and hit the skids."

"Did you lose it all?" Krys asked. "I'm sorry to say this, but as much as I enjoyed it, your music wasn't familiar to me."

"I didn't think it would be," David said, smiling ruefully. "But I am glad you liked it." He paused. "Yes, I lost most everything. Then I came to the attention of a powerful man, you might say a former admirer. He saved me, before I lost it all. But his help came with a price, a big one. But I managed to handle that, after a while."

There was a lot here he wasn't saying plainly, yet she was loath to push, especially as he had to be referencing substance abuse. "Did you go back to music?"

David shook his head. "I went into business management. I'm decent at that, enough so I've made some success."

More vagueness. "Are you here on business?" Krys asked, curious.

"For an important meeting," David admitted, letting out a breath. "Maybe the most important of my life. That old acquaintance has an opportunity I very much want for my own. But I'm not the only one in the running. I've got to convince him to give it to me."

"By using music, which you know he likes."

"Yes," David said, nodding. "This composition has to be perfect. I'll get one chance. The notes have to sway him." He became agitated. "I've rewritten the melody a hundred times. But I don't know if it's moving enough—"

Krys reached out, and took his cool hand in hers. "It's the most moving music I've ever heard. What's your title?"

"Just 'Night Music'," David said, his tone suddenly shy. "I haven't come up with anything better. I've been too focused on the notes themselves." He squeezed her hand.

"But I'm being a bore going on about myself. Tell me about yourself, Krystin."

Krys released his hand, and stood. "I'd like to," she said hesitantly. "But please, come in. I'm cold out here—"

"I'm sorry," David apologized, standing at once. "You likely are cold." He opened the door for her, then followed her inside.

David was oddly formal at times, but he was the greatest gentleman she'd met, beside her father. Krys shut the door after him. "Do you want some wine?"

"No," David said apologetically. "But please have some yourself. I'll take some water, if you don't mind."

Krys nodded, pouring water and some wine into two glasses. She brought them back to the sofa, handing David his.

"To new friends," David said politely, clinking his glass with hers. He sipped, then set it down. "Now please, tell me about yourself."

* * * *

Three hours later, the clock chimed midnight. Krys stopped talking, her face reddening when she realized she'd been going on about herself for a solid hour. But David had been a wonderful listener, asking questions about her life and family. He now knew most of her life story: her wonderful childhood and adolescence, losing her parents in the car accident when she was in college, and her brother's death three months ago. In return, he'd told her of his traumatic childhood with a drunken mother and absent father, his rise to fame, and his own addiction to drugs and alcohol before his benefactor had saved him. What the man had done to save David from himself again hadn't been clear, but whatever had happened, it had worked. David had drunk three glasses of water, but refused anything else.

David stood. "I should go. It's very late."

After connecting with someone in such depth, desperateness not to be alone rose up inside her. Krys bolted towards the stereo. "Wait, we can listen to music or something—"

"No, thank you," David said politely. "I really need to go—"

Krys hit the stereo buttons, the music coming on immediately. To her horror, the song playing was familiar, and the last one she wanted to hear.

"—I'm forever yours—"

"Turn it off," she shrieked, and kicked the coffee table over in her haste. "Turn it off!"

"—forever yours, forever yours—"

David unplugged the stereo as Krys went to her knees, sobbing uncontrollably. Strong arms carefully picked her up. Krys clasped David around the neck as he carried her upstairs, and carefully sat her on the bed. He sat down next to her, then handed her the box of tissues. Krys took two, then blew her nose.

"Tell me why you're so upset," David said softly. "What does that song mean to you?"

Krys took another tissue out of the box, then dabbed at her face.

David waited.

She took a few more hitching breaths.

David clasped his hand in hers. "Do you want me to leave, Krystin?"

"No," Krys said tearfully. "Please stay. I don't want to be alone."

David put his arms around her, hugging her. "Then I'll stay. But please, tell me. You must tell someone. Whatever it is you're hiding is tearing you up inside."

Krys pulled back from him gently, then pulled her sweater off over her head. She pulled off her turtleneck, revealing her white cotton bra. Carefully, she took David's hand in hers, and brought it to her check, rubbing gently.

David sighed, the sound loud in the quiet. "Krystin, I—"

Krys leaned closer, bringing David's hand around to her back, pressing it there with her hand. David, blinked, his fingers feeling the raised tissue.

"What happened?" he asked gently.

"You weren't the only one that made bad decisions," Krys said quietly. "I did, too. The worst one was Richard."

David touched her back slightly. "There is a word there?"

"The beginning of one," Krys admitted. "He wanted me to get a tattoo of his name to symbolize our love. I refused. Later that night, when I was drinking, he put something in my beer—"

"He was lucky he didn't kill you," David said angrily. He let out a breath. "Please go on."

"When I went to sleep, he went to work on me." Krys paused, visibly struggling for words. "But halfway through he sliced too deep with his knife."

"I'm sorry," David said gently, hugging her. He touched the raised welts. "Was there nothing the surgeon could do?"

Krys shook her head. "Sometimes cutting causes this type of scarring. Instead of a little collagen helping the wound to heal, my body produced an overabundance. That caused the scar tissue. It's called a hypertrophic scar. If you mess with them, they only get worse."

"Does it hurt?" David said gently, his hand resting on the scar, but not pressing. "This was long ago?"

"Ten years," Krys said, her smile pained. "The doctors say that in time, it will fade completely. Every day I check, and it always looks the same."

"I'm sorry," David said softly, stroking her back.

"So am I," Krys whispered, burrowing into his chest. "It itches terribly sometimes…"

David moved back, then tilted her chin up with his hand, his cool lips meeting hers. The shock of being kissed made Krys draw breath quickly.

David pulled back, his dark blue eyes questioning, clearly wondering if he'd overstepped in kissing her. Krys reached out her hand to his face, bringing his lips again to meet hers. At first, their kisses were light, the gentle touch making Krys's heart race, and her body tingle. Then David's kisses became deeper, more sensual, his arms pulling her close, his body pressing against hers.

Krys began kissing down David's neck, her lips hot against his cool skin. David took her gently by the shoulders, stopping her.

"Don't think I don't want to, because I do," he said, his tone desire and hope. "But are you sure this is what you want? I don't want to take advantage—"

"I do," Krys said huskily, wrapping her arms around his neck and kissing him for all she was worth. David responded, pulling her astride him, his lips devouring hers.

* * * *

She was going to die if she didn't get some water. Parched, Krys grabbed her robe. Wrapping it around her, she hastened downstairs to the bathroom. Stumbling on the last step, she caught her hip on the door handle and let out a curse at the sharp pain, dropping her robe. She ran to the sink, fumbling for a plastic cup.

There was a loud screech from outside, as brakes squealed. Krys peered out the window blinds as her hands hurriedly filled a cup in the bathroom sink. It was sunny out there today, at least. She gulped down one cup of chill water, then another. Her thirst finally sated, she put the cup down, and turned to leave. Glancing up, Krys caught sight of her back reflected in the cabinet mirror above the sink.

The scar on her shoulder was gone. In its place was new pink skin, the tone slightly reddened, as if by a sunburn.

In disbelief, afraid to look away, Krys reached up her hand, watching her reflection do the same, her fingers confirming that the new skin was real.

What had happened last night? David had to have done this, somehow.

Krys felt the new skin again, then smiled widely, laughing in sheer joy not to see the ugly half word there anymore. She felt better than she had in years. She felt reborn.

* * * *

It took more than an hour for Krys to get over her happy surprise. For years she'd chosen her clothes carefully, coverage her first concern, and also shunned mirrors. Now she couldn't get enough of her naked reflection, loving how young and carefree she felt.

But her body soon reminded her that she'd not really had dinner in two nights, and that the temperature was wrong for naked jubilation, no matter how deserved. With new energy, Krys put on a sweatshirt and jeans over her goose bumped flesh and began making a big brunch, trying to figure out how this miracle had occurred.

David and she had made love last night, several times in fact. He'd been wonderful, both enthusiastic and considerate. She'd fallen asleep in his arms, completely satisfied. But sex—even fantastic sex—wasn't a cure for scars.

Krys thought back as she ate, replaying the night, trying to find the moment when she'd last felt the tightness of her mark. The last time with him, he'd kissed her scar as he loved her, his tongue caressing her warm skin, his mouth gently sucking. The sensation coupled with his lovemaking had been dreamy, erotic, and blissfully wonderful all at once. Krys had wanted it to go on and on, but the climax had crested, sheer pleasure washing over her. When she'd gone limp under him, her cries ebbing along with his, David had given her shoulder a last kiss, then rolled onto his back, bringing her into his arms to hug her tightly. She'd hugged him back, then dropped off to sleep, exhausted. David had left sometime after that, somewhere near dawn.

Unbelievable as it was, David had somehow done this. *How? Was he a sorcerer?* Magic of some kind had to be involved.

Why had he left afterwards? To go sleep in the basement? And how had his kiss healed her?

Maybe he was a vampire, and there was a coffin down there. Krys snorted, then chuckled. That didn't work, as she didn't have any fangs herself this morning. Moreover, there wasn't room for a coffin in that truck of his, unless he strapped it in the truck bed. That would be a sight...

Krys peered outside again through the drapes. David's truck was still there, parked in the same place.

Should she go over and knock? By the clock, it was about one in the afternoon. *But what if he was busy composing?* That opportunity he'd spoken of was clearly important to him. *Damn it, why hadn't he left her a note...*

Maybe he had, and she'd been in such a rush to get downstairs that she'd missed it. Krys rolled her eyes, made an irritated noise, then went back upstairs to look. There on the nightstand was a piece of paper, the writing delicate block letters. Relieved, she picked it up and began to read.

Krystin,

I hope when you wake you will feel happy. I'm equally sure you'll have questions. I will answer them if you wish tonight at midnight. Please come over to the Chalet then, or leave me a note there that you wish me to come to you.

It was wonderful to be with you last night. Writing that sounds trite, but it's the truth. I've been as lonely as you have been, and I very much want to see you again.
In Genuineness, David

"You've got a way with words, David," Krys murmured, shivering in excitement as she remembered his kisses. "But I think I'll let you come to me."

* * * *

While Krys would have enjoyed a few more hours sleep, she also was eager to be out and about. Though her scar was covered with several layers, knowing it was gone made her feel empowered, as if she'd gotten sudden good news that she couldn't wait to share with everyone. Krys walked the trails, making pleasant conversation with a few older couples at the scenic overlooks, greeting the other visitors that crossed her path with a wide smile.

This was how she remembered the park being. This was who she remembered being, this woman who was alive and happy and knew that not only did she have a great destiny, but she was also going to achieve it. However David had accomplished his magic, he was going to get nothing but her gratitude.

On her way back to her cottage that evening, Krys dropped off a note on the door of the Chalet, telling David to come and see her at nine. Then she headed inside, planning on a long bath, and then maybe dinner and a nap, before David arrived.

Krys had just emerged from her bath an hour later when there was a sharp knock at the door. Worried, she got out, wrapped her robe around herself, and went to the front door, moving aside the curtain. There was no one there.

She unlocked the door, then walked out onto the porch. "David?"

A hand went over her mouth, as she was grabbed from behind. "Shush, if you know what's good for you."

Krystin thrashed hard, but the arms around her held firm. Swiftly, she was dragged backward into the cottage, the door slamming hard. Her attacker threw her to the floor, locked the door, then rested a chair under the handle.

Krys watched him from the floor, conscious of being dressed in only her robe. The man was tall and gaunt, his eyes black pinpricks in his white face. Yet his clothing was oddly upscale, his khakis and heavy coat almost tailored.

"Who are you?" she said defiantly.

"That's not important," the man said, going to the window and looking out. "Get dressed. You have two minutes. Or you'll go in your robe."

"I'm not going anywhere with you—"

The man hissed, baring long fangs, the lower two almost as long as the upper ones. "Go!"

Krys ran for the stairs, and up to her bedroom, the man close behind. She slammed into her center room, and shut the door in his face.

"I can break this down in an instant," he said in a low amused voice. "You now have one minute before I do, Krys."

Krys's eyes widened. He knew her name.

"Forty seconds—"

Krys lunged for the closet.

* * * *

"I told you, you were better off being quiet," the man said patiently. "You are the one who screamed. You have only to blame yourself."

Krys glared at him above the tape over her mouth, and kept following him, the rope around her bound hands making her stumble with every few steps.

"This is far enough," the man said, stopping. He turned to Krys and pulled her toward him, grasping her arms, then shoved her up against a tree.

Krys began to struggle, fighting him. With a crack of his hand, he slapped her, the blow making her bite her tongue as tears came to her eyes. Before she could gather her wits, she was securely tied. In fear of what was to come, Krys stared at her captor, motionless.

"Good," the man said, then turned and began to walk off. A moment later, he was lost among the trees.

Relieved, Krys sagged in her bonds. Then a moment later, she straightened with sudden hope at the sight of David coming toward her through the trees. As he neared, Krys's eyes rounded in horror to see the gaunt man rushing toward him, a fancy sword in his hand. She tried to cry out, to warn David, but the tape muffled her cries. In desperation, she kicked out with her leg, trying to draw his attention. The man was almost on him!

In a smooth motion, David drew a gun and fired, the silenced bullet hitting the gaunt man in the forehead with a short "pfft." The man's head jerked back as he fell to the ground, the sword dropping from his slack hand. With a deft move, David grabbed the weapon with his free hand, then severed the man's head in a powerful blow. He sent the head rolling off with a kick of his foot.

Breathing hard, David turned to Krys, letting the sword fall from his hand. She looked into his dark blue eyes with her own scared ones.

David reholstered his gun, and hurried to her side as she began to squirm. "Shh," he whispered, untying her. "You're safe now. Brace yourself." With a fast rip, he tore off the tape.

"Ow!" Krys yelped.

"Are you okay?" David said, looking her over. "He didn't hurt you?"

"Who was that?" Krys said angrily.

"That opportunity I want?" David replied darkly. "Others want it, too." His jaw worked, as he stepped back from her. "I've got to leave tonight, before I put you in any more danger." He walked back to the sword, and grabbed it up. "Can you make it back to the cottage by yourself?"

"Yes," Krys retorted, miffed he would allow her to walk back. Hadn't he just told her there were others, as in plural? What if another guy jumped her on her way back? "Do you want me to call the police?"

"No," David said, wiping off the sword blade on the corpse. "He'll turn to dust by tomorrow morning." He looked up at her. "But the sword won't."

There had been enough mystery and innuendos. "He had fangs, David. I saw them."

169

"He's dead now, Krystin. He can't come back and hurt you. In a few hours, there won't be any trace of him left. That's what happens to all my kind in the sunlight." He smiled sadly. "Just go back to your cottage and forget this ever happened."

He was telling her he was a vampire, even if he hadn't said the word. Impossible as that might make any relationship between them, the last thing Krys wanted was for David to disappear out of her life. "When will you be back? A few days?"

"I might not come back," David said gently, squeezing her hand.

Krys stared at him, her eyes wide in disbelief, her hopes devastated.

"It wouldn't be because I didn't want to," David said quickly. He grimaced. "Oh hell, I'm sorry to say this all so badly. I'm not good with words, Krys. I'm much better expressing myself in music."

Krys just looked at him, blinking back tears.

"Come here," David said softly, hugging her. "I didn't want to spring everything on you at once. I didn't want to heal you last night, to not be with you when you woke. But if it was a choice between healing you and not healing you, I had to take it. Do you understand?"

"How did you do it?" Krys whispered, looking into his eyes. "No more vagueness, David."

"I'm a vampire," David said bluntly, baring his fangs slowly. "My blood and saliva has healing ability. I carefully used both to heal your scar."

Her conclusive jest earlier had been the correct one. She took a long breath, then let it out. "I didn't feel fangs when you kissed me."

"I was careful," David replied evenly. "That you had a few drinks helped." He smiled widely, revealing his fangs.

"Did you drink my blood?" Krystin asked tentatively, not sure she wanted to know the answer.

"A little, yes," David admitted. "It was inevitable in healing you. But I didn't heal you to get your blood."

"I know you didn't," Krys said softly, then she hugged him. "Maybe I should be screaming, or brandishing a cross at you. But you just saved me from that fiend. Last night you did what no doctor could, not with all the latest technology. It makes sense that there's an extraordinary explanation. What you just admitted doesn't change how I feel, or make me regret anything that's happened between us." She kissed David's cheek. "Thank you for what you did."

David hugged her back, all the tension going out of his body. "I'm glad you're not upset. I thought you might have hysterics, especially with being kidnapped."

"I'm happier to be rid of that scar," Krys replied. She looked at the headless body disdainfully. "And I'm not sorry he's dead." She turned back to David, expectant. "So why won't you come back with me?"

"I will, now I know you want me to," David said, looking around uneasily as he took off his long sleeve shirt, wrapping the sword in it. "I thought you might want to end things now, with what's happened. I was giving you an easy out."

"I'm staying in, David," Krys said staunchly. "But I do want the unvarnished truth, all of it, not to mention an escort back."

"You have both, then. I'll tell you the rest when I know you're safe inside walls. Come on back to my place."

* * * *

"Tell me," Krys said, leaning back on the couch across from David. "I'm as safe now as I'm going to be. You know all my secrets. Tell me yours."

"You might as well know it all," David said uneasily, his tension returning. "There is a vampire hierarchy in every country. The United States is no exception. There is a Lord—well, he calls himself Ruler—and under him for each state is another vampire, then under them more lesser-ranked vampires for the cities on down. Danial Racklan—the vampire who was in charge in Colorado—left recently to preside over New York. I want his old spot." He paused. "My benefactor—the one I told you about—is the Lord over all. His name is Devlin Dalcon. He is the one who made me a vampire, years ago. States don't come up for grabs often. The competition will be fierce. Devlin won't play favorites, not when it comes to something like this. My musical ability is my edge; I hope it will sway him in a tight decision. But I'll also need to demonstrate leadership abilities: intelligence, cunning, and bravery. And I'll have to fight the other applicants." David took a long breath, then let it out. "Those can be to the death sometimes, if neither participant will yield." He looked up at Krystin, his eyes scared yet determined. "I can't afford to yield, Krystin. Either I'll come back to you as victor, or I'll not come back at all. But I am going to leave tonight, so I don't draw anymore danger to you."

Krystin wiped at tears that were running freely down her cheeks.

David grasped her hand, squeezing gently. "I didn't want to tell you this, but not telling you was worse, especially if I don't make it—"

Krystin hugged him fiercely, trying to order her frantic thoughts, and lock away her urge to scream at him not to go. She needed to be strong now not just for herself, but for him. She took another deep breath, then let it out, moving back from him and drawing herself up regally.

"I know this is important to you. I can't say I'm not scared of losing you, David." Krystin kissed his lips. "I am." She kissed him again. "Remember I care about you, and good luck." She kissed him a final time. "There's a lot I still don't understand, but I'll take that on faith, for now. My stay's up on Saturday. Call me on my cell if you need to."

David kissed her. "I have the number. Take care, my sweetheart." He hugged her a final time, then left without a backward look.

Krystin watched him drive off, then sank down on the couch, dissolving into tears.

* * * *

The next two days passed agonizingly slow. Krystin checked the phone each hour, hoping for a missed call, but there were none. She walked for miles on the trails, trying to exhaust her body so it would sleep. Yet she still woke frequently in the night, hoping each time to hear David's music wafting in on the night wind. But there was only the sound of the wind in the trees, and the far off rumble of the falls.

* * * *

Saturday morning came. Resigned, Krys awoke, then began to pack. There was no use delaying the inevitable. Even if David was fine, she still had her job to consider.

She was just putting the final pair of socks in the suitcase when her phone rang. She ran to it, looking at the number. It was a New York Area code, but the name listed wasn't David's name. It was a Devlin Dalcon.

Krys stared at the phone. This was Devlin; the lord David had spoken of. There was only one reason he would be calling her. He was calling to tell her David was dead.

She drew a shuddering breath, then hit the green button. "Hello?"

"Hello," a melodious voice said. "This is Devlin. Is this Krystin?"

"Yes," she answered. "Is David—?"

"He's recovering," Devlin said agreeably. "He was badly injured, but you'll be proud to know he succeeded—"

Krys let out a loud cry of relief, sinking onto the bed.

"Not in my ear, please," Devlin said sharply. "You could whisper and I'd easily hear you."

"I'm sorry," Krys apologized, then quickly added "Lord Devlin."

"You do have manners," he answered, pleased. "But please, just Devlin will do. You and I may be on a much more familiar basis before long."

Was he coming onto her? No, he must be alluding to something; maybe to her and David being a couple? "That would be nice," she answered awkwardly.

"I'm glad you think so," he said smoothly. "I've arranged for you to stay an extra week at the park, so that David may spend some time with you there after he leaves here. This is my congratulatory gift to him. I understand it's a very romantic setting."

"Yes, it is," Krys said happily. "I highly recommend it."

There was a pause that stretched into a full thirty seconds, then beyond.

Krys waited in trepidation, unsure of what to do. *Should she compliment him?* "Devlin, I really appreciate your calling to let me know that David—"

"You know what he is," Devlin said, his tone utterly changed from gentle to bitter ice. "If you stay this course, there will be other attempts on you. I guarantee it. David had enemies, Krystin. He has more now he's Colorado's State Ruler. Are you ready for that?"

"I know that," Krys retorted coldly, trying hard to keep a rein on her flaring temper. "He told me this. I—"

"If you stay with him, there are going to be consequences. I am willing to help with some of that, as I've already said. Go into this with open eyes. Wide open." Devlin paused. "Some fates cannot be changed once they begin."

"My eyes are wide open, Devlin," Krys said meaningfully, enunciating each word deliberately loud. "I want to be with David, and he wants to be with me—"

"That's how it always starts," Devlin said with a sigh. "I'll say no more. Expect David in a few days. Adieu."

Krys put the phone down, the dial tone loud. *What had he meant?*

After calling her boss and arranging another week of vacation, Krys hung up the phone and began unpacking, doubt invading her thoughts.

* * * *

Sunday afternoon, Krys watched from the cottage porch as a van parked in front of the Chalet, several couples disembarking in the night air, laughing loudly as they brought their luggage inside.

They looked so happy. Would David and she be that happy, when he returned? There was one thing for certain; they would never even be outside together on a fall afternoon like those couples. If she stayed with David, her world would be the night world: moons, stars, darkness, maybe the occasional firefly. *Could she adapt to that?*

There was also her old life, not to mention her job. It was a safe bet that when David came back, he was going to ask her to go with him back to Colorado. While part of her wanted to, the real truth was she'd only met David a week ago. *While the connection they shared was real, did she really know him well enough to uproot her life for him?* The situation had been life and death, the most romantic encounter she'd ever experienced. *But was that a basis for a real relationship? Could David and she sustain a romance when he wasn't preparing for a fight to the death?*

Krystin wasn't sure what course to take, no matter how many pros and cons she sensibly went over in her mind. Her mind said this could work, but it could also fail. Her heart absolutely told her to go for it, that what mattered was being with David, and the rest would fall into place.

* * * *

David returned the following night, his truck pulling into her driveway around midnight. Krys awoke and came downstairs; opening the door as he slowly came up on the porch with effort.

"Your left leg," she said, taking his hand. "Is it—?"

"It was broken in several places, but its healing slowly," David said, locking the door behind him. He sank onto the couch with a grunt.

Krys sat beside him, looking him over. His face had some bruises, but otherwise he looked the same. She kissed his cheek, and hugged him.

"Devlin said he called you," David said softly, slipping his arm around her. "I'm glad you waited for me."

Krys wiped her eyes, then looked up at him, a smile forming instantly. "What else was I going to do?"

David kissed her gently, then moved back, wincing. "I don't suppose you'd mind if I stayed here with you tonight?"

"No," Krys said. "I'll help you up the stairs."

Carefully, they made their way to the second floor, Krys supporting David's left side. She eased him onto the bed, then closed the window, drawing the curtains, plunging the moonlight room into deep shadow.

"Thank you," David said gratefully.

Krys climbed in beside him. Again, David slipped his arm around her, his happy sigh loud in the darkness.

"Will I be able to leave to eat breakfast in the morning?" Krys asked tentatively. "Will I wake you?"

"I sleep like anyone else," David said, amused. "I'm not going to die overday—sorry, during the day—, or anything dramatic. You leaving or coming in won't be an issue, just please keep the curtains shut."

"Will you need my blood?" Krystin asked curiously.

"No," David replied gently. "I brought some. But I thank you for offering." His lips brushed her cheek. "And before you ask, I'm not hundreds of years old. I didn't see the Civil War, or even the World Wars. I've only been a vampire about thirty years."

"Are there many that are older?"

"Some, like Devlin, are easily two, maybe three hundred, or even older. They're usually crueler the older they are. But maybe you can't help it, seeing the world change and morph into something unrecognizable."

She should let him rest. Yet Krys was too worried over Devlin's warning to keep silent. "Devlin said he and I might be 'on familiar terms, before long'. What did he mean, David?"

"That being with me will eventually kill you," David whispered, clutching Krys tightly. "I dreaded telling you this, even though I knew I had to. I know we've only known each other a short while, but I don't want to lose you." He kissed her cheek gently. "I'm also scared about hurting you—"

"No vagueness, David," Krys said sharply. "How would you hurt me? You forget yourself and drain my blood?"

"I'm not an animal who is starving and a slave to instinct," David said, irritated. "I do not lick blood off the floor, nor do I go wild when I drink some. Maybe there were some vampires who were like that, over the years, but—"

"So you just drink and ho hum, stop when you're done?"

"Yes," David said, affronted. "We usually contract with humans we call donors, though animal blood suffices for someone my age, and that is easily bought. As for humans, we pay them well for their services—"

"From who? Not transients, or prostitutes—?"

"Do you eat a cookie off the floor covered in dirt?" David said scathingly. "Would you have unprotected sex with a man you knew to be diseased, no matter how handsome he was? Of course not. Nothing is more repulsive to me than those stupid movies where a vampire is staring at some girl's neck like it's the Holy Grail and slavering. We contract with people who know what we are that take very good care of themselves—"

She'd offended him royally. *Cringe.* "I'm sorry. This is all new to me. I just feel like I'm at a party I arrived at late and everyone else knows what's supposed to happen but me."

"I don't mean to be so touchy," David said gently. "I'm just tired, and my healing body is painful."

"Let's talk in the morning, then," Krys offered, snuggling into his chest. "Everything else can wait until then."

"No, I need to say this now." David paused. "What Devlin meant is that a human who is bitten repeatedly eventually begins to react to what makes us vampire. You felt nothing when I healed you, or possibly it felt good—"

That was what had made that last time so intense. "It was wonderful," Krys whispered with a sigh, shivering.

"—some call it the vampire virus, some call it magic. But its effect on a human is always the same: once the lethargy starts, the human gets weaker until death comes." He kissed her brow. "But that doesn't have to happen with us. I don't have to take any of your blood, ever."

Could she resist, now that she knew how good it felt? Unlikely. "What if I want you to?" Krys asked tentatively.

"Then we'll be very careful," David assured her. "Get some sleep, sweetheart. I'll be here when you wake up tomorrow. We can figure out the rest then."

* * * *

Krys awoke about ten. David was lying beside her, sleeping peacefully. Carefully, she got up, and grabbed some clothes, then tiptoed out and down the stairs. After dressing, she made herself breakfast and went over her options.

Before David's confession last night, she'd been ready to commit to relocating. But hearing she would probably die as the eventual result was a definite mark in the cons column. Rethinking the conversation, Krys thought she knew now why Devlin had mentioned it. When she got close to death, David was planning on helping her become what he was. He either needed Devlin's help to do it, or his permission...

"Krystin," David called from the other room. "Please come in here. I'd come in there, but there are no drapes."

Startled, Krys got up, and went into the living room. There David sat, a blanket draped over his head and shoulders, sunlight shining in the window behind him.

Krys closed the drapes, then sat next to him, sliding the blanket back. "Why aren't you sleeping?"

"Because I'm scared you're reconsidering," David replied, taking her hand in his. "You'd be crazy not to, after what I've told you."

"Did you come down to convince me otherwise?" Krys said, squeezing his hand.

"I came down to enjoy being with you," David said, looking into her eyes. "If we only have a few days, I can accept that. But I'm not going to waste any of that time apart from you."

God, he was lovable. "Go up and sleep," Krys said affectionately, her heart melting. "I'm just going to pick up more groceries. I'll be back after."

"Good," David said, his eyes mischievous. "Because I wanted to play something for you tonight, if you would like to listen."

"I'd love to," Krys replied eagerly. "Give me an hour, tops."

* * * *

That next week was heaven. David healed most of his injuries that first night, awakening the next with just a small limp. He and she walked each night in the dark, admiring the falls by moonlight, and watching the deer as they came out to feed. They made love in the mornings, then slept late into the afternoons, limbs entwined. And each day at dusk, David would play for her, sometimes on his keyboard, and sometimes the violin, the compositions stirring and magical as the notes flowed over her.

Krys had never been so happy. So what if the moon was in the sky and not the sun? What mattered was she had someone to share her life with and each moment that made it special. Maybe this wasn't a happily ever after. But she was happy now with David. She would trust him, and take whatever consequences there were.

On their last night at the park, David led her in front of the falls, and then turned to her.

"Will you come with me?" he said softly, taking a ring from his pocket.

Krys blinked at him, then at the diamond. The ring was a broken loop, with diamonds set into either end. "That's...I've never seen a ring like that before."

"It was the most unusual design they had," David said sheepishly. "I wanted something special. But I can get a traditional one, if you'd prefer that."

"You want to marry me?" Krys whispered, her eyes still staring at the sparkling ring.

"I do," David said, kissing her hand. "But I'll settle for you agreeing just to come live with me in Colorado, if you'd prefer that for now. I don't want to rush you. But I also can't imagine going back without you, Krystin. I want you with me. But do you want that, too?"

"Yes," Krystin said seriously, putting her hand over David's. "I'm scared about what you've told me, but I also don't want to lose you."

"So is that a yes?" David asked hopefully.

"Yes," Krys said, nodding. "Yes. I love you."

"Good, because I'm in love with you," David said, his face breaking into a wide smile. "Now kiss me, sweetheart." He leaned in close.

"I'm sorry," a voice said excitedly. "But I just wanted to tell you that this was so romantic, proposing right here at the falls. Congratulations!"

Krys and David turned to an older couple, both of them beaming.

"Thank you," David said graciously. "We're very excited."

"Actually," Krys said, rummaging in her purse and producing her phone. "Can you take our picture, please? We'd love to capture this."

"Of course," the man said, taking the phone. "I'll take several. Now just smile, you lovebirds."

David turned to Krys, then kissed her hand gallantly, then took her in his arms and kissed her, the phone flashing again and again.

"There are some good ones," the man said, handing the phone back when they were finished. "You make a lovely couple."

"Thank you," David said, handing the phone back to Krys.

Krys stashed it, then looked up at David. His look was relaxed and confident. "You know, you never told me if Devlin liked it," Krys said coyly. "Your song, Night Music."

"Your song," David corrected. "And yes, he loved it."

Krys stared at him. "My song?"

"'Night Music for Krystin'," David said formally. "I changed the title." He smiled. "Your name added just what I needed to make it remarkable." He kissed her hand. "You are just what I needed."

"So are you," Krystin said, blinking at her filling eyes. "I'm so glad I found you, David."

David took out a handkerchief, and wiped away her tears. "What would you like to do first, my fiancée?" he asked lovingly. "We should celebrate."

"I want you to kiss me, of course," she said sexily. "We'll wing it from there."

Her lips met his once more, her happy bliss making the kiss perfect. At that moment everything was possible, the future shining out before them like an unwritten sheet of paper. Two weeks ago, just the thought of being this happy had been impossible. Now Krys had found not only lasting love, but a new start. Together, she and David would find a way to make it work.

Tears and Rain

Rain poured down on the tall man standing before the newly etched gravestone. The drops that struck his exposed skin sizzled, then became steam.

"I got her for you, brother," Terian said softly.

The stone wept tears of rain that seemed to mock his words, showing them for empty verse. *That's what they were.* Why should Keriam care that his murderer had been punished? He was dead now and no spell known to sorcery could call back a soul from Heaven. Even if there had been one, Terian wouldn't have attempted it. He was half demon. Just the thought of Heaven was enough to give him a headache.

I'd surrender my soul if it would bring you back. But do I even have a soul?

Just a few months ago, Terian's life had been simple, if miserable. Terian had lived with his mortal brother, Keriam, most of his life. His small skill in potions—learned from a sympathetic "white" witch long ago—had been enough to bring in a small income. His brother's new wife, while not exactly compassionate, had been okay.

Then had come his brother's death, a murder that Terian had been sure was the work of the vampire turned entrepreneur, Danial Racklan. Blinded to the danger by rage, Terian has kidnapped Danial's lover Sarelle, and challenged the bloodsucker to a fight. He'd expected to win and be vindicated...or to lose and be put out of his misery. Instead, Danial had hurt him with a blow Terian had never seen coming: that he was not a dhamphir—a half-vampire—as he'd always thought, but instead a bastard mix of human and demon. The blessed blade Danial had used hadn't cut deeply, but the scar still graced Terian's cheek. It was the first wound he'd ever had that hadn't immediately healed.

Sarelle had helped him escape certain death that night. Her kindness had been a surprise, especially as she was afraid of him like most humans were. After Terian had driven away, he'd headed to the closest church. Keriam had never been religious at all; it was his first time being near one. And "near" was as close as Terian could manage; he could not cross onto the grounds of the church, much less go inside.

He stood for a while on the sidewalk, looking at the brick structure forlornly.

"You aren't doomed just because you can't go in," a solemn voice said from behind him.

Terian turned. A priest stood there, hands in his coat pockets. "Who are you?" he said, letting out some of anger, wanting to see the priest cringe away from the feelings of dread his violent emotions always evoked in others.

"Control yourself," the man ordered. "Or you'll make me think I'm wasting my time on you."

Terian took a step back, forcing himself to be calm with deep breaths.

"Better," the man allowed. "My name is Father Ben. I used to be a priest with a human flock." He took a card and handed it to Terian. "Now I tend the larger flock that's scattered." There was something sad about his smile, though it was genuine. "I've found they need a friend the most."

Dr. Stephen Camlyn. "This is a doctor's card," Terian said skeptically, turning the card over to view office hours listed on the back. *Odd.* Half the hours listed were mornings, the rest early evenings.

"A doctor who treats supernatural beings of all kinds. He can show you how to hide your eyes behind special colored contacts that can withstand the natural heat of your body. The fees are reasonable." The priest handed him one more card. "Call Colin, too. He can help you adjust, give you a purpose."

"I don't need anyone to give me a purpose," Terian said, flashing his pointed teeth.

"You have no morality. You have taken human lives."

Was he guessing, or did he know about Alexa? Only ones that killed other people I loved."

"You can pledge to fight evil, or become it," the priest said portentously. "Only you can make the choice, demon."

Terian looked at the card. This had been more what he'd expected. The card was swirled purple clouds, the name Colin Underwood in metallic blue in neat print across the front. But instead of some hype about paranormal investigations or magic, it said, "Existence Coach." Across the back in the same metallic blue was the phrase, "You get one lifetime. Make the most of it."

Terian was tempted to rip the card in two. He'd already lived a human's lifetime, and looked only 20 years old, at most. *What could this man hope to teach him?*

"To lighten up, for starters," a mirthful voice said behind him.

Terian whirled, then struck out with his fist. The man evaded him effortlessly. Terian murmured the words to the only attack spell he knew, calling up the shadows from around him to cloak him in a living cover of darkness. The man's eyes widened, then he murmured words, making his hands into fists, then snapping them open, throwing a still-forming shimmering silver ball of light toward Terian. The light smashed into his shadows, scattering them to leave him revealed before it faded.

"What do you want?" Terian growled, drawing his boot knife.

The man held up his hands in supplication. "Not to fight." He laughed. "That's my card you're holding. I'm Colin. I felt your wish. I've built a sort of homing device into the cards, so I can teleport to anyone who holds a card." He put his hands down, some of his levity leaving him. "Sometimes even that's too long."

"What can you hope to teach me?" Terian said bitterly. "I already know really well how the world works, Colin. I don't need any happy bullshit."

"To teach you hope," Colin said, offering Terian his hand. "And maybe a few more defensive spells, not that Calling Shadows is lightweight."

"You foiled it easily enough," Terian said sullenly, not making a move.

"Because I've studied magic, specifically defensive spells, for close to a hundred years," Colin replied. "That isn't a common spell, so most people wouldn't know the rebuttal. Who taught you?"

"A witch," Terian admitted grudgingly. "She knew I was different, and she was nice to me. She taught me all the magic I know."

"Was she your mother?"

Terian shook his head. "My mother died giving birth to me. I never knew my father. My only family was my brother. He died less than a month ago."

"I can teach you more spells," Colin offered. "I have more than a few tomes you are welcome to borrow, if you're interested. It's all white magic."

A crow scolded harshly from the trees above him, shaking Terian out of his reminiscing. He pulled his coat around his shoulders, then moved off toward his truck. There would be time enough for pondering what his next move would be on the road. Right now, he had to get out of New York State before Theo caught up with him. That werecougar friend of Danial's would kill him if he had the chance.

Terian started his truck, then plotted a route west. Theo likely wouldn't pursue him beyond the boundaries of New York state, his boss Danial's territory. Danial wanted Terian dead, because of his friendship with Sarelle. Sar had saved Terian's life that night he'd fought with Danial. She'd repaid his holding her hostage with kindness instead of the killing blow he'd expected.

She doesn't love you. She never did.

Sar had risked a lot to help him. Terian had returned her kindness by telling her of Danial's secret request for two expensive potions. Demon blood was an expensive ingredient needed for its creation. Half-demon blood was a less expensive option, but needed to be doubled when used in spellwork as a replacement for full-demon blood. Terian thought darkly that he could sell his blood and never have to make another potion himself, if he was inclined.

Sar had brushed his warning about complicated potions aside, refusing to believe Danial was up to no good. When she'd discovered too late her vampire had hoped to start his own immortal family with her as mom, she'd left Danial. Terian had also discovered Danial's plans, and known he had to warn her. He'd found Sar at her old home that New Year's Eve, distraught and mourning a broken heart. To cheer her, he'd given her a late Christmas present of magical wings. She'd been so happy. She'd never suspected he'd laced the spell with a bit of extra magic.

You're as much a liar as Danial ever was.

I needed to know, Terian thought defensively. I needed to know if she could love me.

Sar is good. You're evil. She couldn't love you. That's why Sundown couldn't love you either.

Sundown had been an exotic dancer Terian had stumbled across when he stopped to get some food late one night. Her long dirty blond hair was a ringer for Sar's, even if her personality was completely different. They'd briefly dated and lived together. But as much as Sundown craved the stability of a relationship, her distrust of men was deep. Terian had asked her to commit and Sundown had refused, her learned ferocity lashing out in cruelty.

"Don't you care about me?" he'd said in a small tentative voice.

"It was just sex to me, like I've had with dozens of men."

Terian had known she was lying. His supernatural hearing was acute enough to hear her inside crying as he drove away with his stuff. But he also couldn't heal someone so broken, not without their cooperation. Colin had taught him that.

"Without hope, you are doomed, Terian. Life is hope. If you want to survive, you have to believe that things can get better."

There was nothing left for him here. It was time to leave, to go far away West, like he'd planned a few months ago. Colin's home base was in Denver. Terian needed a fresh shot of hope about now.

* * * *

"There is no comfort in deep-rooted pain," a feminine voice said gently, breaking the silence of the library. "Remembering the past won't heal wounds, it will only keep them fresh."

Terian looked up into deep blue eyes. A beautiful woman stood above him, her long black hair in a glossy braid over one shoulder. Her expression was sincere.

185

"You're a sorceress," he stated.

The woman nodded. "My name is Monica Remmin. And you are?"

Was this a friend of Colin? How had she found him, when Colin didn't know yet that Terian had even arrived? "Terian."

"No last name? Or is that you're working name?"

"Let's say it will suffice for now," Terian said, rubbing his eyes. "Did you come to kick me out of the library?"

Monica smiled. "No. I think you have another hour before they close. I wanted to say hello and ask if you want to join my coven."

Terian looked at her, bemused. "You must sense what I am. Are you sure?" He let his lips part, giving her a glimpse of his many rows of pointed demon teeth.

Monica's smile faltered a little. "I take it that you've been looking for answers. I got word that a half-demon was coming this way with a propensity for trouble."

"I'm not here for trouble," Terian said hastily.

"But it follows you, doesn't it?" Monica prodded. "You've stayed on the move because of what you attribute to bad luck." She leaned closer. "But it's not bad luck, Terian. It's a revenant on your tail."

Terian shook his head in disbelief. "That's bullshit. I've lived for seventy-five years and never seen a ghost."

"That doesn't mean they haven't seen you," she said darkly. She held out a card with an address on it. "Come tonight to my home. I think I can help you."

What was it with people wanting to help him handing him business cards? "Why would you help me?" Terian said, making no move to take the card. "When everyone else I meet usually wants me to keep moving?"

"Because there is more to you than you know," Monica said cryptically. "And I'm meant to help you." She moved to walk away, but Terian leaped up, grabbing her by the hand and yanking her backward. His red eyes bored into hers, the color flooding through his concealing contact lenses. Evil permeated the room, making Monica shiver even as she tried to hold still.

"Tell me and don't lie," Terian growled, showing his rows of pointed teeth as persuasion. "I've had enough lies. What do you want with me?"

"I had a vision of you," Monica stammered. "That's it! I do a spell every New Year's, and ask for guidance for the following year. It showed me several people I knew, and one stranger. You were the stranger. So when I saw you here I knew I had to come over and find out who you were...even sensing what you are."

Terian loosened his grip on her. Monica pulled away, straightening up.

"I don't understand."

"Visions are usually puzzles," Monica said, irritation distinct in each clipped word. "With the other people, I know what I'm supposed to do, because I know them. But with you, I have no idea."

Terian studied her, wondering how much to believe her. Monica gave every indication that she was on the level. *But was she?*

"Come tonight," Monica said again. "Please. No one wants to hurt you here." She turned and walked quickly away.

Terian watched her go, then looked down at the card she'd managed to slip into his hand. He'd go, just to see what kind of witches Monica kept company with.

* * * *

Monica's base of operations was nothing like the witch's lair Terian expected. Her small brick home was cozy with plentiful flowers, and the small one-level red barn at the back had been completely modernized into one plain white room and a set of bathrooms. He sat at a large conference table with twenty other men and women in their early twenties and thirties, most of whom were in casual dress.

"Good, we're all here," Monica said cheerfully. "Please everyone, welcome Terian, who is here by my invitation tonight."

Most of the people murmured a greeting, which Terian returned awkwardly.

The rest of the night was forgettable. Terian would have left after the first ten minutes, but he hadn't wanted to call attention to himself. All these "spellcasters" were of amateur level; young wives trying to win back their straying husbands through love spells, and men with goals of finding a way to beat the odds at gaming tables. Terian left the vapid

187

discussion as soon as he was able. As he walked out, a shadow descended on him, floating ghostlike through the air. At first, he was entertained, thinking it to be some trick of Monica's to impress him into staying. But as it reached him, a sharp odor of lilacs reached him. He fell to his knees, trying to breathe and found his air was constricted. He lashed out with power, and a supernatural shriek rent the air. The scent thickened, then a veil of darkness descended as Terian fell prostrate on the ground.

Keriam was lying on the floor, his face a twisted grimace of pain, his hands claws that had ripped out tufts of carpet as he'd writhed in pain. With a scream, Terian ran to him, gathering the lifeless body to him. Loss and loneliness crashed down on him.

"No!"

There was nothing he could do. He was too late again, too late to save his brother, too late, always too late…

A sharp crack of a gunshot echoed loud in Terian's ears. Then there was the sound of guttural swearing. Terian felt a hand in his. He roused himself just in time to be pulled to his feet by a man who had the same brown hair and facial features as Colin, yet his eyes were as red as Terian's.

"Demon or not, your ass is going to be toast if you don't learn to let things go," the man said grumpily. "Didn't Colin teach you not to dwell on your pain?"

"You're Colin's brother," Terian said in astonishment.

"You're a bright one," the man said with sarcasm, though he smiled. "Half-brother, as you of all people can probably tell. I'm Balt."

What the hell was he supposed to say? Commiserating on their shared demon lineage seemed just as bad as saying that it didn't matter. "Yes," Terian managed.

"Colin told me to expect you," Balt continued, "He's waiting for us, if you're ready to leave. Unless you want that ghost to come back and finish tearing you up."

"Let's go," Terian said, relieved.

Balt took Terian back to a small chain hotel with an attached restaurant on a seedy street of bars, strip clubs, and small motels. Colin was there at the hotel bar, nursing a drink and talking to a tall knockout

188

of a woman dressed in red. She shot Terian a smile as she left. He didn't return it, averting his eyes.

"Sit down," Colin told him, motioning to the bartender. "Bring a beer for my brother and another scotch for me. Terian, what do you want?"

"Nothing," Terian said flatly.

"Bring him a vodka," Balt said over his protest. "He can't bitch about it if he can't taste the alcohol. I'm going to hit the head."

The bartender brought the drinks in a few minutes, while Terian filled Colin in on what had happened since their last meeting.

"Why did you do that to Sar?" Colin asked, clearly disappointed. "I didn't loan you those books to use them like that. I've told you before that you can't force people."

"I wasn't forcing her to do anything," Terian argued.

"You're magic made her give voice to emotions she didn't want to talk about," Colin stated. "That's force."

"I just wanted to know how she felt, so I could decide to stay or leave."

"She told you she was in a relationship with another man. Wasn't that cause enough to leave?"

Terian didn't answer.

"It's the demon part of you that will want to control people," Colin warned. "Demons like power. They like to make things happen."

"My intentions were good ones."

Colin gave Terian a scathing look. "Do I really have to tell you the old saying about good intentions?"

Balt sat down on the stool next to them, taking a long drink of his beer. "I see he's giving you the usual upbeat pep talk. Ignore him. It works for me."

"I'm warning him, because someone had to," Colin said grumpily. "And you'd be better off if you were less flippant about your own situation."

"You'd be better off teaching him a little more magic to defend himself," Balt retorted emphatically. "That ghost last night might have killed him, if I hadn't stopped by to drop off those books to Monica for you."

"Who is she?" Terian said, eager to turn the conversation away from himself. "She made herself out to be a sorceress, but she's more like a poseur."

"She's just young," Balt said brusquely, surprising Terian with his defensive tone. "She can do minor spells like make illusions, and she's a fair healer. She's got the talent for becoming a sorceress to be reckoned with."

"But she cares a little too much about the romance of magic," Colin added. "She's another one that doesn't see her own vulnerability."

"If you're afraid all the time of bad things happening, how are you supposed to enjoy your life?" Balt countered, sounding irritated. He got up and stalked away.

"Don't mind him," Colin said. "He's sweet on Monica, if you hadn't noticed." His tone turned concerned. "But he's right that you need to worry about this ghost. Most don't have enough power to kill a half-demon, but they'll make you suffer. Next time use a dissipation spell. You hit it with that a few times and it'll leave you alone for good."

As much as Terian had wanted to talk shop with his old friend, it was Balt he wanted to speak to now. *Who could give him better advice than someone who was the same sort of being he was?* "Are you staying here? I'm sorry but I need to crash. I haven't slept since I got here."

Colin looked at him, unsmiling. "Go after him, if you want. Just be careful."

Terian gave Colin an odd look, but slid off the stool and went after Balt. The man was chatting up the girl in red who had been talking to Colin inside. He turned as Terian approached. "Terian, this is Rhinestone."

"Hi," Rhinestone said with a big smile. "I asked him who you were. I hope you don't mind." She made a point of getting out her keychain. "I live just down the street. Would you walk me home?"

"Why would he mind?" Balt said a little overzealously, slapping Terian on the back. "He'd be glad to."

Terian looked over Rhinestone with an appraising glance. She was pretty, young, and obviously had getting laid on her mind. And he wanted no part of her. "I'm not sure if that's a good idea. But it's good to meet you, Rhinestone."

Rhinestone looked uncertainly from Terian back to Balt, obviously wondering why he wasn't anxious to take her offer of sex.

"Hold," Balt intoned. Suddenly everything froze still. Rhinestone looked comical, as if she'd begun to speak and stopped. Even the breeze had disappeared, the leaves of the trees caught at odd angles above their heads.

"Impressive," Terian commented, trying to ascertain how far around them the spell reached.

"I'm not a high-level wizard," Balt said with braggadocio. "But I try to push myself as far as I can. I try to live. What's your excuse?"

"I'm doing what I—"

"You need to get whatever pleasure you can, while you can," Balt interrupted roughly. "How long do you think you have to fuck around mooning over a woman you left back east?"

"Eternity," Terian derided. "We're immortal, remember?"

"And what half do we get that from?" Balt smirked back evilly. "Not the human half. The older we get, the more the human half ages. The more our human resolve weakens, the more the balance of power shifts."

Terian's face relaxed from animosity to unexpected confusion. "What are you saying?"

"That being half demon is not like being half something else. The demon side wants to call the shots." His red eyes burned in the gloom. "Sooner or later you'll have a weak moment and that side of you is going to take control."

Fear coursed through Terian, chilling him. "That isn't possible."

"It comes in the night like a dream," Balt said wearily. "The whispers of temptation, the images of depravity, how good the abandonment of your scruples would feel. Then one day you wake up and you're doing those things you imagined and enjoying them."

"If that happens—"

"When it happens," Balt corrected. "Then it's over. There's no healing, no going back, nothing but getting put down like a rabid dog. Demon hunters are more prolific than vampire hunters and werepoachers combined right now. Think about that." He snapped his fingers and the air rushed back, the breeze blowing, ruffling the tree leaves.

"Hey, um—" Rhinestone began.

"I'll walk you home," Balt said, slipping his arms around Rhinestone's shoulders. "We'll leave him to Rosy Palm and her five sisters."

Terian watched them walk away laughing, then headed back inside. Colin was there, standing at the bar, chatting up another statuesque redhead. She also moved away as Terian came up, shooting him a shy smile. This time Terian smiled back, enjoying the surprise in the girl's eyes as she mouthed the word hi at him before heading away.

"Her name is Peaches," Colin said. "Not sure why. You'd think she'd have chosen a stage name like Red Hot or something instead—"

"Balt told me I'm going to turn demon eventually," Terian said. "Is that true?"

"You know, there is nothing subtle about you at all," Colin said, chuckling. "It's bracing, yet also so easy to deal with." He studied Terian. "How old are you?"

"You already know I'm close to seventy-five or so," Terian stated. "Tell me the truth."

"Balt is twenty-five," Colin said, taking a large sip of his whisky. "Already he has a tendency to be on edge almost all the time. He enjoys violence. And every month it gets worse."

Did Colin count sexual appetites for strippers among his brother's faults? Probably not, if he was indulging, too. "You're saying he's turning into a full demon."

Colin nodded.

"Can't you do anything?"

"Like what?" Colin said, wiping at one of his bleary bloodshot eyes. "Go back and make my father not summon a demon for a sexual plaything? Go back and not have him wish for another son, one who was taller and stronger and faster than his thoughtful firstborn?" He repositioned his empty drink glass. "I'm half faerie, because my father tried that first in his quest for power. My mother took me and left him. Balt's mother couldn't leave; she was my father's servant. She finally had him killed to free herself."

"How did you find out about Balt?"

"He found me one night. You remember that priest you met outside that church?"

"Yes," Terian said, narrowing his eyes. "He never told me his name."

"He prefers not to give it. He's kind of a local intermediary." Colin's voice dropped to a whisper. "There's more than the normal concentration of supernatural beings in the bigger cities of the heavily populated states. It's easier to blend in a crowd, because no one looks too close." He paused, as if gathering himself. "Balt came to a small church one night. He'd gotten drunk and beaten a man badly. He'd been in bad foster homes and been abused himself. His control of his demon half was slipping." Colin faced Terian. "He was only sixteen."

"I'm sorry," Terian murmured.

"You and me both," Colin said sadly.

They sat in silence for a while.

"What will you do?" Terian asked.

"I know what I should do," Colin whispered. "If I killed him now, he'd have a chance at going to Heaven, maybe. If I wait until he becomes fully demon, he's got no chance." He drained his glass, then looked at Terian. Tears glistened on his cheeks. "Full demons are immortal, but all they get to do is ferry back and forth from Hell to earth. They spend their lives serving evil people, being tortured, and torturing others."

"How much time is left?"

"Not much."

Colin gave Terian a grief-stricken look, swallowed hard, then grabbed at his new whiskey. He drank it down, then called for another.

Terian got up and left. While he wanted badly to comfort his friend, he was too afraid for himself to be of any use.

You've never had any sign. No dreams of carnage, no tendencies to indulge. Hell, you were a virgin until that first night with Sundown. Maybe some of that was due to the parents' inclinations toward evil themselves? Balt's mother had been a demon and his father an equally bad human. That had to count for something, if both parents behaved like fiends.

You duped Sar. You betrayed her trust.

That had been innocent. He'd never have caused her any kind of pain. He hadn't pushed her for anything beyond the kiss to activate the spell to know her true feelings. Plus he'd shared in the spell himself; after the kiss Terian had been unable to hide his own feelings. *And it hadn't mattered anyway...*

Terian walked outside, catching Peaches walking unsteadily to her car in her 3" heels. When she leaned on his arm and asked him to help her home, he agreed.

* * * *

Sar, I'm okay. I'm learning a lot out here about myself and I hope you're doing well. Here's my address and phone, if you need to contact me. I hope you're well.

Terian paused after the period, wondering what else to write, his guilt bearing down like a fist between his shoulder blades. It had been two full months now since he'd seen Sar. Was she happy? Was she back together with Danial? While he wanted badly to know, he knew it was better not to push her for anything beyond friendship. Colin was right about that. *Just like Bart had been about the girls at the Naughty Nymph...*

"What are you writing, baby?" Rhinestone said, leaning over one shoulder.

"A letter to an old friend," he said easily, kissing her rouged and powdered cheek. "Interested in a shower?"

"I just got dressed," she complained.

"I know," he said meaningfully. Picking her up, he threw her over one shoulder then walked off to the bathroom as she laughed and shrieked.

* * * *

"Have you been practicing spells to dissipate wraiths?" Colin said searchingly, the tinny sound loud in Terian's ear through the cell phone's receiver.

"Yes," Terian responded patiently, trying to shift in his chair to get better reception. "I've learned most of the defensive spells in volume three. If you'll give me the fourth, I'll begin that one tomorrow. All I need to finish is to polish up on conjuring the blue fire. I can get it to form now, but it takes close to an hour. I want to get that down to a few minutes, if possible."

194

"Very good," Colin said with approval. "You're making remarkable progress. Maybe you have some faerie blood in you."

That would be nice. Better than demon blood, anyway. "Maybe."

"Have you tried healing?"

"Not yet," Terian said, not wanting to admit his failed attempts at healing a simple strand of hair he'd cut in two.

"Volume four is the hardest. Demons usually know the most magic of all the supernatural races, not counting faeries. It's the long lived races that tend to amass the knowledge. Human lifetimes generally aren't long enough—"

"What about vampires?" Terian asked. "Are many of them versed in magic?"

"Usually none, unless in life they were a practitioner. The most knowledgeable currently living is Sola, the oathed one of the Vampire Ruler of Canada, Ebediah. But that's very rare. It's far more common for vampires to employ sorcerers long lived like themselves—"

Terian only half listened. Instead he replayed his words to a woman he loved, berating himself each time for having let them slip out.

It wouldn't ever matter how many years had passed, Sar. Not to me. Why had he said that to her, with all the things he might have said? The last thing she probably wanted was another reminder of her mortality. It was obvious that she'd hurried to get off the phone right after. Then to make matters worse, she'd guessed about the potion he'd given her.

Terian, tell me the truth. Did you put something extra in the potion for growing wings?

He'd admitted dosing her with the truth spell. She'd taken it well, all things considered. The hardest truth was that what Terian had done had given Sar a magical dream of her soul mate—or an equivalent—and that person hadn't been him. It had been someone else.

"I've got to go," Colin said abruptly. "I'll call you back tonight."

Terian hung up, then looked out the library window.

I wish I'd never done any of it. Colin was right. It would have been better not to know. The worst had been Sar thanking him for what he'd done to help her find her new guy, whomever he was. *Probably some full blood human...*

"How are you making out?" Monica said, her question breaking

Terian's concentration.

"Good, thanks," he said, flashing her a smile. She returned one, the slight motion putting a spark in her deep blue eyes that heightened her beauty.

Monica had never tried for more than friendliness in the months Terian had been here. He thought it had to be the demon side of him; that it scared her. *Not that he'd had trouble in the love department, as Balt called it.* Rhinestone and Peaches—as well as other girls who worked the unhallowed poles of Papa's Pleasure House and Naughty Nymphs—had been more than forthcoming on several occasions. But they would never be what Sar was to him. They would never be what Sun had been once, either.

Balt kept saying that you had to take advantage of what you were offered, and not pass "the willing" up. But enjoyable as Terian's nights were now, there was a sameness to them that resembled the vapid conversation of Monica's group. The sex was great, yes, but it wasn't meaningful.

"I wasn't sure you'd be here tonight," Monica remarked. "You've been busy lately."

By her tone, she meant his liaisons. "Are you jealous?"

"Don't flatter yourself," Monica snapped.

"Then why would you care?" Terian pressed. "What is it to you who I spend my nights with?"

Monica turned to him, furious. "You know the thin line you balance on? Don't follow in Balt's footsteps. He's going to lead you straight into hell."

"Aren't I already destined to go there?" Terian said drolly. "Being demon and all, you know."

"You're only part demon. You could do something that matters—"

"Oh really?" Terian said cruelly. "Like your self-help group of stockbrokers and desperate housewives? How is that shifting the balance between good and evil in the world, Monica?"

She gaped at him, crestfallen. "They can't help as they don't have the talent you and I have. They're doing the best they can."

"No. they aren't," Terian stated. "And neither are you. Before you get on your high horse about fighting the good fight, you might actually want to spend some time yourself in the trenches."

Monica blinked in shock, then flushed red. "You bastard."

"I'd rather be a bastard than a fake like you," Terian said, gathering his things. "Bye." He walked out, leaving Monica staring after him.

Terian put his things on the passenger side of his truck, then got behind the wheel. He gripped it hard with both hands. *Why did I say that to her? What is wrong with me?*

Angry at himself, Terian drove to his apartment. He pulled in the driveway, only to find someone else was already there in his spot, the engine of the small compact car running.

Terian forced himself to be calm, then got out and approached the intruder. As he drew even with the driver's door, it opened suddenly, making Terian jump back.

"Good reflexes," the young man said. He drew a gun, pointed it at Terian's chest, and fired point blank.

There was no time to duck, no time to do anything but scream as the bullet passed through his heart and out his back. Terian fell to his knees snarling in pain, his hands tight against the wound trying to stop the blood loss.

"Give it a minute," the man said, lighting up a cigarette. "You'll be as good as new."

Terian looked up the stranger with hate.

"I'm Kyle," the man said, taking a little bow. "Demon hunter, if you haven't guessed."

"Why not...just kill me?" Terian managed to say, his panic lessening as he felt his body begin to heal the gunshot wound.

"Because you aren't full demon," Kyle said, matter of fact. "If you were, you'd be dead. I'd have dipped that bullet in holy water, enough to knock you down so you couldn't run. Then I'd have drowned you in it so you burned."

"So what is this," Terian asked, standing warily. "A warning?"

"Yes," Kyle said with a smile. "I understand from mutual acquaintance that you're trying hard to be one of the good guys. But I wanted to let you know that if you decide to go over to the other side, I or one of my brethren will come for you."

These were the demon hunters Balt had talked about. "You'd be safer taking me out now. If you have the stones for it."

Kyle did a double take, then chuckled. "You're just full of self-destruction, aren't you? That must come from the demon side."

"How would you know?" Terian said dully.

"Because I've known a lot of half-demons in my time," Kyle said, his voice losing its camaraderie. "They all went over, eventually. Those with human blood go over first usually, before they're thirty. The ones with other non-human blood can stave off the change longer—"

Terian didn't want to hear this again. *Screw him, and being demon and everything to do with it.* He turned and walked to his house, getting his keys out.

"You're just leaving?" Kyle called after him. "In the middle of our talk?"

"Yes. You need to shoot me, go ahead." Terian went inside, closed the door, then locked it. He lay down on the couch, thinking. A new plan of action was overdue and couldn't be put off any longer.

God, all he'd done since he got here was think and learn magic and have meaningless sex. Maybe that was all Balt wanted out of his life but Terian wanted more, even if Sundown and Sar weren't part of the picture.

Everyone wanted something from him. Monica wanted him to change the world for the greater good. Balt wanted a play buddy, someone like him to share women with and spend time talking about their inevitable doom while getting hammered on alcohol. His lovers wanted some exotic boyfriend or lover and nothing more. And Colin...Colin wanted Terian's help in killing Balt before he became a full demon, so his brother's soul would get a chance to go to heaven.

And how long after I helped kill him would Colin take to decide that I was also better off dead?

Terian didn't want any of those things. Moreover, he wasn't going to do them. He'd been playing at life for too long. The time for acting was over.

He'd stay until he learned the last tome of magic, the fourth volume. Colin said he was making phenomenal progress, so it should go quickly. Then he'd go back East, and try again with Sundown. They had loved one another once. Maybe it could work, if he didn't push her so hard.

Sar…he'd always love her, but she was happy with her soul mate now. Even though that hurt, at least she had to be safe from Danial now. Being friends would have to be enough.

* * * *

Several more weeks passed as Terian flew through the fourth volume of magic, learning some elaborate spells of defense, including one for ripping apart hearts metaphysically.

"I don't know why you're bothering with that, when you easily have the strength to rip out a human's heart with your own hand," Balt said dubiously, studying the page.

"Because it's easier to kill without making a mess," Colin said, looking up from his own book. "There aren't allowances to kill someone if they're evil under human law. This way it looks like a heart attack, at least from the outside."

"If they open the body, though, they'd see the heart was destroyed," Balt replied. "So if you've got to destroy the evidence anyway, why bother making it clean?"

"I'm not learning this to murder people," Terian said, annoyed. "I'm learning it in defense, as a case of last resort."

"Okay," Balt said, holding his hands up. "I'm just making an observation."

"An undue one," Colin added, glancing up in reproach.

Balt laughed, then pushed Terian's book down just a bit, getting his attention. "Do you have some time this evening? There's someone I want you to meet."

Terian rolled his eyes. "The Naughty Nymph get a new girl?"

"Yes," Balt said with a big smile. "And she wants to make your acquaintance tonight at Happy's."

"Sure then," Terian said. "About eleven?"

"That's fine," Balt said.

Terian waited at Happy's later that night, kicking himself for having agreed to come. The bar was crowded with Saturday college kids, as well as regulars. His supernatural hearing was almost on overload, the crack of pool balls melding with the loud talking, live music, and pretzel crunching to create a din.

"Here he is," Balt said at Terian's back. "Terian, meet Patricia."

Terian turned. A gorgeous woman stood there, her expression bemused and seductive. Her platinum hair was cut in a pageboy style, her outfit a very low cut business suit. "Are you supposed to be a nympho CEO?" he asked.

The woman laughed loudly. "You'll make a great demon when the time comes. You've already got down the humor."

Terian went motionless, staring at the woman. She smiled back, her gorgeous blue eyes flooding with red, an ocean of black evil flowing out of her.

She was a demon.

"Don't look so spooked," Patricia said kindly, the evil feeling dissipating. "You've heard the worst about us from the bible thumpers. Being demon can be a lot of fun, so long as you stay on the right side of Hell's rules."

"Which you're going to tell me, right?" Terian said, letting his own heat and blackness billow forth.

"Only if you want to hear it," Patricia said. "Hell's awash in demons, and we aren't soliciting for more. But you're part of the club already, because of your lineage. It's my calling to seek out those on the fence, so to speak, and give them full disclosure."

"Really? Where were you for the last fifty years?" Terian said curtly. "I didn't recently become a half-demon, you know."

"No, but you kept to yourself," Patricia countered. "You knew only very low level magic and you didn't want any part of the human world. Contrary to popular belief, Hell doesn't want just anybody; we want the go-getters, the hard workers, the ambitious and driven. You came to our attention recently, when you began learning more magic—"

The demon prattled on, praising Terian, but he tuned her out. This was just another person wanting something from him.

"There are added benefits," Patricia said with a pointed smile, slipping her finger into her cleavage and stroking slightly.

"What, besides you?" Terian said bluntly.

"What do you want?" Patricia said, still smiling. Her red eyes gleamed like fresh blood in sunlight. "Or who, should I say? I understand that you came out here because a relationship didn't work out—"

"Leave me alone," Terian said, dropping his human mask. He snarled, baring his rows of pointed teeth. "Get out of my sight!"

There was a sudden scream, one of the college girls pointing at Terian. He resumed his mask, but others had already seen him. There was a mass panic, people running for the exit, some of them shouting there was a fire in their confusion. A girl screamed, then went down in the melee, the wet crunch of her broken neck echoing in Terian's ears.

"Lovely," Patricia said with glee. "And she's not remotely devout, either." She turned, heading for the body as the last patrons shoved their way free into the night air. Balt followed her, curious.

Terian stood as Patricia knelt, then jammed her hands into the girl's body. The demon leaned backwards, pulling hard. Then a ghostly figure came free of the body, the indistinct form emitting a whimpering sound.

"None of that," Patricia said with relish. "You had your whole life to make a decision, to believe. It's too late now."

The ghostly figure began to shriek, then writhe as Patricia pulled it close in an embrace.

A shot rang out. Patricia crumpled, cursing. The ghostly figure swayed, then fled back down into the motionless body on the floor, disappearing.

Four hooded men came through the door in a rush, guns drawn and pointed. They surrounded Patricia, while one covered Terian and Balt. "There was only supposed to be the one half-demon," one of them said in confusion.

"Doesn't matter. Do the exorcism, Father," Kyle said, throwing back his hood to reveal himself.

Another hooded man produced a small electronic device and began to read off it, the language Latin. Kyle threw something on Patricia. She flinched, then cursed them. "Do it and see what happens," she growled. "Next time I return it will be for you and your team!" She let out another scream as more holy water hit her.

Balt took a step, and Terian stopped him. "Don't help her."

"That could be us," Balt said, shaking him off. "Don't you get it? They didn't come for her. They came for me."

"That can't be," Terian said. "You haven't done anything."

"Haven't I?" Balt said, his tone chilling.

"You haven't done anything bad," Terian said stubbornly.

"Don't move," the man holding the gun warned.

"You'll shoot me as soon as she's dead," Balt said. Then he launched himself at the man, toppling him and knocking him on his back. The man fired seven times in succession, blowing a huge hole in Balt's back, distracting the priest and Kyle from the exorcism.

Terian watched, wanting to help but not knowing what to do. *If I try to break it up they'll both fight me.*

Patricia rose, her taloned hand slashing out to slit the throat of the priest. Then she went for Kyle, gashing his side as he leapt backward. Balt was on his back, fighting the man who'd traded his gun for a machete.

Sar wouldn't stand here and watch a friend be killed.

Terian uttered the beginning of the spell to tear hearts, then saw the long blade descending. Moving fast, he shoved the man off Balt, then punched him.

"Thanks," Balt coughed, pulling out the tip of the blade.

Terian turned slightly to reply, then felt a heavy blow. He went sprawling, twitching slightly. Balt roared, then came the sounds of scuffling. Patricia was still howling and cursing.

Why can't I move? Terian tried to move his arms, his head, his legs, and couldn't. *Am I dead?*

Patricia lunged for Kyle and he parried her with a table, breaking it on her shoulder. She dropped, then staggered back up immediately, bloodied. "You can't send me to hell without your priest, hunter! I'll be eating your soul tonight—" She lunged again at Kyle. He shoved another table in front of her, blocking her.

"So afraid," she snickered evilly. "But then that's why you hunt us, isn't it? Because you're afraid—" She went rigid, cutting off her words then whipped around as undulating red and black fire washed over her. Patricia let out an unholy screech of agony, then danced wildly, setting fire to everything she touched, even plastic and metal. Then she darted for Colin, who was standing, yelling furiously, words to conjure more fire as black and gold flames formed in his left hand.

"No!" Balt yelled. He darted toward Colin, getting between the burning demon and his brother. Patricia knocked into him, Balt letting

202

out a howl as he wrestled with her, flames rapidly running up his arms. Colin finished the hellfire spell and flung the ball of fire at Patricia, knocking the burning demon off his brother. She convulsed again with the second blast, then collapsed, burning brightly.

"Outside!" Kyle yelled. "The place is going up!"

Terian watched Kyle and his remaining man flee, still struggling to move himself. He managed with effort to finally turn over, straightening his spine. Suddenly he felt the healing return, the feeling come back to his arms and legs. He used a table to pull himself upright. Colin was struggling with Balt, trying to get him out of the rapidly escalating conflagration.

Terian grabbed Balt's other arm. Together, he and Colin dragged the prone giant of a man out of the burning building. They set him down on the wet gravel of the parking lot, rain pelting their faces. Steam rose up from Balt, the remaining flames on him quickly extinguished.

"Always saving my ass," Balt groaned. "Why can't you ever manage to get there before I'm hurt?"

"Be quiet," Colin said, stripping off Balt's shirt. It came off only partially, the left side melted into his flesh.

Terian looked down at the seared and blistered flesh. "Do you want me to help you get him to your home? What do you need? I can bring it here."

"No," Balt said. "Leave it."

"You're not dying here in this fucking parking lot," Colin screeched out hysterically. "Terian, get the car."

"No," Kyle said from behind them, brandishing a gun. "You aren't saving him so he can kill someone else."

Terian hid his left hand, then began to murmur the words to create blue fire as Colin stood and faced Kyle down. "He's my brother and I'm not letting him die."

"He killed a stripper last week," Kyle said coldly. "He's on the verge of becoming demon, Colin. I know he's your brother, but that can't matter."

"You don't put aside your blood," Colin said, advancing. "If you had any family you'd know that."

"I did have a family," Kyle said bitterly, his gun unwavering. "I had a sister. A demon killed her. He was half, just like your brother, until the night he raped and murdered her."

Terian braced himself, murmuring the words as fast as he dared. The fire was forming, but it needed a few more precious seconds.

"I can save him," Colin said, edging toward the car.

Kyle fired, striking Colin in the chest. The man went down hard on his back, his left leg twitching.

The blue fire finished forming, the sheer heat of it making Terian sweat. He braced himself to throw it at Kyle, then felt Balt take hold of his arm, stopping him. "No," Balt whispered. "He's not lying. This is easier…for everyone."

Terian looked down at him in horror. Balt gave him a faint smile, then closed his eyes, relaxing back into the mud.

Kyle walked to Terian, holstering his gun. "Is he gone?"

Terian checked for a pulse. There was none. "Yes."

"I've heard the rain being called God's Tears," Kyle mused. "But I've never heard of it putting out hellfire before."

Terian didn't answer.

There was the wail of sirens in the distance, coming closer.

"Good luck," Kyle said to Terian. "I'm sorry you got in the middle of this, but—"

Everything froze, including the raindrops which hung suspended, millions of them glittering. Then slowly Colin sat up, his eyes glowing red.

"No," Kyle breathed. "You aren't demon, you were faerie half-breed, like me—"

"Not all demons are born in hell," Colin said, baring his rows of pointed teeth. "Some are made from the hells they're forced to endure." He stood carefully, then began murmuring a spell.

Kyle thrashed, trying to flee, but he only wobbled, his feet not lifting from the ground.

"You have hunted for years, unrelenting and unmerciful," Colin said darkly, "I curse you now to be hunted yourself, forever." He spoke a word, and Kyle recoiled, holding his head and screaming. "Run all you want, and you'll be found."

Kyle looked up, his brown eyes terrified.

Tears and Rain

Colin gestured. The glistening raindrops plummeted to earth, the world in motion again. Kyle leapt up and ran, his remaining friend following. They started the car, then drove it off squealing.

Colin came to Balt's side and knelt. He picked his brother up, and began carrying him to his car. Terian watched, then reluctantly followed.

Hours later, Terian stood with Colin near a freshly covered grave. Colin was using the tip of one newly taloned hand to carve the stone. The etching noise was grating on Terian's nerves, though he said nothing.

Colin finished the stone, then set it in place. Carefully, he broke a piece of rosebush off a wild white rose, and pushed it into the earth. With a few words, the demon cast a spell of growth, the branch putting down roots and flowering to a wide mat of white flowers covering the fresh earth.

"It looks nice," Terian offered.

"I know you don't know what to say," Colin remarked, his eyes averted. "I don't either."

"What will you do now?" Terian asked.

"Try to find a lenient master who will let me pursue Kyle in my spare time," Colin said. "I got assurances that would be allowed, but we'll see." He turned to Terian. "What will you do?"

It was time to stop running. "I'm going back to face what I left back east."

"You can feel love," Colin said, regarding Terian will his red eyes. "I feel the same as I did when I was a faerie half breed. I'm wondering now if I ever knew anything about demons, or only thought I did."

"Can I borrow your fourth volume," Terian asked. "To take with me?"

"You can have my books, all of them," Colin answered absently. "I always thought I'd find an answer in magic, but I never did. And I don't think I'll have a home of my own in my new life." He smiled. "And yes, the spell for hellfire is in there, if you look for it."

"I'm sorry it had to be this way," Terian made himself utter. "That sounds lame, but I can't help it, Colin."

"I understand," Colin said, a genuine smile gracing his features. "I didn't either. But what being ever gets what he wants, really? I wanted to

205

save my brother." He laughed bitterly. "I couldn't even save myself."

Balt was saved. He stopped me from killing Kyle. He died without becoming a full demon. Terian held back the words, knowing hearing them would be worse for Colin than not knowing. For if Balt had let Terian kill Kyle, Colin wouldn't have gotten shot...or become demon in a last dying wish for revenge.

Rain began to fall again, dampening their clothes. "It's good we had the rain, or the entire adult part of the strip might have gone up," Colin said jokingly. "What a loss for the bachelors of this town."

"And the library at the end of the street," Terian added. "Not to mention the suburbs beyond."

"I can't think now why I cared about them," Colin said disdainfully. "I spent so many nights holding whores' hands, and listening to married men tell me how they just couldn't love their wives. What a waste of time—"

The bullet hit Colin in his throat, severing his last words. Another hit Terian in the leg, knocking him sprawling. Kyle came charging out from behind a tree, a swing from his machete decapitating Colin.

Terian staggered to his feet, then paused. Two men held a gun on him, with three more assisting Kyle. They began anointing him with holy water, the liquid scalding the flesh of the headless body as it twitched.

"Stop it!" Terian yelled. "Stop hurting him."

"We're trying to save him," Kyle said tiredly. He holstered his gun, then came over to Terian. "I didn't have a beef with Colin. He was a good friend." He looked up at Terian, his brown eyes red rimmed. "I never caught your name."

"Terian."

"Good to meet you." Kyle looked back at his men. They'd erected a small altar and lit candles near it. One opened a bible and began to pray, immediately giving Terian the beginnings of a migraine.

"Walk with me," Kyle said to Terian.

"Why?" Terian challenged.

"Because seeing this is going to hurt me as much as hearing it hurts you now," Kyle said sadly. "Come on."

Terian let out a long breath, then followed. They walked in silence for a while through the trees, then into a clearing with a small stream.

"Can you save him?" Terian asked. "Take back what he became?"

"Probably not," Kyle said, skipping a stone into the water. "But we have to try."

"Balt wasn't a demon when he died," Terian said. "He stopped me from killing you."

Kyle turned to look at Terian, then resumed skipping rocks. "I'm glad of that," he said softly.

"I thought you hated him," Terian said. "I thought you hated people like me."

"I hate demons," Kyle admitted. "I hate how they destroy lives. I never hate half-breeds. They can't help their dual nature, or that the demon side is usually stronger." He dropped his rock. "But I can't afford to have mercy, not when it might mean some innocent person's life. Do you understand that?"

"Yes," Terian said slowly. "I understand that."

"Good," Kyle said, heading past Terian. "Let's go back. They should be done."

The small clearing was empty when they returned, except for the priest standing before the grave. He was just finishing consecrating the ground. He turned as Kyle and Terian strode up. "We sent him to Hell," he said apologetically. "There was nothing we could do. We scattered the ashes near his brother's grave."

Kyle closed his eyes and sighed. "Get everyone ready to go. We've got to head out of town."

The priest nodded, then with a smile at Terian, walked away.

Terian turned to Kyle. "I can feel it, you know," he murmured. "Colin put something on you. There is something inside you that calls to me. It's why I followed you to the stream, even when I didn't want to."

"I know," Kyle said darkly. "I'm going to have a lot of offline followers very shortly, I think, none of them with my best interests at heart."

Terian managed a smile, then stuck out his hand. "Good luck."

Kyle shook it, his expression incredulous. "You're wishing me luck? After everything?"

"You don't compromise or give up," Terian said. "That's something I admire, Kyle." His expression darkened. "But if you come for me like you did for Bart, I'll try to kill you."

Kyle smiled. "Fair enough. I hope I never have to, if that counts for anything."

Terian nodded. "It does."

Kyle let go of his hand, then moved off through the trees.

Terian stood before the grave for a while, reflecting.

I will not give into my demon side. I'm not going to become a monster.

He would go tonight and pack up Colin's books, everything. By tonight he'd be heading back East, back to Sundown if she would have him, back to Sar's friendship if she wouldn't. It was time to stop running, time for his life to be more than just honorable vows he hoped one day to fulfill, or relationships he yearned to have someday. Balt was right. There was only so much time. Terian was not going to waste one moment more.

Terian's hand rested briefly on the cold stone, then he turned and purposefully walked away through the trees.

Heart's Solace

(previously published in Wild at Heart Vol. II Charity anthology 10-2012)

Natasha looked down at the pitiful creature in the small cage. The feline was a large cat, but not like the big cats her father usually kept as pets. This one wasn't a tiger, a leopard, or a lion. He looked kind of like a lion without a mane. She'd have suspected the animal to be a female lion, if she hadn't seen the contrary proof herself.

"You don't belong in a cage," she whispered. "You should be out in your own land, running free. Beneath a wide sky on a grassland, not here in this world of ice and snow."

The battered cat raised its head, its yellow eyes staring into hers. The feline looked almost as if it understood her. Then it put down its head, and gave a long sigh.

Natasha wrapped her long wool coat over her small frame, and then walked quickly on the snowy path into the nearby stable.

Alexey was there, currying her horse, Sasha.

"The new lion," Natasha said. "What kind is he?"

"An American Cougar, otherwise known as a mountain lion," Alexey responded. He gave Sasha a final pat then put away the currycomb. "Your father saved his life, outbidding the taxidermist at the auction. He thinks the beast can be rehabilitated. He's calling him Nadezda."

The Russian word for hope. "But you don't think so?"

"He's damaged goods, Tasha," Alexey said with a frown. "The lion's back legs had both been badly broken in several places, and one of his front legs is also maimed. He may never walk again. Stay away from him. If he doesn't try to attack us, I'll be very surprised."

* * * *

Tasha made sure she was on hand the next day to watch as Alexey put food in the new lion's cage. The creature didn't stir, or even move.

"You have to eat, Nadezda." Alexey said with a shake of his head. "You'll die if you don't. You ate nothing yesterday—"

"Let me try," Tasha offered, coming over. "I'll sit and talk to him."

"Talk to him all you want, but don't open the cage door, or put your fingers inside," Alexey warned. "Your father would fire me if you got so much as a scratch." He headed into the stable.

Tasha sat on some bales of hay near the cage. "My name is Tasha," she began haltingly. "Really, it's Natasha, but everyone calls me Tasha. You're in Russia, if you didn't know. It's close to the end of winter, but we may have some good snows yet—"

Tasha craned her head. The lion's ears had moved slightly. Was he listening?

"—I know people were bad to you. But you're safe now. No one will hurt you here. My father loves his cats. There are two more here, a panther and a bobcat. Both are rescues, like the ones before them. My father has a soft spot for animals, especially lions—"

She couldn't tell if the cat was listening or sleeping, or even if her voice was helping it at all. But she stayed there for an hour talking aloud, just in case.

* * * *

"You're helping Nazdeha," Alexey told Tasha one afternoon. "He's eating better that he was. He'll put back on the weight he needs in no time."

"Will he recover?" Tasha asked, casting a worried glance at the cat. "I've seen the extent of his injuries. He looks crippled to me, Alexey. He crawls like the slightest movement hurts."

"Because it does," Alexey said angrily. "But be encouraged. He is healing far faster than he should be." He offered her a smile. "He'll live for certain. But whether he'll walk again, I'm not sure."

"He will," Tasha stated. "I'll help you however I can."

"Keep talking to him," Alexey replied. "That and time is what he needs most." He paused. "How were your lessons today?"

"Interminable." Tasha drew out the word with deliberate exaggeration, then gave Alexey a wide smile. "I've already completed my high school studies, and am now merely doing advance work in preparation for college. If my father will ever let me attend university. He doesn't want to let me, I think. We spoke on the phone last night for our weekly discussion. This is the second week he hasn't mentioned it—"

"Your father will come around, in time. He is well?"

Tasha nodded, forcing a smile. "His business dealings keep him travelling to Europe, or in Moscow. He sends his love, and hopes to be back for my birthday in September."

"He does love you best of his children," Alexey replied. "I'm sure he will return."

Tasha forced a smile, but didn't respond. What should she say? Her father was a stranger to her, really. She appreciated him very much, but they had never been close. He had never acted like he wanted or needed her affection…

That didn't matter anymore, she told herself. She had someone who badly needed her: Nazdeha.

* * * *

The months passed slowly, and spring became summer, then late summer. Each day, Tasha made sure to be there when Nazdeha was fed, and spent at least an hour talking to him. The mountain lion became a sleek shape as he filled out, and his broken limbs healed. Hesitantly, he began to take hobbling steps about his enclosure. Soon, he was walking with only a slight hitch. But scars still ran over most of his body, crisscrossing the tawny fur.

Tasha had long ago lost her fear of the cougar. Her familiarity was such that one day while putting food inside, she forgot to lock the cage afterwards. After saying goodbye to Nazdeha, she walked up the wide path to her family's mansion.

When the butler opened the front door to admit Tasha, he let out a scream.

A loud snarl sounded from behind her.

With a gasp, Tasha whirled.

Nazdeha was barely a foot away, watching her with intent yellow eyes.

"Don't hurt me," she whispered, her stomach tight with anxiety.

Nazdeha nodded once, and then lay down on the cold stone, rolling onto his back with all four feet in the air. He looked at her, tail twitching slightly.

Tasha blinked at him, amazed. *He had nodded before acting submissive. He had understood her.* The animal before her was no mere cat. It possessed human intelligence.

"Will you obey me, and not hurt anyone, if I let you inside?" She felt foolish asking that, yet also prayed she hadn't imagined the nod.

Nazdeha rolled to his feet then looked at her. Deliberately, he nodded once more.

"Ah!" Tasha said, a wide smile curving her lips.

The door opened a crack behind her. "Ma'am, please come inside. I've alerted the guards—"

"Open the door," Tasha commanded. She strode up to the door, then turned and beckoned to the cat, who came bounding up, thrusting his large head under her slim hand. She petted the large head with both hands, as she'd longed to for months.

Nazdeha closed his eyes, a throaty purr rumbling out.

The butler opened the door, his eyes scared. "Ma'am, you can't let that animal in the house—"

"He is my pet, and he goes where I go." Tasha took on a brazen attitude. "I am mistress of this house, Boris. Now bring me my supper and a large bowl of raw beef. Nazdeha and I are hungry."

"Yes, Ma'am," Boris said, leaning back out of the way as cougar and girl entered the house together.

* * * *

The next few months were magical. Nazdeha was a perfect companion, following Tasha everywhere. They explored the forest, her

212

on horseback, and he in the trees shadowing her. They spent hours lounging in the sun, Tasha reading to Nazdeha as the great cat lolled with eyes closed, her head pillowed on his flank. He slept in her bed, his bulk curled on one side of the great king size bed, Tasha on the other.

The great cat communicated through nods and shakes of his head. He purred when he was pleased or thankful, and distanced himself from her when he was upset. Encouraged, Tasha made an alphabet from large pieces of paper, and laid them out on the floor, telling him to step on the letters, to spell out words for her. "Tell me who you are," she said excitedly, pencil and paper in hand.

Instead of the expected grateful purr, Tasha's efforts instead got her a shake of the head, and the silent treatment for the rest of the night.

Tasha was undaunted by Nazdeha's refusal to communicate beyond yes and no answers. She remained convinced he was a man under a curse, like in fairytales. Several times, she pleaded with him to change his form, to show her the man she knew he must be.

But Nazdeha would only look at her, as if he couldn't understand. Afterwards, he always would retreat away from her and curl into a ball for at least an hour.

Surmising he was trapped in lion form, Tasha stopped mentioning it. Talk of what he had once been only upset him. She had no way to break a curse. That he was here with her was enough for Tasha.

* * * *

Late summer became fall. And with the winter wind came a letter from Tasha's father, telling her he would not be home again for Christmas, but that she was welcome to meet him in Moscow, if she wanted to make the trip.

Tasha tore up the letter. "He knows I hate the city," she said. "Besides, I couldn't take you there, Nazdeha. I'm not leaving you here alone for the holidays."

The cougar nuzzled her shoulder, his loud purr a vibration she felt through her thick sweater.

"Do you need to go out before bed?" Tasha asked. "It's close to midnight."

Nazdeha nodded, then jumped up off the bed, and walked to the bedroom door.

Tasha followed, opening the door so he could leave.

The lion trotted out.

Instead of readying herself for bed, as she usually did, Tasha paused, and then looked out the door, watching the shadow of the lion as it traveled down the long hallway.

Nazdeha had headed for the kitchen, not outside to relieve himself.

Curious, Tasha hurried after the cat, creeping down the long hallway and into the kitchen. A naked man was in front of the refrigerator, his scarred back to her as he ate pickles from a jar. She let out a gasp.

The man heard her and swore, then grabbed a dishtowel to cover himself. "Don't look at me!"

Tasha turned away, her cheeks burning. "So you *can* change form."

"Yes," came the hesitant reply. "Go upstairs, Tasha. I'll leave—"

His voice was rough, either naturally or from disuse. It was the sexiest voice she had ever heard in her life. "You'll do nothing of the kind. Don't you dare change back, Nazdeha. I think I deserve some answers."

"It's Theo, actually," the man said sadly. "That's my real name."

"Follow me, Theo." Tasha strode from the room. "You can borrow some hunting clothes of my father's. Hurry, before you're seen."

* * * * *

A half-hour later, Natasha sat in her bedroom at her breakfast table. Theo was across from her, fully dressed, his expression distressed.

"Nothing has to change," she said finally. "I always knew you were something more than you pretended to be. Stay here with me."

"I can't sleep here in your room anymore," Theo snapped. "Your servants will notice me, if they haven't already. They'll tell your father, who would be none too pleased, I'm guessing."

"They'll say what I tell them to say."

Theo shook his head. "Not for something like this. You're only seventeen, Tasha, and that's only by a few days."

"My sister was married at sixteen," Tasha interrupted. "I'm not a child, Theo, so stop treating me like one."

"You don't know me at all," Theo spat out, getting to his feet and pacing.

"I know you could have easily taken advantage of me in the last six months," Tasha said softly. "You didn't. Now I understand why you excused yourself in the morning and evenings, when I was dressing. You were being chivalrous."

Theo gave her a look. "I'm in my late twenties, Tasha. You're right that I'm a man as well as a cougar. But I'm not going to hurt a young girl who doesn't know better, even if I am horny as hell."

Tasha looked away, her face aflame, trying to get control. *He'd said that to shock her. That was all.* "Where will you go?"

"Home," Theo said, his tone hopeless. "I've been gone a long time. Close to a year now. God, I'm not looking forward to that."

What person wouldn't want to go home? But that was good, as Tasha wasn't letting Theo go. *Not now. Not ever.* "If you must go, let me help you, Theo. I can arrange passage for you—"

"No," Theo said. "You've helped me enough already. I was planning to slip away in the night, but I'm glad you found me instead." He came over, and knelt before her, cupping her face in his hands. Gently, he kissed her forehead. "I'm very grateful to you, Tasha. Part of me wishes I could just stay here with you. But I can't. I've got to go back to the U.S."

"Why?" Tasha asked, eyebrows drawn into a frown. "You clearly don't want to go back. You're afraid of what has changed since you've been gone."

Theo nodded. "Yes. But I have to. Besides, I've come to care about you. People I care about usually get hurt. I don't want you to get hurt, too." He smiled briefly, his gaze meeting hers. "Maybe it won't be so bad."

Tasha looked deep into Theo's blue eyes, and promptly fell in love in that magical split second.

"I have to go," Theo said, moving towards the door. "Goodnight, Tasha."

"No," Tasha argued, latching onto his arm. "Change form if you feel you have to. But please stay with me." She hugged him tightly, delighting to feel his hard muscles under the thick cloth. He was so solid...so comforting.

Theo didn't reply.

"You haven't spoken to anyone for so long," Tasha continued. "Don't you want to tell me about yourself? You listened to me for so many months. You know all my hopes, all my dreams, practically my whole life story. Tell me yours, Theo."

"You won't want to hear it," Theo whispered, even as his arms slipped around her, hugging her close. "It's ugly and awful."

I love you. I want to know. I have to know. "Tell me, please."

"All right."

* * * *

The next morning, Tasha woke early, and lay in bed, looking at Theo lying next to her. She pulled blankets over them, and then cuddled close, pretending that they were married, that they had just spent their wedding night together, and that today was the first day of their life together.

Nothing had happened, of course. Theo had been the perfect gentleman, making sure to sleep with all his clothes on outside the bedcovers. Tasha had hoped for a kiss, had even dared to kiss Theo on the cheek, hoping he would get the hint. But he had been wrapped up completely in his story, his eyes haunted as he relived the horrors of the past year, and before.

He had told her his past; his childhood of privilege, his brief college days as an art major; his fights with his parents, who wanted so much more for him; his fiancée Casey who he'd lost after being attacked, his acclimation to being a werecougar; and finally, his collusion with a vampire to become a sort of bodyguard.

After that, things were hard to understand. Theo had clearly been hiding something, if not several somethings. He talked of witches and demons, vampires and werefoxes. He had mentioned no names, just vague events. Only two things were completely clear to Tasha. One was Theo's life was in danger. He had been sold into slavery by his enemies. Several people—powerful people—still wanted him dead. The second was if Theo left here, he would almost certainly be killed. He would never make it home.

Tasha had to find a way to make him stay, no matter what. *But how?*

216

She would talk to Alexey. He was her only real friend here, plus he was a man himself. He should be able to give some insight.

Leaving Theo sleeping, Tasha dressed quickly, and hurried down to the stables.

* * * *

"That is the craziest story I've even heard," Alexey scolded, when Tasha finished.

"You don't believe me?" Tasha crossed her arms over her chest, her eyes flashing.

"I do," Alexey said, nodding. "But only because I know you, Tasha. You would never make this up—"

"What should I do?" Tasha interrupted. "I have to stop him. He'll leave and be killed!"

"You can't make him stay here against his will." Alexey shook his head. "He's not a character from a fairy tale, Tasha. He's not a prince in disguise."

"He mentioned supernatural beings," Tasha said quickly. "They will kill him if he leaves. I have to save him, Alexey." She paused then blurted, "I love him!"

"I can see that, child," Alexey murmured gently. He touched her check with his callused hand. "So much a young woman, yet still so much a girl. These things can't be forced, Tasha. He must do what is right for him."

"He's too scarred by what he went through to know what's right!" Tasha said, her anger rising. "Why won't you help me save him?"

"I couldn't, even if I wanted to." Alexey pressed his lips into a firm line. "I've never met a supernatural being. I have never wanted to. Your best bet is to convince Theo to stay with logic, not with emotion."

Furious, Tasha stalked out of the stable, and then ran up to the house. Dark clouds were coming across the mountains in the distance, lightning flashing.

Tasha hurried inside and went down the hallway to her room.

Suddenly, a shadow appeared before her, blocking out the light.

She let out a cry, cringing backward.

"Don't be afraid. I mean you no harm…Tasha."

The voice was raspy, like dry paper crackling. "How do you know my name?" she challenged. "Who are you?"

"A friend," the figure said. A wrinkled hand held out a paper. "Call me when you are ready."

Tasha didn't take the proffered paper. "Ready for what?"

"To save your love, of course." The figure disappeared as suddenly as it had come.

The paper lay on the floor, testament she hadn't imagined the figure. Leaving it there, Tasha ran to her room, sure Theo would somehow be gone. But he was as she had left him, asleep in her bed, snoring slightly.

He was so handsome…

The phone rang shrilly. Tasha bolted to it, grabbing it up. "Hello?"

"My daughter," her father's voice said with a loving note in this voice. "You are up early."

"I was hoping to go riding," Tasha answered, her words tumbling out. "Alexey is saddling Sasha now."

"Your ride can wait. I have some good news." He paused. "I have arranged for you to be married this coming Christmas."

All the blood drained from Tasha's face. "What?"

"He is a doctor at a university of veterinary medicine. He will make a wonderful match for you, with your love for animals—"

"What about my college plans?" Tasha managed to speak around the lump in her throat.

"You will never need to work," her father said, his words were clipped and sharp. "There is no need for you to attend college, Tasha. Don't be afraid. Arkady is an older man, and he will put few demands on you, save for children—"

No. Not now. Especially not now! She was in love. If she was going to marry anyone, it was going to be Theo. "That sounds lovely, Father," Tasha said quickly. "Alexey is calling me from outside. Let me call you back this evening. I want to hear all the details."

"Tasha—"

She hung up on her father then raced to the piece of paper. On it was just a phone number. She crossed to the phone and dialed.

The voice that answered was the same. "You waste no time. That is good."

"How much to help me?" Tasha said. "It must be tonight. There is little time."

"I want nothing but Theo's safety," the voice said, followed by an amused chuckle. "He is safest staying with you, wouldn't you agree?"

"Yes," Tasha said. "But he won't stay." *Say it.* "He doesn't love me as I love him."

"He will," the voice said with surety. "He already is affectionate with you. It is not hard to give that affection a push to make it blossom into love. I will give you something to help that happen."

"What?"

"Heart's Solace. It's a spell to help those with broken hearts forget their troubled past and find love again. The powder can be readily mixed with alcohol—"

"I won't hurt him," Tasha said.

"This won't hurt him. He will die if he leaves, that I promise you. Don't you want to save him?"

And myself in the process. "Yes. Can you bring it by tonight?"

"It will be on the front doorstep by nightfall."

There was a sudden sound of the dial tone. Tasha put down the phone.

This was the right thing. It was the only way.

But Theo wouldn't be the only one to take Heart's Solace. She would take it, also. If she was willing to trust the man she loved to a sorcerer's spell, she had to trust herself, too.

* * * *

The powder was there at dusk, on the step in an envelope. Tasha poured the packet into the bottle of wine, then brought it into the bedroom where Theo waited, a duffel bag at his feet.

"I have to go," he said, raking a hand through his blond hair. "Thank you again for all you've done for me. I wouldn't have come back to life without you, Tasha." He gave her a heart-melting smile.

It was now or never. They would either die together, or live happily ever after.

Tasha poured the wine into two glasses. "Will you toast to me before you go?"

"To what?" Theo said, taking the glass. "I've never known you to drink, Tasha."

"I'm getting married," Tasha said, smiling unevenly. "To our new lives." She clinked her glass to Theo's, then drank it down.

"Congratulations." Theo emptied his, too. He set it down, then staggered slightly, holding onto a chair to steady himself.

Tasha swayed then sat down heavily on the bed. Her head was spinning, and she felt slightly sick.

Theo came over then went to his knees before her. "Are you all right?"

"No," Tasha said, wiping at tears. "You're leaving and you're asking me if I'm all right? Don't you know I love you?"

Theo stared at her a split second, his lips parted. Then he embraced her, his strong arms surrounding her, his lips meeting hers in a rough, passionate kiss that took Tasha's breath away. She kissed him back, and then they were embracing on her bed, her arms around him, running up his muscular back, his lips devouring her hot skin.

"Will you marry me?" Theo whispered.

Tasha froze, then looked up at him. Had he really said that, or had she imagined the words?

"I love you," Theo said again, cupping her face in his hands. "I know you're not eighteen. But I want to be with you—"

"You're thinking of your America," Tasha said with a laugh. "Here in Russia, the legal age of consent is sixteen, Theo. Having just turned seventeen, I'm certainly of legal age—"

"You didn't answer my question," Theo said lightly, kissing her neck.

"So long as you aren't leaving," Tasha teased.

"I'd be a fool to leave you," Theo said, kissing her again.

Tasha kissed him back, her arms around him, blissful. Neither she nor Theo noticed the shadowy figure watching, or saw his smile as he faded away into nothingness.

About the Author

Tara Fox Hall's writing credits include nonfiction, horror, suspense, action-adventure, erotica, and contemporary and historical paranormal romance. She is the author of the paranormal action-adventure *Lash* series and the vampire romantic suspense *Promise Me* series. Tara divides her free time unequally between writing novels and short stories, chainsawing firewood, caring for stray animals, sewing cat and dog beds for donation to animal shelters, and target practice.

Other works by the author with Melange Books, LLC

Return To Me
Surrender to Me
The Origin of Fear in Spellbound 2011 Anthology
Night Music in Midnight Thirsts II Anthology
Partners in Midnight Thirsts II Anthology
Kink in Wicked Christmas Wishes Anthology
The Oath in Wicked Christmas Wishes Anthology
Bedtime Shadows Anthology
Make Me Behave Anthology

The Promise Me Series
Promise Me, Book 1
Broken Promise, Book 2
Taken in the Night, Book 3
Taken for his Own, Book 4

Coming Soon
Latham's Landing, An Anthology